This Song Is About Me

PRAISE FOR MELISSA DE LA CRUZ

"De la Cruz mixes biting satire with suspense and throws in a few more surprises. Readers will be riveted as long-simmering secrets come to light."

—*Publishers Weekly*

"Stylish, sophisticated, and sharper than a four-inch stiletto . . . As always, hits it perfectly."

—Lauren Weisberger, *The Devil Wears Prada*

"A reigning queen of the genre."

—*Kirkus Reviews*

This Song Is About Me

A NOVEL

MELISSA DE LA CRUZ

Little a

This is a work of fiction. Names, characters, organizations, places, events, and incidents are either products of the author's imagination or are used fictitiously. Otherwise, any resemblance to actual persons, living or dead, is purely coincidental.

Published by Little A, New York

www.apub.com

EU product safety contact:
Amazon Media EU S. à r.l.
38, avenue John F. Kennedy, L-1855 Luxembourg
amazonpublishing-gpsr@amazon.com

ISBN-13: 9781662533693 (hardcover)
ISBN-13: 9781662533686 (paperback)
ISBN-13: 9781662525360 (digital)

Cover design by Lucy Kim
Cover image: © Pete Thompson Photography / Gallery Stock;
© Ekaterina Goncharova / Getty

Printed in the United States of America
First edition

*For Mattie, who continues to be
an inspiration in every way*

PROLOGUE

Amid the glitz and glamour of MTV's Video Music Awards in New York City on a balmy night in late August of 2018, international pop icon Ryan Holding disappeared off the face of the earth.

Many people talked with Ryan that night. Audiences all over the world saw her sit regally as she always did, in an electric-blue blazer that matched her startling eyes, with diamonds on the shoulders and a signature red lip as she applauded the other artists with her wry smile.

At precisely 10:17 p.m. Eastern time, Ryan ascended the stage of Radio City Music Hall to accept the award for Video of the Year, which officially made her the most-awarded female artist in MTV history.

The video that had earned her the honor, "Hear Me Now," played on the enormous screen behind her as she addressed the crowd. It was a visual feast—vaudeville costumes interspersed with hypnotic modern dance, nods to old Hollywood and early cinematography all set across a lush set that captured the timeline of her career, from her bluegrass roots to her cross-genre collaborations to her most recent achievements in Los Angeles.

Ryan stood at the microphone with her silver astronaut trophy in her hands. Some have said she looked sad in that moment; others have named her expression as resolute.

Still others, scared.

"I can't tell you all what this means to me," she said. Her voice had long since lost its rural Massachusetts accent, but a hint of it seemed to creep back into her *a*'s. "Every day, I find it hard to believe this life is mine. But I hope—I hope it's all been worth it."

She stared into the crowd for a moment—seven silent seconds, to be exact—as she stood before them.

It's a moment that has been analyzed by fans, conspiracy theorists, discussion boards, and journalists alike. What was she thinking? Was she looking at someone? Was she on something? About to say something else? For those seven seconds, it seemed that all of Radio City Music Hall held its breath.

Then Ryan shook her head and said, "Thank you, New York. Thank you."

She descended the stage to thunderous applause.

And then she disappeared.

It was an event with cameras everywhere—mine included. As a celebrity photojournalist, I'd run in the same circles as Ryan; I'd seen her rise to fame and photographed her peers.

But despite all the press and red-carpet clamoring before, during, and after the event, I was the only one to capture Ryan's photo as the crowds were leaving. *The* photo. The one of Ryan amid the music industry's finest, framed against the curved stairs of Radio City's grand lobby, looking back over her shoulder.

I happened to catch her right as she was looking toward the camera. I'll always be proud of that.

She's going down to the lower level, not up or out, in the photo—counter to the current of people moving toward the exits.

No one knows where she went after that.

In the six years that have passed since the 2018 VMAs, Ryan Holding has not been seen in the public eye. Her social accounts remain in place, untouched. Her band has broken up. Her Malibu estate sits quiet.

Was it foul play? A publicity stunt? A conspiracy?

Nobody seems to have the answer.

~

What follows is the first comprehensive published study of Ryan's life and career up to the point of her disappearance, through the eyes of key witnesses to her fame: childhood friends, ex-lovers, colleagues, media personnel, bandmates, producers—even Ryan herself, through her myriad and well-documented media appearances, interviews, documentaries, and original content.

By following the firsthand accounts of those who scorned and worshipped her alike, in their own words, I hope to create a portrait of Ryan that goes far beyond the public-facing character she presented to her fans and to shed light on what could have happened to her in the final moments of her fame.

Even casual fans of Ryan will be familiar with the fact that she was somewhat of a mastermind with a proclivity for symbolism and clues placed carefully for her fans to find.

While my work in this project draws heavily on what internet sleuths and Ryan's devoted fandom, the Ryde-or-Dies, have already made clear, I will also document the evidence in Ryan's final VMA video in the hopes that it will provide the answers to our many, many questions.

Because something tells me she wants to be found.

And I intend to find her.

PART I

ONE

ELYSE JAMES, *AUTHOR*

Who is Ryan Holding?

You already know the answer to that question. Most readers on this earth will be familiar with such a famous name, and while I hesitate to overestimate how widely this book might be published, Ryan herself has topped the charts in upward of seventeen countries.

If one were to conduct the briefest Google search, they would be overwhelmed with the sheer amount of information and opinions on this pop star, even discounting the flood of investigative material of recent years that covers her disappearance.

And much of that investigation concerns her final music video, set to the single "Hear Me Now."

For the uninitiated, Ryan's video was primarily shot in the historic State Theatre in downtown Los Angeles, one of the surviving movie palaces built in the 1920s. It opens on Ryan alone on the ornate stage in a simple blue dress, with her banjo, under a massive papier-mâché model of an old oak tree. There is a small table next to her that holds a glowing crystal ball.

Ryan begins to sing: *Just a whisper in the night / That's how all of this went down / People say I chose my path / It was the other way around.*

She reaches the end of the first verse, and the music swells as her band joins her, silhouetted and backlit behind her on the stage. At the same time, the movie screen above them flickers to life and begins to play old footage of Ryan's shows and media appearances. The two scenes continue to play out concurrently and, at first, parallel each other: Ryan performs at a bluegrass festival on-screen while below, she mirrors her own movements and wears the same silver minidress and cowgirl boots as she sings. The band behind her grows closer and increases in number as other people crowd the stage, just out of the light; and then, as footage of Ryan's first arena show plays and Ryan sings *And you wanted me for your own,* the arms of the crowd reach out and yank her into the darkness as blue strobes flicker.

The lights rise again, and the stage is lushly decorated: marquee lights and chintz furniture, the band fully lit and dressed in old Hollywood style with Ryan looking like a femme fatale in a dark-red sequined dress at the center, hand on an old-fashioned microphone. Concert footage continues to play above her, along with clips caught by paparazzi of her dates with famous men.

And I wanted you for my own, she sings.

As the song plays, it can be seen that Ryan is gradually rising above the stage on a platform, and the camera cuts to the back of the theater, where water has begun to trickle down the aisle. A group of women, dressed to the hilt, gather below Ryan's platform and sneer at her. The water rises. Soon it's lapping around the red velvet seats in the audience, and objects can be seen floating in its churn: an old flannel shirt, a red Solo cup, a toy boat with the name ANGELINE on its side.

A young man appears near the bottom of the platform and reaches out his hand. Ryan takes it to bring him up with her, but instead he yanks her hard and nearly pulls her off. The screen above briefly shows Ryan being interviewed outside a hotel in the rain, and the blue strobes flash even brighter than last time. Water begins to flood from the balcony, from the box seats. Another sneering woman in a bright-orange dress stands in front of the box's drenched velvet curtains and pours buckets of water over the railing.

Onstage, Ryan is now in a long black gown with an ornate lace cape, silvery white, as the water laps at the platform. She begins the bridge—*I've been here singing my heart out / Can you hear me now? / Will you hear me now?*—and the deluge engulfs her at last, lifting herself and her band off their feet and into the depths.

The singing becomes muffled and distorted as Ryan tangles in her heavy clothes and instruments float around her: a fiddle, a banjo, a set of drums. The cape is caught on an electric guitar, and Ryan is able to yank free as the chorus returns loud and clear. She reaches out to grasp the crystal ball and clutches it close to her chest before kicking hard and swimming upward.

In the ornate ceiling, she locates a hatch and pushes against it, swinging it open as the music swells and abruptly stops as Ryan climbs out into an empty field in rural Massachusetts alone, now back in the light-blue dress. The crystal ball rolls to the side as the camera slowly pans away, silent but for the distant sound of wind and birdsong.

~

Obsessed as it is with her, the world can't seem to make up its mind about Ryan Holding. She's an American sweetheart. She's a sex symbol. A prude. A slut. She's single-handedly destroying the climate. She's the most involved human rights activist we've ever seen in Hollywood. She's authentic, just like us. She's a Chinese psyop. She's immortal and looks suspiciously like that satanic cult leader from the '70s. She's gay. She's Republican. She's the epitome of white feminism. She receives unfair, disproportionate criticism because she's a woman who makes music for women, and everyone secretly hates and envies her for her unfathomable global success.

But let's start at the beginning, before Ryan was any of that.

When her story began, she was an ambitious young girl growing up in the idyllic suburbs of Hamilton, Massachusetts.

I visited the town in the fall of 2019 when I began my interviews for this book and found it hard to believe—but fitting, maybe—that someone as prolific as Ryan would come from such a tucked-away place with hardly a Main Street to its name. No more than twenty minutes outside Salem and twice that from Boston, Hamilton has a cozy population of seventy-five hundred and owes its fame to Ryan. Its residents live on forested back roads and must travel to nearby Wenham for any restaurants or shopping.

It was here in this woodland that Ryan was raised by her schoolteacher mother, Barbara, and banker father, John, who sadly passed away from cardiac arrest shortly after Ryan's disappearance.

Her mother, now living in a very exclusive retirement community in South Carolina, is almost impossible to reach. In the single instance that she deigned to take my call after the many messages I'd left for her with the tight-lipped front desk, Barbara had shared only a few short words: "Leave my daughter alone. Do you hear me? I have nothing else to say to you people."

"Do you know where she is?" I'd pressed. "People care about her. They just want to be sure that she's safe."

"You think so? You'd be wrong," Barbara said. "They don't give a shit about her."

And she hung up on me.

I didn't exactly disagree with her. A lot of people—millions, in fact—might genuinely claim to care about Ryan's well-being. And they may truly believe they're being sincere. But would that still be the case if she'd *chosen* to step away from the spotlight?

The line I fed Barbara was just another iteration of the phrase that had been thrown around many times across the internet: *The fans have a right to know.* People feel personally responsible for Ryan's rise to fame. No artist would ever be successful without the audience that celebrates them, shows up to their concerts, buys and listens to their records in order to put them at the top of the charts time and time again. It's a working relationship—akin to ghosting your job without notice.

But it's also a parasocial one. A career in which your entire life is on display.

I'm a private person myself, and my line of work suits me. I get to put others in the limelight while generally staying out of it. I've seen time and again how celebrities become products, human commodities. And although it's my hope that Ryan disappeared willingly, I've also developed a greater understanding of the sheer amounts of money that change hands when you live in that stratum of wealth. It gives the illusion that you're protected, impenetrable. But look at the cases of Selena, of Brad Pitt's assault on the red carpet, of Kim Kardashian's Paris robbery at gunpoint. And while those attacks were perpetrated by people lower in prestige than their victims, we hear even less about the crimes of megamillionaires and billionaires. Money is an excellent tool for keeping things quiet.

Ryan may have been the richest female musician to date. But there are other fish bigger than she is, and they're powerful enough to make anyone disappear.

~

Out of everyone I interviewed in Hamilton, the person with whom I wanted to speak most was almost as difficult to reach as Barbara Holding had been. Her name is well known to any Ryde-or-Die, who must often wish to be in her place: Mari Stevens, Ryan's oldest and closest friend.

She'd dodged my messages across several different platforms, finally sending the brief DM "You have to fucking stop" before blocking me entirely.

I'm no stalker. But any journalist worth her salt would know how to find Mari's address—public information—and at least attempt a visit to Hamilton in the hopes of casually running into her at Crosby's.

The town that fall was beautiful—misty, wooded lanes with overhanging trees the color of scarlet and gold, little roadside coffee shops, and farms with chalkboard easels advertising fresh eggs and pumpkins like an aesthetic Instagram fever dream. The lyrics of "September Rain" came easily to mind—*You drove me down that autumn lane, September long ago / I drank you in like gentle rain and never thought of snow.*

I started at Mari's house and drove up the long, winding lane looking for signs of life. The houses here are modest but set atop large plots of land with plenty of privacy. When I reached the end of the drive, I came to a quaint green cottage with white shutters and flower beds in the front yard.

At the door there was no answer.

I waited in my car thirty minutes, forty-five. When I got sick of turning the engine on and off for warmth, I pulled away to regroup.

I drove past the house where Ryan grew up, long since sold for more money than it was likely worth. It's a two-story colonial on an acreage, facade now modernized with slapdash board-and-batten and startling black shutters and trim.

I personally found Mari's house much cozier.

The wide oak tree in the front yard is referenced lyrically in Ryan's first album, in "Honeywine": *I loved you deep and tall just like the oak in my front yard / You left me alone and hollow with your crooked, wooden heart*; and visually in her final music video, where a gnarled papier-mâché representation looms over Ryan as she plucks her banjo on an ornate stage. The final part of the video, in fact, was filmed right there in Hamilton.

I was just wondering whether I should check the grocery store for Mari when my phone buzzed in my pocket.

When I lifted it to answer, I was surprised to see her name on the screen.

"Mari?" I answered.

"It looks like you're in town," she said. Her voice wasn't exactly friendly, but it at least wasn't as hostile as I'd expected.

"I am," I said. "I just stopped by your house, actually."

"I'm well aware." She let out a long sigh. "You still want to talk?"

~

Below, along with our other key witnesses, I present Mari's story in her own words.

MARI STEVENS

No, I don't know what happened to Ryan. That's the first thing I want to say, so I'm saying it. I changed my mind about talking to you because . . . I don't know. I just miss her.

I think what you're doing is a cheap cash grab, if you do in fact want me to be completely honest. I don't want to say that I've given up hope, but I don't know how much good any of this is going to do. I mean, it's been a year. What's the rule—the first forty-eight hours in a missing persons case are the most important, and after that, the chances of finding them diminish exponentially?

By the time anyone realized Ryan was missing after the VMAs, like *missing* missing, it had been longer than that.

Maybe I decided to talk to you because . . . I still feel like that's my fault.

I was with her that night, yes. Ryan was supposed to ride with the rest of our group to the after-party, but she told us to go ahead because she wanted to stop back at the hotel and work out some lyrics that were in her head. That wasn't unusual—she would run off at all hours of the day and night, try stuff out, record something that she'd been working over. I figured she probably got some ideas from everything surrounding the awards show. So I let her go, and I went on with my night . . . I should have known something was wrong. Picked up on signs. Trusted my gut. She was . . . off, in a way.

But I didn't act fast enough. I—

I don't know. It's hard to talk about. I haven't talked to anyone but the police, really. You must know that. It's a big part of the reason I moved back here, to get away from it all. I never liked LA in the first place. Plus, it eventually became apparent that I was out of a job, running Ryan's marketing team and having nothing to market. And I'm not going to say that the cost of living is much cheaper here, but what with buying my parents' house at a discount and investing my savings from Ryan's tours, I'm pretty comfortable. I do the marketing for North Shore Music Theatre now. It's nice.

But . . . it's easier to miss her here. Or to feel like that whole whirlwind was a bizarre dream, and now I'm back where I started. Some days it feels like I could just walk down the road to her house like I used to—I'm sure you know how close it is. You probably already drove over there. Did you see what they did to it? It used to be this beautiful brick, with lanterns by the front door . . . Yes, they put that shitty plywood right over the brick.

Anyway.

Ryan and I met at the tiny elementary school in Hamilton. She was the new kid in fourth grade, since her parents had just moved into town. I remember seeing her in front of the class, all twiggy with this curly red hair up in a thick ponytail. I thought to myself, *These girls are going to eat her alive.*

I'd had some trouble with my classmates, see. Kids can be really cruel. I don't even remember how the bullying started, but there was a group of girls who would pick up on the dumbest, most insignificant things—the ones that just happened to be the very thing you were most insecure about. Like, I have a birthmark on the back of my neck. No big deal, right?

But for whatever reason, this little clique decides it doesn't like me, so one day when I was wearing my hair up, one of them shouted, "Look at Mari's neck! Gross! Is that dirt?"

"It's just a birthmark," I said.

"It looks like dirt," said another one. "You look like Pigpen from Charlie Brown."

It wasn't an insult that was even very clever or creative. But dammit, they called me Pigpen from that point forward, and it bothered me so much that I wore my hair down every single day, even in gym class, even when it was ninety degrees in our classroom with no air-conditioning in August.

So you can imagine the kind of treatment I thought Ryan would get.

And I feel horrible admitting this—I already admitted it to her long ago, and she forgave me, so I can say it here. But I was irritated when she sat next to me at lunch that day. I thought, *Oh great, she's just going to make it worse for both of us.* Because that's how it worked, right? The law of the jungle and all.

And sure enough, those girls walked by and immediately said something like "Look, Pigpen's got a new friend!"

"Pigpen and Pinky!"

I saw Ryan hesitating with a half smile, trying to work out what was going on. I could feel my face going red in that way I hate—I've always wished I could control it, but in any stressful situation, I look like a beet.

"I love Pigpen," she said, giving me a meaningful glance. "I read him in the comics—he's so cute! But who's Pinky?"

"Pinky, like from *Pinky and the Brain*?" one of the girls said, like she was talking to someone impossibly stupid. "You look like that skinny lab rat."

"Oh!" Ryan said brightly. "I haven't seen it. Is it a good show?"

The lead girl made a face. "Everybody's seen it. Do you live in a hobo shack or something?"

Like I said—not clever.

Ryan just shrugged. "I don't watch a lot of TV."

The girl smirked at her. "That's pretty weird."

I was feeling a lot of secondhand embarrassment by that point, but Ryan gave her a wide, genuine smile. "I know, right?" she said. "I'll have to watch it and tell you what I think!"

The girl frowned. "Whatever."

The group gave up and walked away, hardly giving a backward glance; Ryan watched them go.

"You really don't know *Pinky and the Brain*?" I had asked, still being kind of snotty. It was a weird mix of emotions—irritation that she had brought this on us, surprise by how she'd handled it, and relief that the attention hadn't been on me.

Ryan turned back and looked me right in the eyes. "Duh, I know *Pinky and the Brain*," she said in a much different, more down-to-earth voice than the bubbly one she'd been using before. "What I *didn't* know is how many assholes there would be at this school."

I stared at her. Even in the years afterward, I barely heard her swear. I think she picked a very choice moment to employ *asshole*, to show me who she really was.

And then I burst out laughing.

She did too. And from that point forward, we were best friends.

Apart from the little shits at school, we had a good childhood; sometimes there's this perception that the best art comes from people who have suffered in life, but Ryan and I were happy kids. We rode our bikes to school, swam at Ipswich, had sleepovers, and made friendship bracelets. She was always humming, coming up with little melodies even back then. She would write out poems and songs in this little pocket notebook that she carried with her *everywhere*. It was packed with these wrinkled, dog-eared pages that were almost illegible with pencil and pen scribblings that, to be honest, were so, so angsty back then. An all-American green-eyed girl with that wild hair I always envied, who came from a comfortable background and caught fish off the Walnut Road bridge in the summer—what did she have to be angsty about?

But Ryan was very into Emily Dickinson's poetry, and her mother was born and raised in Kentucky, where she lived until she moved to New York for school. So Ryan was introduced early on to all that bluegrass music. I swear, the first thing she downloaded when she got an MP3 player was "House of the Rising Sun" by Doc Watson. I don't think she knew what it meant—I mean, I hope she didn't, at that age—but she was raised on those old folk songs.

It resulted in her being this strange, sort of ethereal kid. Walking around in her own world, listening to these mournful songs in her headphones, all wrapped up in her notebook. She was tall and lanky, even back then, and it made her stick out in groups. Ryan didn't have many friends, and neither did I—we leaned on each other—but that didn't mean she was shy.

She was one of those weirdos—I say that very fondly—who would break out into song during recess or sing to herself while she was at her locker. This did mean, unfortunately, that she was the target of more than a few unkind comments. But she generally let that roll off her back. And here's the thing—she had the talent to do so.

I remember we had a middle school talent show, just an informal thing, and Ryan brought the ukulele she'd gotten for Christmas. I saw the faces of some of the other girls when Ryan walked up to play, like, *Oh boy, here we go.*

But where anyone else at that age would have strummed simple chords and sung Alanis Morissette or something, Ryan fingerpicked the most delicate, haunting melody. It was one she'd written herself. It was never published, but I remember it. I always thought she should try to rework and record it: *Meet me under the willow, the willow / When the full moon is high / Hear me call on the air when the wind blows / I'll be there by your side.*

Eleven years old. She wrote that. Near rhyme and all.

A lot of the people who criticize Ryan now don't listen to her music. It's easy to look at her fame, which—let's be honest—is almost obscene, not that she can really control that. But if you actually attended her shows, listened closely to the lyrics, understood what she was doing and the musical tradition she's rooted in—she proved herself every time.

The girls in our class stopped making fun of her after that day. I know for a *fact* that Stacy Hiester asked for a ukulele for her birthday the very next week.

But, of course, Ryan's instrument of choice was the banjo.

For more on that, you'll want to talk to Frank.

FRANK GREENFIELD, *Ryan's first teacher*

Oh, Ryan. She was a whiz on the banjo. I've been thinking of her lately, just as I'm having my grandson help me clean out the studio before I move into assisted living at Gardner Park. He tells me I could sell any of my instruments for a fortune now that people know my name. I say, what do I need a fortune for?

He says, *Well if you wouldn't use it, I could.*

He's a good kid.

But I couldn't part with any of those instruments—not for money, anyway. Probably donate them. I've got guitars, banjos, ukes—used to own a shop after my old jug band broke up, you know, and I dealt to plenty of folks out in New York and all up and down the seaboard. Not to be mystical about it, but every instrument carries a little piece of its player.

Ryan understood that. She had a real respect for that banjo she received on her eleventh birthday. It was her mom who bought it; she came in the shop and told me she had a little girl who was killing it on the uke and ready to branch out to something new. Well, guitar is the next clear choice.

But no, Barb said her girl was a little different. Thought she'd like a banjo. The two of them enjoyed listening to a lot of bluegrass and jam bands together. So I showed her the models I had, and I always offered a free lesson with the purchase of any instrument—so long as it was one I could play, anyway.

Ryan came in that very next week. This waify ginger girl carrying this banjo that was almost as long as she was tall. But she had this determination to her I rarely saw. Most kids, they're just playing for the fun of it, yeah? Not Ryan. She was bright and bubbly, all right, don't get me wrong. But when we sat down to it, she approached the chords and hand positions with all the focus of a concert pianist down at Carnegie Hall.

I remember thinking, *What's your plan, kid?* Because you could tell she was in it for the long haul.

She seemed to like the lesson well enough; she kept coming back for more, and her mom signed her up for a regular schedule. We worked through all the basics quickly. She'd managed to teach herself everything she knew about the ukulele—not impossible, but pretty impressive for a kid of that age—and although there were a few hand positioning techniques we had to course correct, she caught on quickly.

In fact, if I was pressed, I'd say that was her one fault: being so eager. The banjo is not like the guitar. Rather than strumming, the playing is based on fingerpicking, or what we call those "rolls" on the strings to form individual notes instead of chords. You've got to go real slow on the rolls when you start out to avoid any mistakes—because if you make mistakes while you're building those skills, your brain will have a hell of a time undoing it as you get faster and faster.

Slow down, slow down—that was probably the phrase I said most to Ryan in those early days. And she'd laugh and laugh and just keep going.

But she made it work. Before long, we were picking out songs together for her to try playing. I was surprised by her taste. She really began to nail songs with simpler melodies: "Hear the Wind Blow" or "Little Sparrow." She'd sing along with them, too, in this light and wistful voice.

And that's when things began to get interesting. Because Ryan started bringing in her own songs to workshop with me.

MARI

Ryan never shut up about those banjo lessons, I swear. I say that lovingly. She'd always be reading off lyrics to me, bringing them to Frank, asking what I thought about this melody or another.

But I could feel her excitement—all those scribbles she'd had in her notebook were finally getting an outlet somewhere. It was hard to understand what was actually happening in her creative process to us as twelve-year-olds back then, but I think the mentorship with Frank, someone who knew music and knew what he was doing, forced Ryan to really *look* at her songs and pick out the better ones from the little-kid ramblings. Then that batch got refined and refined even further.

I mean, I say all of this knowing she was no major musician at that point. She *was* still a kid, just messing around and trying to make something that sounded cool. It was just that she was taking it more seriously than other kids her age might have, and she was lucky that it was Frank on the other end of her questions about songwriting and performing and working in the music industry.

I don't call myself a musician, and sometimes I pinpoint that to a third-grade piano lesson when my crabby old teacher told me I had technical skill but no emotion in my playing. I mean, who says that to a third grader?

But Frank was nothing if not encouraging. I went with Ryan to his shop one day. It's that cute little place on Union, used to be an old barn. And I was just messing around with a secondhand folk harp he had while Ryan was talking to him. I still remember, Frank came over and said it sounded good.

"Is that Pachelbel?" he asked.

"Oh yeah," I said. It was just something I remembered from piano lessons; I didn't realize I was managing to play any recognizable tune.

"That's one of my favorites," he said. "You're welcome to play that harp anytime you're here."

So I did. I followed along with Ryan on a lot of her lessons and just hung out while she and Frank played, and he'd give me a few pointers at the end. After a few months of it, I was able to play a pretty decent "Canon in D" just by ear. And Frank came over and said: "I don't want to risk this harp going to anyone else after you've spent so much time with it. I think you'd better take it with you today."

My parents were up in arms when I got home, but I didn't know any better. He said to take it, so I did. They tried to call him to either return or pay for it, but Frank told them it was a run-down old model and I'd been the first one to show interest in it in years; he was trying to clear inventory.

But that harp was in perfect shape. Still is, right over there in the living room.

Ryan was over the moon. "We can play together now!" she'd said.

We had some good jam sessions, but harp and banjo isn't a common pairing for a reason, and it was harder for me to transport my instrument. Of course, you'll have heard me on some of her later recordings, after I had some actual lessons, and you'll remember that she somehow convinced me to play onstage for "Keep Me" years later—god, I still have stress dreams about that show.

But it became clear that we got very different things out of playing. It's fun for me, relaxing; if I have a hectic day with North Shore, I'll come home and just play for an hour or two in the evening. I get a lot of comfort from it.

Ryan, on the other hand . . . I don't know. That banjo was like a tool for her, a way to work out all this noise that I gradually realized was constantly in her head. Her face when she played—it's hard to describe. I sometimes thought of it as her and the instrument locked in a wrestling match, with Ryan working the strings harder and harder to see if they could measure up to the song only she could hear, and the strings in turn testing the limits of her skill. She *wanted* something out of it, something big, and she was never completely satisfied by what she got.

Ryan improved scary fast. I think even Frank was a little unnerved by it.

FRANK

Boy, she was flying. Within a year or two of our lessons, I started to think—at this rate, this kid will outpace me by Christmas. And you know, younger musicians always have that elasticity on their side; their brains are better wired to pick up a skill, and do so quickly. But Ryan was a special case even with that in mind, and I knew she'd soon outgrow my dusty little studio and need a better way to challenge herself.

I had a bulletin board in the back of the shop, just a place where local musicians could tack their business cards or band flyers or notices about instruments for sale. Ryan often lingered by it, I saw. She'd been so fired up to play with Mari, but I know that sort of petered out—I don't blame Mari. It seemed like everyone in Hamilton was having a tough time keeping up with Ryan. What she wanted was to be part of a musical community.

So I was poking around for opportunities to help make that happen for her.

And one afternoon, I opened my mail to find a very interesting brochure.

And I got an idea.

TWO

HOLLYWOOD REPORT MAGAZINE, "In Her Own Words" profile, November 2012
RYAN HOLDING

I think I was just thirteen when I went on what I like to call my "first tour." Before then, I'd played in my bedroom, for my friends, for my teacher. And there was something very special about that. I had room to experiment, to be bad; I bounced a million awful and unoriginal ideas off my little circle, and I'm lucky they still supported me through that.

Honestly, I once wrote a song about feeling like a frog stuck in the mud. I mean, sure, in the right hands it could've worked—if Three Dog Night did it, maybe. But not me. One of the lyrics was something like "My legs are meant to swim, but I can't move an inch"—like, whew! It's a good thing I got that out of my system.

But that's what you need to do as a creative, right? You have to have the freedom and support to let things be "good" or "bad" so you can find the voice that's really yours. And it's going to sound really strange and unfamiliar at first—because you've never heard anything exactly like it before.

At the same time . . . you can't work in a vacuum. I hear so many of these really tough, singular artists being all, *I work alone. No one understands me. My sound is so unique.*

Okay, sure. Except everything we make is informed by all the musical traditions that came before us; our music exists in conversation with other artists. You're not special, buddy.

Bluegrass made me understand this more than any other genre would have. Hazel Dickens, Doc Watson, Elizabeth Cotten, Flatt and Scruggs—and Arnold Shultz even before them, who developed the thumb-style picking we still use today. They're all building off this old American music and then off each other. They pay tribute to each other's sound. And it grows and grows: Singers like Dolly Parton and Olivia Newton-John built careers off bluegrass and folk. It lends itself to community with others and these incredible cross-genre opportunities.

It's an amazing thing, it really is. It's very close to my heart.

But back then, like I say, I didn't have any of that community. I have my first teacher to thank for changing that. And my parents. And my friends.

The whole bluegrass community, in fact—I'm a lucky gal.

MARI

So, I want to be clear. Everyone who talks about Ryan's privilege, her silver-spoon upbringing, the chances she got that no one else had—I mean, I'm not here to go on record and tell you that they're *wrong.*

I think, in a lot of ways, that's the point of most famous people. That's why they call it a "lucky break." Anyone who's successful in life, in any field, has arrived there because they had the skills to do so *combined* with opportunities that weren't available to others. It's nature *and* nurture. There are also plenty of people in the world who have opportunities that aren't available to others, and they do *nothing* with them.

Ryan took the opportunities presented to her. And one lot in life in which she was extremely lucky was the fact that she had supportive, open-minded parents.

I was actually having dinner with Ryan and her family the night that Frank called about the River Rocks festival. She and I were setting the table while Barb made spaghetti, and it was John who answered the phone.

"How are you, Frank?" he asked, which was our cue to start listening—the call was definitely about Ryan, and possibly me, if Frank was on the other end.

I remember him saying something like "Oh. Well, that sounds—you just mean to attend, right?" He'd frowned into the phone and then said "Oh" again, glanced back at us. We pretended we weren't paying any attention.

"Well, I don't know," he said at last. "We'll have to have a talk about it and let you know . . . All right . . . All right . . . You too."

Ryan and I shared a glance and hurried to sit down at the table as fast as we could. John looked perturbed as Barb dished out the spaghetti and joined us.

"Ryan," John said as we picked up our forks. "You have any interest in going to a bluegrass festival?"

"Sure," she said. "But only if I can play in it."

And John looked at her very levelly. He hadn't even begun to eat his dinner.

"Did Frank say anything to you about this?"

"About a festival? No," Ryan answered. Although John and Barb looked skeptical, I believed her; I would have heard about it too.

"Which festival?" Barb asked.

"It's called River Rocks, Frank said. Down in Rhode Island. I don't know anything about it, but Frank told me it might be a good opportunity." John shrugged.

"That could be fun," said Barb. "I don't think you've ever heard any live bluegrass, have you, Ry?"

"Never ever," Ryan said. "When is it?"

"End of August. The tickets aren't cheap." John rubbed his chin. "But . . . Frank thought you might be able to go as a performer."

"What?" Barb said.

And Ryan grinned.

"She's barely thirteen," Barb protested.

John opened his hands to avoid blame. I just sat there with my head going back and forth like I was watching a tennis match and wondering what the odds were that I'd be allowed to go to Rhode Island too.

"There's a new-artist stage," John went on. "Sounds like they have young talent perform sometimes."

"What do I have to do?" Ryan asked.

John finally looked back at her. "Record a tape, I think. And if they like it, there's an audition in June."

"I'll get started, then," Ryan said.

"Hold on, now," said Barb. "Your father and I have to talk about this. We need to check this thing out, make sure it's going to be a—well, a wholesome place for young ladies. Heck, we need to look at the calendar to see if we can even make those dates."

"Do what you need to do," Ryan said, spooling a massive bite of spaghetti onto her fork.

That was her, to a T; she didn't want to wait. She wanted everything to move as quickly in reality as the vision that was materializing in her head. I could almost feel the energy radiating off her from the other side of the table. In her mind, I knew, she was already on that stage in August, unleashing her music into the breeze off the Atlantic.

FRANK

She crushed the audition tape, of course. I helped her with the application form and let her use the little studio and mic equipment in my shop to record two songs of her choosing. She wanted both of them to be original, but I encouraged her to do at least one cover—the judges would want some point of comparison. We'd been working on "Travelin' This Lonesome Road" by the Osborne Brothers, so she went with that.

I've talked a lot about her string skills, but not much about her voice. I know so much has been said about it—hell, they've had folks down at Johns Hopkins write articles about her vocal cords by now. But it was just real pretty even then, sweet and clear. A Massachusetts kid through and through, but Ryan managed to nail that traditional bluegrass vocal break that's such a hallmark of the genre. Maybe it was in her blood, with Barb being from Kentucky and all.

It was still a young girl's voice, but it had some weight to it. She sang like she was really thinking about the words coming out of her mouth. How many kids genuinely grasp the feeling an adult would have, listening to a song like "Lonesome Road" about being all alone while storms are raging. But she did, somehow. Or was at least able to represent what she didn't fully understand.

She did do a couple of takes to get a recording she was happy with. After the third or fourth time around, Ryan ended the song and did this firm nod of her head, and I knew. To be honest, all the takes had sounded like winners to me.

"That sounds real nice in your range," I said.

And she looked straight at me and told me, "Well, that's why there should be more bluegrass singers who are girls!"

And I laughed. Not *at* her, not at all, but—well, she did like to speak her mind. And she wasn't wrong.

With the next piece, I let her go ahead and record one of her own songs. I'd worked with her a little bit on some of them. I know this book you're writing isn't about me, but I'm not too humble to admit I had some success back in the day. I was the leader of my jug band, and we did do the festival circuit and some New York shows on the songs I wrote. Got a couple of awards for them, nothing to puff me up too much, but enough for a steady gig schedule. I was happy to help Ryan out with chord progression, hooks, bridge ideas, the like.

But the lyrics were all her own. I'm not touching that—and I didn't need to. She would come in with her tattered old notebook and just write about what was on her mind that day, the things that happened in school, and so forth. But she had a way of framing them so poetically—I mean, Ryan's what happened when you took the lyricism and depth of Bill Monroe and packaged it in the perspective of a thirteen-year-old girl.

She still had a normal life, back then. I'll say this: When I suggested River Rocks to the Holdings, those festivals were as far as I ever expected or intended Ryan to go. It was my opinion that she needed a community and an outlet for her obvious talent. But the way she soared was nothing I could have predicted.

Should have, maybe. I think we all underestimated her.

Now, I'm no "hater," as my grandson would call me. And wherever she may be, god bless her, I still say I'm Ryan's biggest fan. But I—I do feel responsible. Would I have set her on this path if I knew it would cost her her childhood, the best of her teenage years—any sort of a normal life?

No. No, I don't think I would have.

I don't know. Maybe there was something in me that knew I couldn't stop her as I sat in that little studio listening to the song she recorded.

It was "Providence." Yes, the very one that appeared on her first album. I got to hear it before anyone else. It was a little different back then, but those verses—it was poetry beyond her years.

It's just you and me, William / How many years will we be young? / I'll keep you with me down this lonesome road. / It's Providence that brought me here / The same that sends you off, I fear. / I hope you'll wait for me on Wickenden.

William was—well, you know. He was that boy she ended up having so much trouble with down the line. The melody was something she'd been playing around with for some time. I know she adapted it to name the venue location for River Rocks, and I thought that was pretty clever of her. A nod to "Lonesome Road" to make for a nice pairing on her audition tape, a little homage to River Rocks' home. And it was pretty heads-up for a kid like that to grasp the double meaning of *Providence.*

"Have you even been to Rhode Island before?" I asked her. "How do you know Wickenden Street?"

Ryan grinned. "Looked at the atlas for something that would rhyme."

She recorded the song in one take. And she let it be what it was.

Of course, at those last concerts before her disappearance, she sang, *It's just you and me, William / How many years will we be young? / It's getting old to walk this lonesome road. / It's Providence that brought you here / The same that makes us strange, I fear. / You left me all alone on Wickenden.*

So, you know. The lyrics evolved to reflect what had happened.

THREE

JUSTIN WILLIAM AYERS, *RYAN'S FIRST BOYFRIEND*

Look. I already know I'm going to be the villain in this story, okay? But I'm just a regular human being who was swept up in this—in this web of Ryan's fame.

It wasn't a life any of us expected to live. Take the brains of kids, teenagers, going through puberty, and then throw them into nationwide visibility, throw them into mass attention, throw them into amounts of money they have no idea what to do with.

I'm not going to make excuses for any of my actions. I'm also not going to make any apologies that, quite frankly, I don't think I'm under any obligation to give.

All I ever asked for was my fair share. All I ever wanted was basic cut-and-dry recognition where recognition was due.

When I didn't get it, I had to take matters into my own hands.

But I'll get to that.

Yes, I am the William in "Providence." That's my middle name, that's the nickname she used for me all the way back then.

We sort of started dating, if you can call whatever thirteen-year-olds do "dating," the summer before her bluegrass thing in Rhode Island. She wanted it to be a secret. Thought it would be "thrilling" and "romantic." You'll learn this about Ryan, if you haven't already: She liked to make *way* too big of a deal out of things, have them her own way, create all this theatrical, elevated drama that was unsustainable for normal human relationships.

So maybe she was born for the life she ended up living, who knows.

But I'd never liked a girl before like I liked her. So I went along with it.

She always liked to call us star-crossed lovers. Ryan had these big plans she used to tell me about—*I'm going to travel the world, I'm going to make music, I can't stay in Hamilton forever*—and she would always dangle them over me like she wasn't sure I was in her future. I was like, dude, I'm thirteen, I don't really care.

I mean, I did care a little. Obviously.

She made everything feel kind of magic, even back then. I will give her this: For as huge as she got, for as much money as she made, Ryan never stopped being a great listener. The summer before she started doing all those festivals, Mari was gone with her parents on a trip to the Grand Canyon, and Ryan and I spent nearly the whole week together. Her parents probably knew there was something going on between us, but for all she told them, we were just friends—and the thing is, we were really good friends. She was cool; even though I liked country more than bluegrass, we had a lot of common ground. We both loved *Buffy the Vampire Slayer*. I told her that I wanted to be a writer when I grew up—I'd never told anyone else before. She read my stories and didn't laugh at them, and I read her songs. We had a lot of respect for each other.

I wish that was still true.

There was one day that week, Saturday, I think, that Ryan and I rode our bikes out to the Pingree Woodland trail and hiked from there. Mari was coming back the next day, so I wanted to make an impression. There's a marshy stream that flows through there, and we walked along it until we found an old stone bench to sit on. I was working up the guts to tell her something when she started first.

"I got into the festival," she said. She was talking about River Rocks.

"That's awesome," I said. "I'm really proud of you."

"I couldn't have done it without you," she said. "Because I wrote the song in my audition tape about you."

Do you have any idea what it feels like for someone to write a song about you? It's a special thing. It's like—wow. Someone liked me enough to put all this thought and creativity into something brand new, something that has never existed in this world before.

Except that wasn't quite it.

I want you to realize the difference, the one that took me forever to grasp: The song was written *about* me. It wasn't written *for* me. It was written *for* the audition tape, *for* the judges, *for* the purpose of advancing Ryan's chances at a career. Some old guy in Rhode Island got to hear that song before I ever did.

And yeah, it's her music, she can do what she wants, but there's a difference. There is.

I, on the other hand, had done something *for* Ryan that I wanted to share with her. I'd written her a poem.

THE poem.

> How do I capture your hummingbird heart?
> It's always moving, full of art
> I'll do what I can and return to the start
> To try to make you mine.

There's more, but you get the gist. And when I was done reading it to her, I asked her to be my girlfriend. She answered by leaning over and kissing me on the lips. My first kiss, there in Pingree Woodland. And no one ever knew.

MARI

Of course I knew about the kiss. It was *her* first kiss too—do you think my best friend wouldn't tell me something like that?

Justin is an asshole. I don't want to talk about him yet, but let me just put it like that: asshole. I didn't give much thought to him then—I knew about their "secret" relationship too. Maybe I had some lingering jealousy around Ryan, who knows. I'm only human. But I'm still glad he didn't come to Providence with us for the festival.

I was lucky that my family's Grand Canyon trip didn't overlap with River Rocks, because I honestly think I would have made my parents leave me behind otherwise. I could not *wait* to go. It was a three-hour drive down on Friday, and we skipped dinner because Ryan wanted to get to the festival ASAP. When we made it to the grounds just outside, you could already hear the music from a distance. It was . . . thunderous. I realized I hadn't been expecting much from a genre that wasn't rock, and before you come for me, remember that I'd only been listening to Ryan alone on her banjo all these months. But with those musicians together . . . it was unlike anything I'd heard before. They were *whaling* on the strings, singing at the top of their lungs—the crowds along with them, with all these wild harmonies and whoops. There was the main stage and two smaller ones, but people were spread all over the grass, jamming with each other in little groups or watching the performers.

"Why didn't I bring my banjo?" Ryan said next to me.

And then Frank came out of the crowd with a hot dog, waving to us and saying he was glad we made it.

"You see that big old stage?" he said to Ryan, pointing at the tall band shell with strings of carnival lights between its high rafters and the oak trees that dotted the park. "Tomorrow afternoon, that'll be you up there."

I remember watching her as she followed his gaze, the evening starting to fall around us. The fireflies were beginning to come out.

And she looked like she had come home.

~

I don't think Ryan slept that night. I, too, found myself pretty restless. At one point, becoming aware of the change in my breathing, Ryan whispered to me: "You awake?"

"I've hardly been to sleep," I whispered back.

She was quiet a moment. Then she said, "What if it all goes wrong tomorrow?"

"What could go wrong?"

Ryan looked at me through the darkness. "My strings could break. I could faint. I could forget the words."

"You *wrote* the words," I said. She was going to sing both songs from her tape, and a third—"My Tennessee Mountain Home" by Dolly Parton—that she'd used for her in-person audition in Boston. "And you know the others by heart."

"Not always. I forget sometimes, even when I'm playing for Frank."

I studied her for a moment and realized she was genuinely scared. From standing up to that clique to her ukulele performance at school to her weird relationship with Justin, I hadn't seen her scared before. *This* is what she was afraid of failing at.

"Then just play for Frank. He'll be there," I said. "And play for me."

She closed her eyes and took a big, long breath.

"I think I can do that," she said.

~

Ryan's mom had to just about force-feed her in the morning.

"I am not letting you get on a stage in ninety-degree weather without having at least a little bit of protein," I remember Barb saying as she heaped the scrambled eggs from the hotel breakfast onto Ryan's plate. They were horrible eggs, dry and kind of gritty. Ryan was looking green as she tried to choke down a few forkfuls.

Yes, it was forecasted to be a high of ninety-two that day. When we stepped out of the air-conditioned hotel to load Ryan's banjo into the car, I could tell that for the first time she might have been genuinely doubting the decisions that had gotten her to this point. Her eyes were flat and staring straight ahead, her mouth in a thin line.

I only saw that look a few more times over the course of Ryan's career. But that day, it was there.

FRANK

Ryan didn't initially seem nervous when she and her crew came walking across the grass, but when I asked her how she was holding up, she just nodded, kind of looking through me. I thought maybe it was dawning on her that all these people here were going to be staring at her and watching her every move. River Rocks wasn't a huge festival by any means, but a couple thousand people was far more than the handful she'd performed in front of before.

Funny, isn't it? Ryan's played for a hundred million since then. But that day in Providence, the bluegrass crowd in the park must have felt like a stadium.

"Do they have any water backstage?" Ryan asked, sounding numb.

"Water, Gatorade, of course," I said. "Let's get you set up."

We got her tuned up while another young man performed his set, and I sat with her backstage while her parents and Mari went to watch.

"You feeling okay?" I asked. Her face was almost totally drained of color. I was feeling a bit nervous myself by this point. What if she had a rough experience and never wanted to play again? That would be okay, but I'd had such high hopes for her first bluegrass jam. I wanted it to be fun for her. I told her, "It's a tough day to perform. If you're not feeling up to it, I want you to know—that's completely okay."

She sort of snapped out of her stupor and looked me right in the eyes then. "I'm up for it," she said. "I'm fine."

Then she walked onstage, and I said a little prayer under my breath.

MARI

Ryan had picked her outfit very carefully, but I don't think any of us counted on the heat. She'd worn a short-sleeve cotton dress with blue-and-white flowers all over, and a denim vest, which she handed to me before she went backstage. I'd set it across my lap while we sat in the grass, and it felt like a lead blanket.

There was a guy older than us, maybe in his twenties, performing before Ryan went on, and he was *good.* His fingers were flying on the strings, he was whooping and hollering, stomping his feet on the stage and everything. The crowd was getting into it despite the heat too. I was a little bit dazzled by him, I'll admit it, but it also gave me this sinking feeling, of *Oh shit. Ryan has to follow this.*

And his set ended, and the crowd applauded and quieted.

Everyone waited, shifting on the lawn.

Suddenly this music started playing, and Ryan came onstage while strumming her first song, reaching the mic and pausing the strings just as her voice rang out sweet and clear across the park, singing about that lonesome road.

She drew it out a bit, letting the final note linger with her natural vibrato and giving a little *whoop* at the end. She called out loud and clear, "Well, hey there, River Rocks!"

Ryan restarted the first three notes of the song and came right back down on beat, stomping her leather-sandaled foot on the stage. A genuine, full-hearted cheer went up from the crowd, and they began clapping along with her.

There she was, looking completely at ease with her hair all around her shoulders, heavy and curly and thick in the humidity. I'd told her I could help her pin it up, but no, it was part of her look.

She was right to keep it that way. That hair became her signature.

FRANK

I was real proud of her. So proud.

I hold that my encouragement didn't make a bit of difference—Ryan pulled that confidence from somewhere within herself. You can't teach stage presence like that.

She moved seamlessly from the first song to "Providence," her own song. I hadn't coached her on the order, but she'd had the instinct to start strong, bring it down to something slow, and leave them on a high note. She barely even waited for applause when she finished "Lonesome Road," looking for a minute there as though she was entirely absorbed in her own world, picking out a little melody while she tuned a bit.

And when the audience was quiet, she began: *These sunny days a stubborn shadow's slipping 'cross my mind / The afternoon's a dream when I'm with you. / But I can see the ocean calling through these Norway pines / And I know what it's calling me to do.*

Her voice was cool, haunting. After the lively first song, she had her listeners in the palm of her hand for that mournful little piece she wrote. Watching from backstage, I swear I didn't see a muscle move the whole three minutes she was singing. Hell, even the guy in the taco truck back by the other vendors was leaning out to watch her, his elbows on his stainless-steel window counter.

You couldn't look away when she was singing like that.

MARI

When Ryan finished "Providence," I swear—no one moved. No one breathed.

And then she started "My Tennessee Mountain Home" just like the first one, a cappella, hands resting on the body of the banjo, using that same sort of lonely voice she'd used through "Providence," drawing out the words about sitting out on a front porch in the summer.

But as she went, she let her voice warm and lighten. And then she began fingerpicking again, pushing the tempo faster. She leaped up an octave on the second chorus, and I got goose bumps even in that August heat. Some people broke out cheering just for that.

By the time Ryan had reached the final refrain, the audience was singing along—she was encouraging them. She picked the final notes on the banjo and got a standing ovation.

I saw the mask slip, just a little, as relief flooded her face. Then she recovered and took a deep bow, throwing her hair back once again.

FRANK

I knew I'd created a monster when Ryan ran offstage with this huge grin and this look in her eye. She wasn't just happy about the performance—she was hungry. She wanted more.

MARI

The heat didn't seem to bother Ryan the whole rest of the day as we walked around the festival and watched the other acts. Nickel Creek was the headliner Saturday night, and Ryan sat there on our picnic blanket with her arms wrapped around her knees, drinking in every song.

We drove back to Hamilton very late that night. Between the excitement and the heat and being outside the whole day, I was exhausted. I fell asleep just about the second I plopped down in the back seat of the Holdings' Toyota.

But somewhere outside Boston, I woke up and looked over at Ryan. She was wide awake, staring out the window with her chin in her hand.

~

Three days later, she came over to me at lunch and smacked a folder down on the table. School started just after River Rocks, although it seemed to me that Ryan had hardly noticed we were back in the classroom. She said, "I made a deal."

She was looking very smug about it. "With who?" I asked.

"My parents." She opened the folder and showed me the pile of brochures and flyers she'd certainly taken from Frank's shop, advertising different festivals and bluegrass events all up and down the Eastern Seaboard.

"The hell is all this?" I asked.

"They agreed that any event I can get into, they'll take me. That includes all these fall festivals, the Salem Halloween ones, the holiday shows, and then next spring and summer when things start warming up again . . ."

I had stared at her. "You'll never have time for all this," I remember saying.

But I was wrong.

JUSTIN

Things really started to ramp up after Ryan did that River Rocks festival. I feel like I hardly saw her that eighth-grade year, which was tough, since I'd thought we were about to get closer.

It was like every other week she was gone. I still don't know how she got her parents to agree to it, but maybe they were starting to see dollar signs in this thing. Ryan wasn't just entering in festivals, but in competitions—and she was winning the kind of money that was unthinkable to a couple of middle schoolers.

A hundred bucks at Salem Days. One-fifty at Long Island Sound for the second-place prize, *three* hundred for first at Raleigh Rumble. She let me tag along with her and Mari sometimes, which is the only reason I knew I wasn't totally dumped—yet.

I'll be real with you. She was . . . spectacular.

I remember watching with this sort of slack-jawed awe. And I'm serious, I was happy to cheer her on. That was my girlfriend up there, playing like her hands were on fire? Hell yeah, it was. Mari and I made signs and got up in the front row. She would blow me kisses, and I just felt . . . yeah. I've never felt anything like that since then.

But that was only when she—and my parents—let me come with. When Ryan wasn't going to Boston or Albany or Poughkeepsie, she was scrambling to catch up with schoolwork or preparing for another audition cycle.

It got worse in the spring. I should have seen it coming, and maybe I had, deep down, but when Ryan asked me if I wanted to go for ice cream at Crosby's, I was just happy that she wanted to spend time with me again.

It was a sunny but cold spring day. I remember I was excited to see the leaves coming back on the trees because it meant that baseball season was coming. Ryan had come to a lot of my games the summer before River Rocks. I was hoping she'd do that again.

She was just as good at listening as she'd always been, but she'd become . . . I don't know, distracted. Ryan used to ask about *me*, how things were going in my life, but she just sort of—stopped.

I know how it sounds. I can hear her legions of fans coming at me like little yappy rabid dogs—*Oh, boo-hoo, he's so sad a beautiful, intelligent woman wasn't* interested *in him as a middle schooler!*

Yeah, it did make me sad. I was a kid, and she was my first girlfriend, and I really liked her.

So it shouldn't have surprised me when she had her mint chocolate chip, and I had my butter pecan, and we were sitting on top of the picnic table outside like we always did, that she turned to me with this really sorry look on her face.

"So . . . I'm going to compete in the Raleigh Bluegrass Festival in June," she said.

I knew what that meant. More practicing, more traveling. But I wanted to be supportive. "Hey, congrats," I said. "I know how hard you've been working for it. Can I come?"

"If you want." She looked down at her sneakers. "But the finalists go on to compete in Nashville in July. And . . . my dad is going to

Austin for work—Austin, *Texas*"—I remember she said *Texas* like it was impossibly far away from where we sat on Walnut Road—"so I'm going to try to plan something there too."

I nodded. Tried not to look at her. "Going to be a busy summer."

"Yeah."

That summer had already been looming over both our heads. We were going to start high school in the fall, and although that just meant moving to a different building down the street to Hamilton-Wenham, it felt like a huge leap. Some of our classmates were heading to Bishop Fenwick or Salem Prep, and it felt like we'd never see them again. It was already a lot of change.

Ryan went on, "Look, William . . ."

I wanted to save face. I preempted her and said, "Okay, so I guess I might not see you that much. If you want to just call it for now, that's—that's okay with me. I'll always be cheering you on from the sidelines."

"I'm really sorry," she said. "Maybe down the road, if things are different . . . we could try again someday."

I nodded. She leaned over and kissed me on the cheek; I remember the way the cool mint smelled on her breath.

Then she got up and walked home without me. We didn't talk again for years after that day.

But I held her to her word. I did.

FOUR

Reddit user u/Hear_Me_Now:

I think the bluegrass community is covering something up, tbh. I mean, she *belonged* to them as a kid. She spent all her summers at those festivals. Also . . . Ryan's talked about that guy who followed her to all her festival appearances in interviews. How do we *know* that wasn't Simon McCarthy?
Yes I realize that should have come up in the McCarthy investigation but u don't understand how many years passed between those incidents. And I think Ryan's team wanted the McCarthy stuff to blow over as quickly as possible.
But I mean, this could be a case of someone who's really obsessed. Who's to say there's not some connection between them?
Just food for thought . . .
#RescueRyan

FRANK

I couldn't believe how much Ryan took on that year. One festival after another—the poor kid hardly had any summer vacation left! But I can't deny that she was making a name for herself on the circuit. She grew her hair out even longer, and I think that really helped cement an "image" in people's minds; she was a force to be reckoned with up there, all those messy auburn curls around her skinny shoulders and her throwing it about every which way, not missing a note on her strings the whole time.

Ryan had a real energy. A lot of kids can perform, get up onstage, and get kind of overwhelmed by the adrenaline and forget what they're doing, but Ryan never let it get out of check. She had stamina.

I was pretty impressed by her. And even though I was already feeling guilty about putting her on what was looking to be a career track at the tender age of fourteen, I did help her out with a secret project that summer.

You see, she had big plans for Austin. Not only did she manage to snag a spot in the Texas Bluegrass Association's summer jamboree, but she wanted me to help her make a demo tape.

"And just what are you going to do with this demo tape?" I asked.

"What do you think?" She just grinned at me. "Pass it around."

I looked at her long and hard then and checked myself as well. I wanted to tell her *Slow down, now*, just like I used to when she was first learning her instrument. A dozen thoughts flashed through my head: *What are we really doing? Is it a good idea to pass out demo tapes? Could someone take advantage of this wide-eyed kid in Austin?* At best, I figured people might take them and forget about them in their glove compartments or junk drawers—amateur demos are a dime a dozen in Austin.

At worst, some bad actor could take her eagerness and naivete and use it to scam her.

"Now let's think this through," I said to her. "Have you talked to your parents about doing this?"

"Sure," she said. "But not Mari, not yet—I'm worried she'll think it means I'm going to move away. So don't mention it around her."

Oh, that little sneak. It was a long time before I realized it was the other way around.

No, Ryan had *not* told her parents. But Mari was always near when they came by the shop, so I was none the wiser.

~

We recorded a nice tape—well, I should say CD, there I'm dating myself—together. It was four of Ryan's best songs, all of which ended up appearing on her first album. We began with "June Bug," always fun, and the one that showed off her mezzo range and vocal control the best as she's flipping up into her breathy register on the chorus. Then "Providence," of course, for a slower burn, then "Salem Swing," certainly her edgiest to date at that time. I had to hazard a guess it was about those mean girls in her class. *You like to step on my toes / You like to curse my things. / Luckily I'm a dancer / I'll teach you the Salem Swing*—those lines always got me. Wouldn't want to be on the receiving end of Ryan's wrath, no sir. Not that I could ever imagine her angry.

We ended on "Let Me Know," that sweet little upbeat song. I'd thought it might be a nod to whatever producer might be listening: *I'm still in your corner / I'll see you at the show. / If you'd care to walk me home / Then won't you let me know?*

I was prepared to help her with the rejection when she got back to Hamilton.

Well, shows you how much I know.

MARI

I played my part well. There were even a few moments I hammed it up in front of Frank: I *bet you'll* hate *Austin, Ryan. It's so hot there. You'd never move to Austin without me, right? This is just another festival?*

I could always tell by the look on his face that he'd bought her story. Back then, I didn't really understand Ryan's reasoning; her parents were happy to take her to the festivals. I thought they'd be fine with the idea of the demo CDs.

There had been a recent weird incident at a festival in Pennsylvania where an older man had come up to Ryan after the show. I wasn't there to see it. Barb and John were talking to the stage manager, and the man sidled up when their backs were turned and said something like, "I've been catching you at these jams ever since Salem Days, and they just don't make pretty young ladies like you anymore. You ever think about making a website for yourself? Posting your shows?"

Poor Ryan was trying to be nice. And honestly, it didn't sound like a bad idea just as Myspace was starting to become a thing—but it's easy to look back now and know what his intentions were. She said she'd think about it, and then he started pushing her to give him her number so she could text him the shows. Ryan said she didn't have a cell phone, he said he'd buy her one . . . so on and so on. He didn't shove off until John came over and told him to get lost.

I think that freaked her parents out a little. The Austin festival sixteen hundred miles away probably sounded pretty good just then.

When Ryan told me about the incident, I asked her, "Were you scared? I mean, it's true. You're up onstage for all these people to see, and anyone can buy a ticket to a festival."

She didn't look at me. But she shrugged and said, "Cost of doing business."

And I said, "You sound like Frank."

"That's because it's his phrase."

I'd laughed. But the night Ryan disappeared, I just . . . I thought about that man. I know it sounds dramatic to call him her first stalker, but I stand by it.

That was so many years ago, and I don't think some *Southie* schlub like that would've had what it took to kidnap a pop star. But you never know what people are capable of.

Anyway, all that is to say—I know now why the Holdings might not have wanted Ryan to be going around Austin, Texas, handing out her music and information to everyone she met. The CDs did have John's number on them, but the stickers said: "Ryan Holding, Hamilton, MA Bluegrass | 978-555-8853." There was also a photo of Ryan taped to the back of each, a Polaroid of her and her banjo she'd had me take in front of the old oak in her front yard and then copied at the library. A real sicko could've tracked her down if he wanted to.

But at age fourteen, as dumb kids from a town of less than eight thousand people, I didn't think about *any* of that. Listen, I trusted Ryan with my life. She was my best friend and the most interesting person I knew. So when she told me we were getting on a bus to tool around downtown Austin while John and Barb recovered from the flight in the hotel hot tub, I said, "Where's the stop?"

She'd packed dozens of the CDs in her little denim backpack and led me down Twelfth Street. Leave it to Ryan to understand the Austin bus lines. I guess she always had an eye for details like that.

We wouldn't be able to hit all the studios, but she managed to get us near the capitol, and we walked to a cluster of them on Fifth Street from there. Republic Square, Studio 22, Tough Grit—I mean, the girl had done her research. And in every single lobby, she walked right up to the front desk and said, "Hi there! I'm Ryan Holding from Hamilton, Massachusetts, and I'm putting my own spin on bluegrass. Would you please deliver this to Mr. *X, Y, Z*?"—she'd even managed to learn the executives' names—and then she'd pop one of the CDs on the desk.

"How many do you think you'll hear back from?" I asked her after the third or fourth stop.

She'd pressed her mouth into a thin line. "One, if I'm lucky."

That surprised me. In my fourteen-year-old mind, I was sure she'd have offers piling up in no time. But looking back now, it was an incredible bit of realism on her part.

I wonder how many of those CDs actually did end up in the trash.

MERLE GONZALES, *former executive at Studio 22 Records*

You'd better believe I'm kicking myself. God, I think about it every day. I was actually down in the lobby when she came in—I remember that day because I had terrible heartburn. Decided to see if I could walk it off while the TUMS kicked in.

So I'm getting my steps in, and all of a sudden these two little girls waltz through the doors, totally unaccompanied, and head straight over to Doris. She talks to them for a little bit, takes something from them, and then they're off.

I go over and say, "What the hell was that?"

She shrugged. "They left a CD for you."

"For *me*?" I started laughing. I mean, yes, I did produce records. But before or since, I'd never seen anyone *that* young try to pull something like that.

I don't want to be mean; it was . . . well, it was a very intentionally done album. The photo on the back was a nice touch. But it looked like a kid's art project. Like I said, I was having a rough afternoon, it was a slow day, and I felt like I could use some amusement. So I popped it in my desktop upstairs.

It was good, I'm serious. I had to admit even then that it was a thoughtful demo and that her songwriting was more than a few degrees better than I had expected.

But . . . she was a child. It was too much of a gamble. Apart from the sticky situations you can find yourself in when it comes to contracts and ethical standards at that age, who knew what her work ethic was? Would she be able to follow through, or would she get sick of the industry real quick and turn into a headache and a waste of my limited time and resources?

Had I been presented with a thousand other talented fourteen-year-olds, I would have turned them down again and again. It was the principle of it.

It's the only thing I can tell myself to soothe my regrets.

MIKE ROSETTI, *CEO of Tough Grit Records*

I threw it away. Didn't even listen to it. Biggest mistake I've ever made.

MARI

Ryan didn't expect to hear anything right away. We stopped at the post office last, where she mailed the rest of the demos to the producers we couldn't visit in person, and then—by some miracle—managed to make it back to the hotel without too much suspicion from the Holdings.

"We walked to the 7-Eleven for slushies," Ryan said when they asked where we'd been. "It was farther than we thought."

She played the festival the next day and shone as always. Played all the songs on her demo tape along with her favorite covers to enthusiastic applause.

Ryan, her parents, and I were all packing up our hotel room the next day, late morning, when John got a call on his cell. He paced around the room for a signal, and then said, "I'm sorry, you're *who*?"

Poor John.

And then he glared at Ryan. He said, very stiffly, "Thank you for your call. I need to talk to my daughter about this." Then he hung up the phone and said to Ryan, "What did you *do*?"

She looked at him very innocently. "About what?"

"You know about what, young lady. Why is someone from Madcap Records calling me about bringing you in for a test session?"

Ryan stayed nonchalant, but I saw her eyes light up. "Oh, is that who that was? I sent some demo CDs around town. I thought it was a good idea in case any of them wanted to see me play on Saturday."

"Whoa, whoa, whoa," said Barb. "Ryan, why didn't you talk to us about this first?"

Ryan had looked down then while I sat awkwardly on the edge of the hotel bed, watching it unfold. I think she did feel bad about sneaking around her parents, but she had known she couldn't risk them shutting the plan down. Austin was a big opportunity.

"Well, I'm calling them back and telling them we're leaving town today," John said.

"No!" Ryan looked up. "Dad, there are no major record labels in Massachusetts—not for the music I want to play, anyway. This was my one chance to see if anyone who's a real *professional* might be interested in my music. Can't we at least try?"

"Ryan, this person could be scamming us," John said. "He could want something unsavory from you. You are fourteen years old, for god's sake. There will be plenty of time to try again when you're older. Right, Barbara?"

"Here's the thing, John," Barb said.

"Dear lord." John sat down on the other queen bed and put his head in his hands.

"We're here now, it does seem like a pretty unique opportunity, and we can all go to check this thing out. If we get even a hint of something not being right—even just a whiff—we'll walk. No decisions have to be made right now."

"And our flight? And work tomorrow?" he said.

She shrugged. "Flights are cheaper on the weekdays, anyway. At least call back and see what they want."

John looked at her a long moment. Then he handed her the phone and said, "You do it," and shut himself in the bathroom.

SKIP MCINTYRE, *founder and producer at Madcap Records*

Here's what I always said I wanted, from the very beginning: I wanted *fresh*.

Special. Unusual.

Madcap was small back then. I broke ground with my partner, Andre, after we'd both quit our jobs at the bigger labels in search of something new. Different. We knew it'd be an uphill battle to carve out a name for ourselves among those other giants, but we had a few artists on our side who agreed to sign with us, and in those days, the competition in Austin wasn't quite so fierce. Significant, yes, but the major labels were still out on the coasts. And the tech-bro revolution in central Texas was more than a decade out.

From the very beginning, I wanted to find our niche. Andre and I agreed: We didn't want to take on just any singer who could work a crowd and carry a tune. We'd pooled together some decent seed money and decided that if we wanted to compete, we'd cultivate the type of talent that other labels might pass over at first blush. Quality over quantity, you know? We could afford to look a little closer, take our time.

We were starting to make a little name for ourselves around town for the underdogs we were taking in. Like Sinclair Dupree, he's the one who went by the stage name EsDee, the elderly gentlemen from Alabama who made some really excellent hip-hop records. There was the jazz pianist Candy Elliot and the young rapper Límon from Venezuela. Eccentrics who could really strut their stuff. People who had staying power, not just a flash in the pan.

So when Ryan's demo came across my desk, I stopped to listen. I listened to it five times in a row on that Friday evening, back-to-back. Then I called in Andre.

"It's a risk," he said. "She sounds real young."

I didn't know her age at that point; I'd asked our receptionist, who said the girl seemed like she could still be in middle school. But the talent on the CD was undeniable. Complex fretwork, beautiful lyrics, unpredictable chord progression—you'd think you knew where the song would go next, and then it would take an entirely different direction, just to come back to that satisfying resolution when you needed it. Sure, I thought someone might be writing the stuff for her. But if not . . . then she could be something special.

The message that this girl, Ryan, had left with the receptionist was that she'd be playing at Austin Bluegrass Jam the next afternoon. Shit, I didn't have anything else to do that day. So I thought I'd take a look.

I'll never forget it.

I got to the Bluegrass Jam around 2:30 p.m., heat of the day, right when everyone's energy was starting to lag. People were out in that bright sun, mopping their brows, looking around for a cold beer.

And then she comes out.

Skinny little kid with all this huge hair, sparkly silver dress flashing in the light, looking like she can't even feel the heat. I felt the mood in the crowd shift at the same moment I started to doubt my little trip out there; I mean, she was *young* young. If you'd have told me she was twelve, I would have believed you.

And then she started to play.

It's hard to explain—it wasn't that she had the air of an older performer, necessarily, although she did just exude this confidence and self-assuredness beyond her years. Confidence is one thing. But this was a charisma that was all her own.

Our youngest artist on the label at that time was Límon, who was twenty-two, but I'd still seen plenty of kid acts in my day. I find them hard to watch. They're cute, fun, sure, but it's like I can always *see* how hard they're trying. It's too desperate. Kids just don't have the experience of artists who have spent decades performing; they really want to be good, and some of them *will* be good, great, even—with time and practice—but at that moment, they just aren't there yet.

Ryan, though . . . she belonged up there. I'm sure it took plenty of effort to get up in front of those hundreds of people, but she didn't look it. She was just having a great time.

I called Andre after I got back from the festival and talked things through with him.

"What's the harm in waiting a few years?" he asked me. "Why not wait until she gets a little more experience under her belt and then really polish her up?"

"Someone will take her if we don't," I told him. "I heard she spread those CDs all around town." I was on good terms with Studio 22's tech guy and had asked around a bit.

"You think they'd take a what—thirteen-, fourteen-year-old?" Andre said. I heard the doubt in his voice.

"They will once they see her perform."

"I wouldn't do it if I were you," he answered, and I felt a little jolt of anticipation because I knew he'd resigned himself. "But . . . I know you, and it sounds like you've already made your decision."

I can't lie. I called the number on Ryan's CD right after we finished talking.

FIVE

MARI

Skip was like a younger, edgier Frank who had tattoos and chewed a lot of gum because he was trying to quit smoking. He had the same music philosophy: Don't rush things, take the time to make the thing you're producing *good.*

It was really lucky that Ryan ended up with a producer like him. Things happen for a reason, I think.

You already know where this went. Of course she did great in the test session—I got the impression that it was more to see whether she and Skip could work together than to gauge her skill. He seemed to have already made up his mind that she had talent, and it sealed the deal when Ryan came in all professional and friendly even at her young age, cracking jokes with Skip about Austin traffic and the dry heat. Just like an interview.

He had her sing a few things for him—not recording, just to listen—and asked her to try changing keys, swapping out one lyric for another, and so forth. I think he wanted to see whether she was willing to be flexible and work with feedback.

After about forty-five minutes, he thanked Ryan and asked if he could talk with her parents separately. There was a studio assistant who brought us snacks and chatted with us while we waited, but Ryan could hardly focus enough to have a conversation; she kept looking toward Skip's office door. She had a paper Dixie cup in her hands and was slowly crushing it and bouncing her leg.

We figured that Skip wouldn't have brought the Holdings to his office if he wasn't interested. Looking back, it was really decent of him to talk with Barb and John first. He could have easily told Ryan to her face that he wanted to sign her, forcing the pressure on her parents in the same way those toy commercials do. *Tell Mom and Dad to buy Barbie's tropical beach house today!* or whatever. But I think he was treading very carefully.

It was more than half an hour before they reemerged, and I remember John just having this totally blank look on his face and Barb being dazed. Both of them were blinking like they couldn't quite remember where they were.

And Skip shook all our hands, said it was nice to meet us, and that he would be in touch. To her credit, Ryan didn't push it just yet. She only said, "I hope to work with you again soon!" and looked Skip straight on with those green eyes of hers.

The second we were back in the rental car, though: "So? What did he say?"

John answered, "We'll talk about it when we get home. There's a lot to talk about."

"You have to give me *something*!" Ryan pressed, and honestly, she was right. I was buzzing back there too.

"He was impressed by your music and your work ethic," Barb said. She was cracking quicker than John; I remember catching this faint smile on her face when she said it. Barb was dazzled, in a word.

"We'll leave it at that for now," she went on. Ryan nodded and knew what that meant. She grabbed my hand in the back seat as we drove to the hotel, and I held on tight.

~

I'm pretty sure the Holdings' first call when we all got back to Hamilton was to their lawyer. From what Ryan told me, they spent more than one evening that week at his office, talking late into the night. It turned out that Skip had presented them with a contract and encouraged them to take as much time as they needed going through it and discussing it with Ryan. When they finally got through the first phase with the lawyer, they sat Ryan down and had a long, long family meeting.

She told me about it breathlessly over lunch the next day, how they talked about what each of the different legalities meant, but also what would happen if Ryan actually signed.

She did, of course.

And that changed both of our lives for good.

JUSTIN

Ryan didn't even tell me that she was moving to Texas. I had to hear it from Matt Danvers, who said she'd be gone by the Fourth of July. I remember having this image of Fourth of July fireworks in Texas and how everything would be bigger and better there.

She didn't say goodbye to me.

FRANK

I was sorry to see her go. To see all of them go—I felt like I'd gotten to be good friends with the Holdings over those early years. But Ryan was on the warpath, and she had important things to do. I gave her a little care package with all the extra strings and fingerpicks she could want, plus a few treats from around town to remember Hamilton by.

I think she might've got a bit choked up during our last lesson. I know I did.

MARI

Of course I tried to convince my parents to move to Texas, and of course my parents, born-and-bred New Englanders, were appalled by the idea. I knew it was a long shot, anyway. But even though Ryan and I crammed every bit of quality time we possibly could into the end of our eighth-grade year, it felt like I blinked and suddenly we were lying on our backs on a picnic table in Patton Park, throwing Skittles up in the air and trying to catch them in our mouths the night before Ryan left for Austin.

"I don't want you to go," I remember saying. It kind of came out of nowhere, and I immediately felt terrible—like I wasn't supporting her dream, like all I cared about was keeping her stuck in Hamilton for the rest of our lives so she could go to high school with me and come to my harp recitals and watch *Eternal Sunshine of the Spotless Mind*, quickly becoming our favorite movie, over and over again.

But she surprised me by saying, "I don't want to go either."

I remember sitting up on the table and looking over at her, but she was staring straight into the blue sky. "You don't?" I asked.

"I don't and I do," she said. "I'll miss the pine trees. I won't know anyone. And I won't have you."

She slid her eyes over to me when she said it, and I saw that they were full of tears. The whole time I thought she'd been thrilled to move; all she'd talked about nonstop was the town house her parents were renting and the music equipment she had to pack and the weather that would never feel cold—at least to us Hamiltonians. I'd even tortured myself with the idea that she might be glad to finally get out of our quiet little town.

"But there's just something in me that says if I don't take this chance, I'll never get it again," she said. "I don't know what it is. I have all these ideas—so many ideas, Mari, and I have to get them out somehow. I have to *do* something with them. If I just sit on them and waste them, it gives me this itchy, horrible feeling. And then

I listen to other people creating stuff and think, *I could have done that.* Or *I could do better.* And it makes me feel . . . guilty, I guess. That I didn't try harder."

I nodded. It wasn't something I could completely relate to or understand, but as I got older, I recognized that feeling in other artists I met. I've thought a lot about the compulsion to create over the years. Ryan's wealth was beside the point, especially at the outset; there was no guarantee that she could make any money off of this, at least no more than she was already gathering with festival winnings. A near fifteen-year-old wasn't equipped to understand income in that sense, anyway.

Ryan was driven by something beyond herself. And it was powerful enough to force her past fear and discomfort to become something that was truly exceptional.

It was the last time in my life that I viewed her as a kid just like me.

SKIP

Ryan Holding moved to Austin in the summer of 2004, a week before her fifteenth birthday. I primarily communicated through her parents at that time; I said to her father, take a week, a month, whatever you need, have her settle in and enjoy her summer for a little bit.

Nothing doing. Ryan showed up with her mother to my office the following Monday and wanted to schedule some studio time.

"I'm free now," I told her. "Let's head up and hash this thing out."

Barb brought a book of crosswords and a copy of *Woman's Day* and sat quietly in the corner of our studios while we talked.

"You're eager," I told her. "Didn't you want to take some time to celebrate your birthday?"

She shrugged and said, "We went out to dinner. It's more important to me that I don't let you change your mind about all this."

I chuckled. "We signed a contract, so I'm not going to change my mind. At least not until I see how your first album performs."

Out of the corner of my eye, I saw Barb raise an eyebrow. But hey, I wanted to set expectations early, and Ryan looked like she could handle it. I do my best to never, ever be unkind and to be the best possible advocate for all my artists. But this was a business relationship, a transactional one, and any new sign-on would go through a probationary period in my book until I could trust them. I would hope that Ryan held me to the same standards—her parents certainly did.

For her part, Ryan nodded at my comment. So I went on and said, "Here's what I'd like to get out of the next year or so in plain terms in case no one's laid it out for you yet. We'll produce an album together, your debut album. It sounds like you're an adept songwriter, but if you get stuck, we've got folks to help out. I'll work on getting you some more appearances. Festivals, yes, but some meatier gigs if we can swing it—opening acts whenever possible." I watched her face for any confusion or hesitancy as I was making my little speech, but she seemed to be tracking. Then I said, "But it's also very important to me what *you'd* like to get out of the next year. What do you want out of this opportunity, Ryan?"

She didn't stop to think, didn't miss a beat. She looked at me with clear green eyes and said, "Everything."

"Everything?" I repeated.

"And more." She had the faintest smile on her face when she said it.

That was Ryan—she always had me on my toes. She was earnest and self-deprecating at the same time, serious and focused and laid-back all at once. Sometimes I thought I knew what she was thinking, and then something entirely different would come out of her mouth.

I don't . . . I don't mean to talk about her in the past tense so much. I know why you're here, and I wish I could help. But all I can do is tell you about the Ryan I knew and the career she had up until the end.

RON SANCHEZ, *Ryan's classmate in Austin, Texas*

Yep, I went to school with Ryan Holding. We were lab partners. Even if it was only for the better part of a year, that'll be my claim to fame until

I die. I bring it up at parties. The farther from Austin I am, the more of a reaction it gets—she ended up having a lot of random connections with people around here. My sister-in-law's dad was the one who rented Ryan's parents their town house. I think my connection is better, though. I got to actually know her.

I mean, sort of. She was real sweet even if she wasn't around a lot. Not the type of person you'd think would end up a billionaire. But she did keep to herself. I always felt like I was the one doing all the talking—rambling on about some stupid sketch I saw on *Saturday Night Live*, describing what I had for lunch, reading off the lab instructions to her. It was about halfway through the semester that I realized she was asking *me* a lot of questions and not really answering many of her own.

Like, I knew she was kind of a different duck. We all did. A lot of people around school had parents and family that worked in the Austin music scene, but no one was actually building a *career* in it—especially not freshmen. But Ryan was in and out of class a lot, and constantly did makeup work, so it was pretty obvious she was up to *something*.

It made for a little bit of bullying, nothing major. One kid, David Zaminski, would sort of holler at her when she came in late to her locker—*Did Ryan have a special appointment again? Wow, so nice of you to join us, Ryan!*—but for the most part, she was left alone because people didn't see much of her. The general story was that she was working as a backup singer on a Kidz Bop CD or something. No one guessed that she was producing her *own* album, even though she was constantly scribbling in this little notebook she carried around. David tried to grab it from her once, but she swung her backpack around so quickly that she knocked it out of his hands and ran away. I was pretty impressed.

So I asked her at lab, "What's in that notebook you carry?"

"Just stuff." She shrugged.

"Is it poetry?" I said.

"Sort of."

"What do you like to do in your free time?" I kept going and dared to broach the subject. "When you're not doing music or school stuff? What do you like?"

She glanced at me and then looked back down at our pipettes. She said, "I don't really *have* free time."

"Oh, come on," I said. "There's gotta be something."

She smiled. "I always thought *Mario Kart* would be fun."

I was blown away. "You've never played *Mario Kart*?" When she shook her head, I said, "You'd love it. You can come over and play sometime if you want. I just got *Grand Theft Auto* for Christmas, too, and it's next level."

"That sounds cool," she said. "I'd do that."

It never happened, of course. She got busy again, and I brought it up once or twice, but nothing ever came of it.

That's okay. She was still a nice person.

SKIP

One thing I do wish I'd pushed harder for in those days was to have Ryan spend more time with people her own age. We got into a routine: She got out of school at 2:45 p.m., and on Mondays, Wednesdays, and Fridays, she'd come to the studio to work until six. I don't know what she did most Tuesdays, Thursdays, or weekends, but judging by the pace she was cranking out songs, it was probably just more of the same.

I did tell Barb, hey, make sure she takes time off to live her life a little, yeah? I didn't know when Eastside held their prom, but it seemed like something she should go to—and I think she did. I want to say I remember her writing something about it for "Eastside Blues." Not the happiest song, so I'm not really sure what transpired, but still.

My ask wasn't completely altruistic. You've got to build up real-life experiences in order to write songs about them, and I didn't want her to be drafting lyrics as a total shut-in.

I think, though, that Ryan was reluctant to really get close to any of those other kids. She was already set apart, kind of going through school with one foot in the classroom and the other in the studio. If I was less generous, I'd say it almost gave her a kind of martyr complex.

"These kids aren't going where I'm going," Ryan told me once. "They don't understand what I'm trying to do. That's okay; they can live their normal life, and I'll live mine."

I had to hide my smile. It was such an angsty thing for this bright-eyed kid to say. "You don't think you can live a normal life?" I asked her.

She shrugged. "I don't want to."

Ryan didn't know just what the future held or how long she'd be at Eastside—which proved to be a fair concern, since Barb started talking about homeschooling near the end of that first year. Ryan's schedule just needed to be more flexible than it was, especially once we started booking shows.

But it was worth it. I could tell. Ryan worked with one of the best songwriters that Andre and I had been able to poach from our old labels, Jas Jeon—or Jasmine, I should say for the official record, but I've only ever called her Jas or JJ—and they just refined, refined, refined together.

JASMINE JEON, *songwriter, Madcap Records*

Ryan was such as sweetheart. I shouldn't say "was," but, well . . . it's been a long time since any of us have seen her.

I loved working with her. I've written for Nickel Creek, Miranda Lambert, Darius Rucker, but honestly—Ryan was my favorite. I've never been able to work so closely or have as long of a tenure with any other artist.

We got a pretty good thing going, where she always had the reins and I was there to step in when she needed help. Her understanding of songwriting back then was simple but solid. We did a little bit of homework together; I had Ryan bring me in the lyrics of five songs she really admired.

Not just liked for their sound, but for their words and message—the kind she wanted to emulate—and we studied them together, really picked them apart and questioned why they were structured the way they were.

She had a great knack for slant rhymes. I cowrote six of the ten tracks on her debut album, but my favorite line in all of them was hers: *And I believe you loved me, yes / But you don't know what love is yet.* That's from "Eastside Blues." But she knew when to come in with those satisfying perfect rhymes, too, like with "Shoes on the Dash"—*He's got gospel on the radio / I've got my sneakers on the dash / We're runnin' on a gasoline dream / And a shoebox full of cash.* Just a lot of fun, unpredictable, fresh lines.

Ryan drew from a deep well of ideas. She'd come in with ten different hooks already in her head, and we'd riff on the banjo while she just talked through what happened in her day.

I understood and agreed with Skip's desire for Ryan to keep up a regular life, a social life, outside the studio, but my reasoning behind that was—she's a kid. I didn't share his concern about plumbing real-life experience for songwriting material. A better writer than I once said that, honestly, making it through childhood is all the lived experience you need to be able to accurately convey emotion, conflict, yearning. I mean, have you seen these teenagers? We're not going for realism here in the music industry. Save that for documentaries. We're going for *drama*, for lyrics that make you *feel* something, and teenagers have it in spades.

Ryan was no different.

SKIP

She had a great eclectic mix in that eponymous album, a really interesting fusion between her Massachusetts roots and the Texas flavor she was starting to pick up.

I had a mind to get her more enmeshed with the Austin music scene, but while we were working on the first album, the separation was intentional. Don't go to too many shows, I told her. Don't worry about getting to know the community just yet. Focus on your stuff first. There will be time for the rest.

And I can't take full credit, but I think it lent her an incredibly unique sound. There are pared-back nods to New England alongside the tracks with a little more twang—a smash of Texas spice. Ryan was keen on adding more mandolin and whistle to the former, and some electric guitar to the latter.

I mean, what a cool fucking fusion. I couldn't have asked for a better album.

The only question was whether listeners would agree with me.

~

We chose "Providence" and "Shoes on the Dash" to push as her first singles, the same two that bookended her album. They were just great songs. A little longing and melancholy in the first, and a feel-good summer jam in the second.

What I really wanted was to build up enough momentum to hit a glide. I've never been great at analogies, but—you know when you're cutting paper with scissors, cutting cutting cutting, and then something catches and *kshhhh*—the scissors are gliding effortlessly? We hadn't hit our stride yet, and I wanted Ryan to start feeling the benefits of all the work we were putting in.

I wanted to start feeling them too. I wanted to know that our investment would pay off.

JASMINE

Skip and I finally got Ryan to release her grip on the tracks in mid-May 2005. That girl was something else—some songs she could whip off like nothing. But others—"Eastside Blues" and "Highway 71"—she just wanted to keep marinating and marinating on until she got it right.

Skip pushed the team to mix and master the album as quickly as possible without sacrificing quality. He wouldn't admit this at the time, but I knew what he was doing. It wasn't hard to guess that he wanted *Ryan Holding* to go out into the world as close to July first as humanly possible so we could maximize the eligibility period for the 2006 Country Music Awards.

Saying that out loud would've been jinxing it. I mean, it was crazy—Ryan was just a little girl, we'd acquired her so recently, and Madcap was still so nascent itself.

But she brought an energy to all of us that made us believe, in our incredible hubris, that it just might be possible. Ryan learned everyone's names, from Bonnie, our receptionist, to Guy, our bookings manager, to Evan, our lowly runner, and she always said hi if she saw them, even if it was a quick wave from behind the sound booth. It would be easy for the more cynical among us to dismiss that as naivete, but in an industry full of assholes . . . she was a breath of fresh air.

A whole bunch of the staff gathered in the conference room to listen to the final playthrough—more than Skip would usually have allowed.

Ryan sat very still and kept her arms crossed, elbows on the table, eyes down.

No one said anything the whole time except for a few looks and nods to each other from across the room. I liked it, and I could tell that Skip was satisfied from the way his jaw kept still—whenever he was stressed or irritated, he'd work it like he was chewing his nicotine gum, even if he didn't have a piece just then—but it was really important that Ryan liked it too. That's a major milestone for an artist. You have to be proud of what you're putting out or else it's going to be that much harder to sell it and perform it.

When the last few bars of "Shoes on the Dash" ended, everyone stayed quiet. I mean, you could hear a pin drop in that whole room. Everyone was holding their breath.

Ryan kept her eyes down, and Skip looked at her, hands folded on the table, from beneath his brows.

Then she looked up at him in the same fashion, raised her eyebrows, and grinned.

She nodded, and I swear the room broke out into cheers.

There's no such thing as a perfect album. Of course there are always going to be notes you'd like to change, words you wish you'd arranged differently—and that's okay, that's the beauty that comes with live performance, when you *can* make those adjustments and experiences, keeping the music dynamic and alive.

But *Ryan Holding* was damn close to a perfect debut. And it was the most fun final playthrough I've had the pleasure of attending.

JUSTIN

I remember the first time I heard Ryan's voice on the radio. It was so, so weird—I'd had my license for a week and was driving my dad's truck to Ipswich with the stereo blasting. I always shut it off when I got close to our house, but out of earshot of my parents, I cranked that sucker.

I was just pulling into town when "Providence" came on. I had to slam on my brakes because I nearly sailed through a three-way intersection.

There was Ryan's voice, just how I remembered it.

And she was singing about me.

It's just you and me, William.

I had to buy her album. I was sort of embarrassed by it, so, you know, I didn't tell anyone. But I listened to the whole thing again and again. And it was the first time I began to feel . . . I don't know. This is going to get me slandered, but it's how I feel. It was kind of an ownership, you know? I mean, those lyrics were about *me*. My relationship with her had given her the material for all these songs. *When I need reassurance, you're the only one / I'll be waiting for you on Highway 71.* That was me. We'd talked about how, if I ever visited her in Austin someday, I'd fly into Austin-Bergstrom International Airport—which is on Highway 71.

I'm not crazy.

People really, really crucify me for this. But they don't know what it feels like to have songs written about you—recorded, professionally mixed, published songs—that someone else is making money off of.

It just—I don't know. I was the first time I kind of thought, *Huh.*

MARI

My mom flew out with me to attend the launch party. It was maybe the most excited I've ever been. Not only did I get to see Ryan again for the first time in *way* too long—although we racked up our parents' phone bills with plenty of long-distance calls—but I'd get to go with her to, like, *the* swankiest party my fifteen-year-old self could possibly fathom.

She and her mom picked us up from Austin-Bergstrom International in a company car from Madcap, which was already unbelievable. And—this is why I love her—she wouldn't let me ask any questions about her life until I caught her up on everything I was doing: on my harp lessons, on Frank, on all the gossip around Hamilton-Wenham and our old classmates.

We had our first sleepover that night in a long time, but it felt like we'd never been apart.

And yes, we watched *Eternal Sunshine of the Spotless Mind.*

SKIP

The break I was hoping for came in September, when I got a call from a connection of mine. He'd recently started working with the band Dust and Roses, the country group who'd won a well-deserved Grammy the year before, and he said they were looking for an opener for the

Northeast leg of their spring tour. The South was covered, he made that clear, but they were looking for local voices that would be a nice nod to the regions where they were traveling. And would Ryan Holding be interested in taking it back to her roots?

Would she *ever* be.

SIX

NBC10 BOSTON NEWS, *AIRED FEBRUARY 7, 2006*

HOST: I'm here with young bluegrass star Ryan Holding, who's been making waves in the Austin, Texas, music scene with her two hit singles "Providence" and "Shoes on the Dash," along with her eponymous album, *Ryan Holding*, released last summer. Now, she's headed on tour with country music group Dust and Roses—but into familiar territory. Ryan, you're from our own town of Hamilton, Massachusetts, just a short drive from this very studio. How does it feel to be back home?

[Ryan smiles and tucks her thick hair behind her ear, smoothing her hands on her blue jeans.]

RYAN: It feels good. It's hard to believe I'm here, honestly.

HOST: Now, you are the youngest musician that Madcap has ever signed to their label, and as far as I'm aware, certainly the youngest to ever tour with Dust and Roses. Have you gotten to meet the band?

RYAN: Oh, definitely. They're all really sweet, taking me under their wing and stuff. They got pizza delivered right to the stage after the first rehearsal, and we just sat together and talked about how we got to this point. I've been so lucky to have a lot of teachers—my first banjo teacher, Frank, but then my producer, Skip, has taught me so much, and

my co-songwriter, Jasmine—everyone at Madcap. And now the Dust and Roses crew. I know I'm still starting out, so there's so much to learn.
HOST: It sounds like you're on the right track. What are you looking forward to most about being back in the Hub?

[Ryan laughs.]

RYAN: Honestly, I carved out some time between shows to see my old friends again. I'm looking forward to that more than anything. Oh, and maybe a lobster roll!
HOST: I don't think Texas can beat that. Ryan, I have your album here with me, and I'm going to give our audience a good look so they can find it at their local record store and wherever CDs are sold. And while we're admiring this album, can you tell me a little bit about the art?
[The host presents the album, which features a photo of Ryan with her banjo between two monolithic stones, taken at Enchanted Rock's peak in Texas. Then, the host opens the CD case and points to the lyric booklet, which is covered in white doodled lines on a black background. Ryan smiles demurely, and her tone is innocent.]
RYAN: I'm not sure what you're talking about.
HOST: Well, some have said that there's a secret message written in the doodles here. I haven't cracked the code myself, but that looks like *storms*, and I think I might see *roots* down here . . .
RYAN: Would you look at that! You must have really good eyesight.
HOST: I'll neither ask you to confirm or deny—it sounds like our audiences will have to look for themselves. *Ryan Holding* is out now, and you can see her perform live with Dust and Roses at the Orpheum Theatre on February 11.

MARI

There were three different versions of the secret messages. They were all quotes Ryan lived by: "Storms make trees take deeper roots," by Dolly Parton; "I was determined to carve out a music of my own," by Bill Monroe; and "Keep the music ringing"—that was something Frank always said. She spent a day making the doodles herself and getting them just right before they sent the design files off to the printer.

SKIP

It was genius. Everyone wanted to get their hands on those CD booklets to see what the secret messages were, and back then, the way to do that was to buy it. I'd say that idea alone nearly doubled sales.

Her numbers didn't skyrocket like some of the other artists I'd seen at the big labels, but it was good, steady growth. And the tour could only improve that.

Reddit user u/RyanComeHome_90

Ryan's team claims there are only three versions of the RH secret messages in the CD booklets. Not true. One of the lots that shipped to retailers in Boise, ID had a different message and many have taken pictures of this evidence—comment below if u have a booklet.

THAT version says "Storms make trees carve out a music of my own." You can also clearly see the word "ALLEGE" in the loopy script. Is it a misprint? Maybe, but if it is, why was Boise the only place to receive those booklets? Why did the tree in Ryan's childhood home feature so heavily in "Hear Me Now?"

Plus the photo from u/countryjamz of the woman at Albertson's in Caldwell who appears to be Ryan has NOT yet been debunked. Caldwell is just a short drive from Boise. Stay alert.

#RescueRyan

MARI

Dust and Roses was when Ryan officially began homeschooling. The Northeastern tour dates stretched across two months, and between that and the other gigs she was playing, it just stopped being worth it to be enrolled at Eastside at all.

I was so excited to have her back in Massachusetts. I mean—it wasn't exactly how I'd pictured it. I maybe hyped myself up too much. She came to Boston, not Hamilton. She only had, like, two days before she had to join Dust and Roses again in New York. It made me wish I'd made even more of our time together in Austin for the launch party—it was a very different feeling now that she was touring, and of course she didn't want to let her headliner band down.

The launch party was a celebration. This time . . . I could feel the secondhand pressure.

It was sweet, though. Ryan reserved box seats for me, her parents, and Frank at the Orpheum. Before the show, she had us all come backstage. She had her own greenroom, and we had to wear badges and be escorted by stage techs and everything. It was *legit* legit.

"I know it's not much," she said. "But I wouldn't be standing here in this freezing-cold dress without you all, so I wanted to give you something."

It *was* cold backstage, and Ryan was wearing a metallic silvery dress with a million pleats that swished every time she moved and hung off her frame with these skinny little spaghetti straps. Matching silver cowgirl boots were on her feet. A whole team of people had done her hair and makeup, and she had thick black eyeliner winged way out and huge false lashes, like *pow*. Onstage it looked normal, but up close I could hardly recognize her. Her hair, in these perfect red ringlets, was voluminous and wild. It was the look that would define her for the next six years.

Ryan picked up three CDs for each of us. She gave Frank the one with his quote, her parents the Bill Monroe, and me the Dolly Parton.

Inside each lyric booklet she'd written a thank-you message—mine said, *I stand by you forever.*

SKIP

I got Ryan all set up backstage and then headed into the house to see the lay of the land. I was hoping I could get a sense of whether anyone was here for Ryan, *just* for Ryan, with Dust and Roses being an afterthought.

No offense to them—they had a great following by that point in their career. But Ryan was my priority.

Man, I bet you'd never seen so many cowboy hats in Boston. Definitely more of a bluegrass city, if that, but I had to chuckle to myself when I saw the Stetsons and leather boots. Country fans never fail to surprise me—they can and do exist where I least expect them to.

I'd staked out a spot on the mezzanine to do my surveillance, taking in all the couples and the yuppies and the middle-aged guys like me.

And then I saw something interesting.

There were a couple of young girls in the front, maybe ten, twelve years old, wearing silver cowgirl boots. No, not just two girls—there was another, and another, some with their moms, some with what must have been older siblings. In fact, I counted no less than twenty-two middle school girls from my lookout on the mezzanine, and that was in the orchestra level alone. Not all of them had silver cowgirl boots, but I spotted silver ribbons, vests, et cetera.

I remember thinking, *What's up with that? Are Dust and Roses doing a school partnership I don't know about?*

Well, silly me. Because just imagine what happened when Ryan walked onstage.

All those little girls started *screaming*.

Ryan smiled wide and waved like she was a goddamn pageant queen. And when she opened her mouth? Yep, those girls knew every word.

I tell you—I just started laughing to myself. How had I missed it? Pigheadedness, I guess, I'll admit it: Maybe I just didn't expect young women to be interested in bluegrass. I don't know; in my mind, I think bluegrass, I picture a grizzled old man up in Appalachia. Joke's on me, the man who was literally producing the bluegrass music of a young woman. Just goes to show about biases and the like, I suppose.

That crowd couldn't get enough. They even chanted her name when she finished up "When in Texas" and ran offstage.

And I stood back there leaning against the wall, plotting, asking myself, *Skip, how are we going to harness this?*

ELYSE JAMES, *author*

It was on the Dust and Roses tour that Ryan's path first crossed with mine. I was a student at the University of Pittsburgh on scholarship at the time, and although I was majoring in communications, I was trying to get a photography business off the ground and working my way up by securing press passes to all the live music and events around town.

My brother, he . . . well, he was still in high school at the time. He never would have admitted it, but I knew he thought my side gig was cool. He was always asking if I had an extra pass, what it was like to see the performers up close, and so forth. He was taking guitar lessons and—while no one can match the ambition I've seen in Ryan—shared a similar drive.

We grew up in a duplex in the McKees Rocks neighborhood. When I came home for family dinners, I'd catch him fiddling around in his room with his unplugged, secondhand Mitchell, looking out the window onto the Ohio River. I knew he had dreams of making it out of our industrial little backwater someday. So I took him along with me to concerts whenever I could.

He was with me when I shot the Dust and Roses show that Ryan opened. Country wasn't quite his style—he very much identified with Bruce Springsteen back then—but he wasn't about to turn down a free ticket to the New Hazlett.

I, too, remember being intrigued by the number of young girls I saw up front. All decked out in silver accessories to match Ryan's style. There was a tiny girl on her dad's shoulders right near the front, wearing an equally tiny cowgirl hat.

What stuck with me, more than anything, was how Ryan genuinely acknowledged this group—how she seemed to meet every eye in the room when she strode onstage, already breaking into "Shoes on the Dash." She couldn't have, it's silly to think so—but I swear she winked at me before she got to the mic.

My brother must have thought the same.

I've heard about how connected Ryan is to her fans. Throughout the course of her entire career, she never seemed to get aloof like other major stars or to take her audience for granted. Maybe she knew, back then, that it was their collective power that could launch her into stardom, and she was going to do all she could to earn their attention.

Or maybe she was just having fun.

Either way, when she stretched her arm out to touch the reaching hand of the little girl in the cowgirl hat during "Highway 71," I captured it.

Two young bluegrass fans looking for all the world like the fresco in the Sistine Chapel.

The *Pittsburgh Post-Gazette* bought my photo to use in a write-up about bluegrass's revival in young female audiences. *Entertainment Weekly* asked permission to use it a week later.

And as Ryan's career grew, so did mine.

JASMINE

I don't know what kind of magic Ryan managed to work on the Dust and Roses tour, but by the time she got back to Austin, Skip had booked her a tour of her own. San Antonio, Phoenix, San Diego, LA, Vegas, and San Francisco. He joked that it was the "Southwest Sans," which personally reminded me of a Taco Bell order, or maybe a font, but someone thought he said Southwest *Sands*, and I guess it caught on.

That photo from the Pittsburgh show, the one with the little girl in the silver cowgirl hat, did wonders—even my auntie called and told me how cute it was, and was that the young bluegrass lady I was working for?

Yes, Gomo, that's Ryan. That's Ryan to a T.

I think she knew exactly what she was doing with that photo.

SKIP

Kshhhhhhh. Glide, baby.

GAVIN ARMSTRONG, *lead singer of Montana Line*

Ryan Holding's crew brought us on as openers for the Southwest Sands tour. That was back when Ryan was still country. I don't mean no disrespect—people change, and I guess their music can too. I don't want to say she sold out. I guess I just mean . . . we had her first, you know? I know some folks in my genre find it easy to think she sold out on all of us. It's a real tight-knit group, and that's only gotten more true in, well . . . in our current political climate, should I say. There's a mindset in the industry that country's gotta stick together. And some would say Ryan gave it up down the road.

But I remember that tour. She was just a half-bit of a girl, she was, but what a spitfire. Me and the guys were young, too, barely in our twenties, so it felt a little weird to be opening for someone who could've been your kid sister. I mean, we were happy for the opportunity—don't get me wrong for a second. No one knew us from Adam in those days. But Ryan really had her own way of doing things, and for a bunch of guys who were already trying to do everything we could to be "cool," well—it was different.

Different, but . . . great.

Part of it was that she was so normal. Our first rehearsal, she comes in wearing Hollister sweatpants and a hoodie, and you're like *Wait, is this her? Is that Ryan?* She was always professional in demeanor, but you could tell she was still learning to handle fame, this being her very first brush with it. Still not *quite* big enough to be recognized on the street—and neither were we, not by a long shot—but big enough to find on any country station or Best Buy CD rack.

It hadn't made her self-conscious yet, if that makes any sense.

KYLIE CAMERON, *model and singer*

One thing that Ryan would do at her early shows was pick audience members by random, and on their ticket, they'd get a little june-bug icon—you know, like the song. That meant they had VIP access.

It wasn't like my shows, or, I mean, *any* shows, where you had to pay extra to get the VIP ticket. No—it was totally democratic, totally random.

And that kind of pissed me off, you know? Because this girl was starting to be a big deal, even though I didn't know what the hell bluegrass was. But she had this bomb-ass dress in that *Entertainment Weekly* photo, and I *wanted* a dress like that. Silver was having a huge comeback because of her.

And I wanted to meet her. I wanted to know what was going on in those VIP meet and greets.

I was just modeling back then; I didn't have any music industry cred, so I didn't have any connections who could get me backstage like I do now. In fact, I got into music *because* of Ryan. She's really been so influential to so many people. But the only way I could get to that backstage was if I bought someone else's little june-bug ticket, and those were quite hard to come by.

Ryan did a really good job of building this . . . intrigue. A young girl breaking into the bluegrass scene, becoming mainstream with a genre that no one on the *Billboard* Hot 100 had thought about in—I don't know, decades? But her singles started showing up there on her

Southwest Sands tour. What was her deal? Where were all these little bluegrass fans coming from?

And, listen. People can be . . . well, just mean. Look at Olivia Rodrigo. Look at Charli XCX. Anytime you start to see someone totally unknown—*especially* a young woman—skyrocket upward, people are all like, What's the catch? Why does *she* deserve it? Tale as old as fucking time.

I'll admit I hung out with a lot of those people. I'll admit that I *was* one of those people. You don't know catty and petty until you've clawed your way up in the modeling industry, and I had to earn my stripes somehow. The word around our circle was that Ryan's whole wide-eyed, girl-next-door thing was nothing more than a schtick. You don't grow that fast without stepping on some necks, and this all-American persona of *Who, me? I'm just a girl! I'm so excited to be onstage, and I love baking cookies and watching movies with my best friend!* drove some of my friends batshit.

Maybe it felt like an insult. We'd learned early on that we had to be tough in our industry, we had to take a lot of abuse. And here she was acting like it was all cupcakes and butterflies and . . . she was having *fun*. Or seemingly so.

I told myself that I was hate-reading the magazine articles about her, hate-listening to her songs, hate-buying a ticket to her show and getting there early to see if anyone would exchange a june-bug ticket with me. I went alone except for my own security guard. None of my other friends were interested back then.

But there was something else when I finally got to my seat, VIP ticket in hand from some eleven-year-old who'd been gullible enough to trade it for a hundred dollars. I felt my pulse jump when she came onstage playing all those crazy jangling notes and whooping it up, getting the crowd to clap faster and faster and stomp their feet until I could hardly see her fingers flying over her strings. I remember having this image of my grandma, but, like, my grandma at my age, listening to something like this or even playing it herself and feeling . . . alive.

It was fun. Plain and simple. I was enjoying myself.

I still expected something exclusive when I headed to the VIP lounge after the show; I don't know what. Carved ice, sushi, champagne—even though she had just turned sixteen and I would only be nineteen the next month. So when I had my ticket scanned by this massive dude in all black, I was, well . . . surprised by what I saw.

There was no huge line to see her. There was no security or roped-off area. Ryan was right there and had changed into a flannel T-shirt, and she was playing *Guitar Hero* on a projector screen with a couple of fans competing with her and the rest cheering her on. I just stood there and stared.

It was like no other VIP lounge I'd ever been to. There was a big archway decorated with fake bluebonnets and a wooden sign where you could take pictures, yes, but there were also craft-services tables full of pizza rolls, nachos, brownies, sodas. It wasn't until I grabbed a plate that I realized how hungry I was, and I was there stuffing pizza rolls in my mouth when Ryan came over to grab a 7UP.

"Hi!" I said with my mouth full. "Such a great show! I'm Kylie Cameron."

She smiled. "Hey, thanks so much for coming, Kylie! I'm so glad you liked it, that means a lot."

I could tell she didn't recognize my name. I mean, that's fine, I wasn't *major* major back then, but it did take me down a peg. I mean, I was in a *lot* of magazines. And I had a second where I felt all that judgment swell up again at her fake-looking smile.

"Yeah, I model with Marco Barbieri, so I was able to get tickets through them," I said. "I was surprised at how hard it was to get backstage; usually that's pretty easy for me. I don't know what I was expecting, but . . . it wasn't this."

I widened my eyes a little and raised my eyebrows. I was trying to be mean.

But Ryan's own eyes got big and she gushed, "Oh wow, Marco Barbieri? That's amazing! Wait—I totally recognize you! I think I've seen your picture at Kohl's?"

I mean, no. I never modeled for Kohl's. But between looking at her quizzically and saying, "Um, yeah, I guess," and her going on about how cool it was that I came, I realized—oh, you're just like this. You're just genuinely nice and normal, and not at all used to fame.

So I knew I had to take her under my wing.

JASMINE

I don't mean this to sound patronizing; Ryan was an extremely talented young woman at the time and didn't need my approval. Or anyone's, for that matter—she was coming into her own. But listen, I've never had kids, and I felt very protective of her, and . . . I don't know. I was just very proud of her, especially at the start. Like she was my daughter or niece or something.

She didn't have a lot of experience with fame, no. But that gave her the freedom to sort of do whatever the hell she felt like doing without being wrapped up in what the "right" way to act was. She wanted pizza and ice cream in her VIP lounge, she did it. She wanted to make Valentines with her fans during the February shows, have at it.

Ryan did things in her own unconventional way, and it only brought people closer and closer to her.

SKIP

I had to be careful to stay levelheaded as record sales rose and Ryan's shows began to sell out. *It's a good sign,* I told myself. We've got a good thing going, and we're going to stay the course.

Ryan and Jas were beginning to work on her second album, too, and I didn't want us to get ahead of ourselves. I wanted her sound to stay raw and hungry and uninhibited. No time to rest on laurels.

But when I got the call that she was nominated for New Artist of the Year by the Country Music Association, I gave the whole studio the day off and took us out for ice cream.

MARI

Ryan was scary calm the whole afternoon leading up to the CMA Awards. I'd flown into Nashville a few days before, and we went to the zoo, the Johnny Cash Museum, the Parthenon. She seemed glad to have some time off and asked a lot about what was new with me. I told her that I would get my license in January, and she said, "Oh my god, I forgot."

"Forgot what?" I said.

"Forgot to learn how to drive."

I laughed, but she looked totally bewildered. "There's plenty of time, isn't there?" I said. "You've been busy."

"Yeah," she said.

"But you're having fun, right?" I said. Something in the way she said *Yeah* made me ask. "Because . . . it should be fun, right?"

She shrugged. "It's work. It's not always going to be fun. It's a lot of pressure."

"I bet." I hadn't understood how she could get onstage in front of a hundred people, much less the thousands who were attending her shows now and would be in the Gaylord Entertainment Center tomorrow night. That couldn't be me.

"But it's what I wanted," she continued.

"And you still want it, right?"

"Of course."

But she said it too quickly. I narrowed my eyes at her, and after avoiding my gaze for a minute, she sighed.

"Have you ever taken a spin class?" Ryan asked.

"What? No." I frowned. "Like with the bicycles?"

"Yeah," Ryan said. "Kylie made me come with her to one. It's not like a regular bicycle. It's got this super heavy weighted wheel on the front, and they strap your feet into the pedals so you can't slip off. Then you pedal faster and faster until the heavy wheel is going a million miles an hour and pulling your feet along with it, and you feel like if you stop, it's going to break your legs."

"That sounds awful," I said. "Why does Kylie do that?"

Ryan shrugged. "All the model girls do. It's good exercise."

"I'll stick to jogging."

Ryan was quiet for a moment. Then she said, "Sometimes my career feels like that. Not always, but sometimes. And I wonder if I made the right choice strapping in, way back at the beginning."

"Your legs won't break, though, right?" I said. I was stuck on that. "It can't *really* be dangerous, or they wouldn't let you do it, right?"

"Maybe." She looked ahead down the park path. "It's really hard to get your brain to believe it, though."

I didn't understand what she meant by it. I do, now, but at the time I left it at that. In fact, all throughout my Nashville trip, she seemed to want to talk about my life more than anything, rather than her own. I couldn't tell if she was just that interested in learning permits and harp recitals, if she wanted an escape from her day-to-day, or if she was worried about coming off as self-absorbed. Maybe it was a combination of the three.

It got better, later on, when we started to work together.

~

Ryan had this whole after-party lined up with industry contacts and Madcap people and "friends" I'd barely heard of—it would be the first time I met Kylie Cameron and the entourage of girls who were starting to follow Ryan around—but she wanted to get ready with me. It wasn't quite the same as when we'd hung out together before her album-release party; the makeup team who worked with Ryan for all her shows came to the hotel where we were both staying and got us both ready. I was stunned when I looked in the mirror. Like, stunned—I looked at least three years older, and they'd done all this complicated stuff to my hair that somehow made it look completely natural, just . . . fluffier and softer.

We still blasted music and popped popcorn and ate Fruit by the Foot while Barb ran around fretting about her crow's-feet. I was kind of surprised—Ryan was listening to a lot more Top 40 by then and not nearly as much bluegrass. I mean, I didn't mind, it's what I listened to too. But it was kind of funny to sing along to Christina Aguilera and Fergie with her instead of the Stanley Brothers.

Listen, I don't want it to sound like I was upset with her for changing, and I don't want it to sound like all I did in between my visits to Ryan was to pine for her. I had my own life back in Hamilton. I had a boyfriend and a soccer team and plenty of things to do. And I'd had a pretty honest conversation with myself when she first moved away that things probably wouldn't be the same again.

She was still the Ryan I knew, just . . . capital *R* Ryan now. It was an interesting change to observe.

And I had an inkling that if she won that night, she'd see yet another transformation.

JASMINE

Well, you already know what happened. Our girl got what she deserved! And she called all of us onstage with her, the sweetheart. I thought that was a real class act.

CMA AWARDS, *ABC broadcast footage, aired November 2006*

RYAN: Oh my gosh. Oh my gosh . . . I seriously can't believe this. Wow, it's heavier than I thought. This is an incredible thing to hold. Thank you—thank you, from the bottom of my heart, I really am stunned. But I don't deserve this by myself—Skip, Jas, Andre, come up here! Yes, come up! I would not be a new artist of any kind if it wasn't for this amazing team, all the folks at Madcap, Mari, Mom, Dad, *Frank*, and of course a million other people I'm forgetting.

I didn't even prepare because I thought there was no way I would win this. Thank you, thank you, I'm more honored than I can say.

JUSTIN

Call me delusional, but I guess I counted myself in the "million other people" she forgot. It would have been nice to be mentioned, though.

SEVEN

KYLIE

We had the rager of the century after those CMA Awards. It was like Ryan had never been to a real party before! Like, dear lord. Get outside, girl.

All my people were hesitant about a quote-unquote "country" party, but I was like, hell, let's lean into it. Themed drinks. Skimpy denim shorts and flannel. Tumbleweed tequila sunrises—don't ask me, they put Frosted Mini-Wheats in them or something—and pigs in a blanket. Rodrick, the guy I was dating at the time, brought a tin of edibles and codeine and called it cowboy candy.

A bunch of my LA friends flew out for the CMAs, and we rented a big house in Nashville. Professional DJ, catered Smokey's Bar-B-Que, the works. Some of them stayed behind to get a watch party going while the rest of us were at the Gaylord, and when we all got back with Ryan and her friend in tow, it was cranked to a hundred. I got her a red Solo cup and a vodka cran immediately.

But when I handed it to her, she said, "No, thanks, that's okay."

I'd—listen, I'm not proud of it now, but—I laughed at her. I said, "What? You don't want it?"

"No," Ryan said. "I'd take some lemonade, if you have it."

I laughed again and her friend gave me a dirty look. She didn't want anything, either, I guess. I asked them why the hell they didn't.

"I'm seventeen," Ryan said, smiling.

"Ryan," I snapped at her. I pulled my friend Desiree over. "Do you know who this is? This is Desiree LaBelle. She does commercials for American Family Insurance."

"That's really cool," Ryan said. "And?"

I'd rolled my eyes. "*And*, she's literally zonked on cough syrup right now. Aren't you, Desee?"

"Hmm?" Desiree said. She had that look in her eye.

"Yeah," I said. "So you can keep your clean-girl image and still have *fun*. Everyone does it. I'm here to tell you: Age stops being a number when you literally have a career."

"Good to know," she said. "I'll keep that in mind."

I can't be 100 percent sure, but I don't think she touched any food or drink for the rest of that night.

SKIP

I wouldn't have faulted Ryan for doing as much celebrating as she wanted after that CMA win, as long as she was being safe. John and Barb were starting to take a very . . . well, let's just say it was a hands-off approach by the time Ryan reached seventeen. I get it. There's no parenting book out there that'll tell you how to raise your teenage daughter who's bringing in more income than the two of you combined.

Barb was more like her accountant by then, managing all the money that was coming in and out and working with a financial adviser to invest it.

John . . . I think John started to check out. He was overwhelmed, if I had to guess. It's not easy seeing your little girl become the center of—well, all the attention, good and bad. We had a few long talks, the three of us, about what it means to be a public figure. They did share with me about the man who'd followed her from festival to festival, yes. And as a rule, we provide security details to all our artists and make sure there are quite a few layers of separation before anyone can contact them directly.

But it's just an occupational hazard, I stressed to them. The bigger your audience, the greater the likelihood you'll get a wacko here or there. Barb seemed to accept it, but I know it was hard for John.

Anyway. Ryan did take some time off, which I was glad to see. Spent some time with Mari and started developing a circle of peers on her level, which was even better. I asked her how things went the day after one of their parties.

"Awful," she said. "They all suck."

I had to laugh. "Aren't there thirty-something of you running around with Kylie Cameron? Every single one of them sucks?"

"Every single one."

"Listen," I said. "I'm not saying you have to spend any more time with them than you want to. But it might help to think of them as coworkers if you can't think of them as friends. It's good to have connections."

Connections were how Andre and I built our business. It was what Madcap ran on—that and Ryan, slowly but surely.

"Less talk, more producing," she said. "Did you want me to do another album, or was the first one enough?"

I laughed again. "If either of us ever want to retire, I think we'll have to write a few more songs," I said.

"That's what I thought."

In many ways, the sophomore album is even more important than the debut. Now you've got eyes on you. Now you've got anticipation. You've managed to get their attention with something shiny, and they're wondering if you're capable of doing it again.

If you're not, you're done.

JASMINE

If Ryan was a perfectionist while writing *Ryan Holding*, she was obsessive about *Firebird*. I talked to Skip a million times—don't ever say that thing to her, don't even mention the word *shiny.* No metaphors. You're only going to get in her head.

I think Ryan felt the pressure instinctively, though. It's tough going it alone. At that point, we still kind of had a revolving-door band backing her; I know she was wanting better camaraderie with her musicians that just wasn't there yet. One of Skip's goals, which was somewhat contingent on the success of album two, was to put together a good, strong backing band with long-term contracts. Maybe even get some dancers, because Ryan was showing a theater kid's affinity for making up her own moves on the spot and working the crowd.

We had to solidify our foundation before having those conversations. But I told her not to think about any of that—your job isn't to focus on anything but your music.

There was one day in the studio when Ryan was almost doubled over with the effort of lyric writing for "Didn't You Realize." She was literally hunched over her banjo. She was stuck on the chorus and didn't like any of the rhymes I suggested for *realize*. I noticed that she had a habit of tugging at her earlobes when she was stressed, and she was yanking on her left one pretty hard just then. So I said, "Hey, kiddo, let's take a walk."

She stared at me, wide-eyed. "We're not done."

"We're not getting anywhere," I said. "So come on. Fresh air always helps."

We walked all the way to Jim-Jim's Water-Ice on Sixth—god, I still miss that place—and got Italian ice together. Melon ball for me and strawberry kiwi for her. And I said, "I know you're not having writer's block. I saw you with your notebook all throughout the Southwest Sands tour. So what is it?"

Ryan didn't answer for a little bit. Then she said, "I've got a lot of material, yeah. But it all sounds . . . different."

"Different how?"

"It's not like my first album," she said. "And my first album was what got me here—I know I don't have to do the same exact thing again, but that's what everyone *liked* the first time."

"That's true," I said. "But they also liked *you*. They liked what you did with the music that was authentic to you. And this album will also be authentic to you."

She took a deep breath and sounded exasperated. "A lot of what I wrote is about being on tour. About meeting new people and going to parties."

"So? Write what you know; it's good advice for a reason."

"Going on tour is not very bluegrass." She took a big scoop of her water ice, and I realized we'd gotten to the crux of the problem. "Doc Watson never wrote about being offered pills by someone who models sunglasses for a living."

I stopped short and said, "You didn't take any, did you?"

"Pills? No."

I'm twenty-four years sober this year, I'm damn proud to say. And I owe that to Skip and the environment at Madcap, where having a seventeen-year-old as a coworker really contributed to that success.

"Those things will mess you up," I told Ryan. "I'm fucking serious, it's not worth it. Okay?"

I wanted to drive my point home. She looked embarrassed and said, "Yeah, I *know*. Okay."

"Okay, good," I said. "So I can pretend I didn't hear that if your mother ever asks."

"She won't." I remember Ryan stirring her ice very aggressively.

"But anyway, you're wrong," I said. "Haven't you heard 'The Junkie's Prayer'? 'Mama Tried'? There's such a thing as dark country. Not that that's what you're writing, but you know—your bluegrass can be whatever you want it to be. A traditional genre plus mixed with your own experiences and modern ideas—that's what makes it original."

She'd recovered a bit from my scare-you-straight. "That's true," she said.

"And don't tell Skip I said this," I went on. "But say you put your heart and soul into this album and it flops. So what? If people don't want to hear what you have to say, do you want their money anyway?"

Ryan laughed. "I mean, yes."

"Sellout." And I elbowed her.

But she whipped off two songs—"Whiskey and Wine" and "Candy Girl"—when we got back to the studio.

Reddit user u/candygrrrl_1997

I'm sorry but it's so obvious to me that Kylie's model friends did something to Ryan. Ryan took Kylie from them, she got with a lot of their boyfriends, she made a lot of enemies. I mean, these girls were mega powerful. You don't think they could have paid someone off to take her out and hush it up? Ur kidding yourself.
#RescueRyan

HELLADONNA, *New York–based pop artist*

I dunno, I always steered clear of Ryan Holding. Sure, she's prolific. She's worked hard. I'll be the first to say that her output is insane—like, the girl must be *tired.* Ryan is a lot, in every sense of the word.

But here's the thing: She never struggled. Not like the rest of us.

Sure, everyone has their own journey, whatever, but I've never seen anyone shoot to fame as fast as she did. Ryan worked hard, but time and again, she *never* faced rejection. Open doors at every turn. You want to learn the banjo? Boom, here's an instrument and lessons every week. You want to travel around the country playing festivals? Boom, we can afford that. Move to Texas for a record contract?

Boom, no problem, sweetie, we'll just uproot our entire lives so you can follow your dreams.

I worked at the bodega down the street to buy my first Casio keyboard. My parents thought music was not only a phase but a terrible career path. I was scraping *pennies* together. I played late-night bar shows forever and got total radio silence back from my demo tapes before I clawed my way into the industry. You're talking to Victor!a for this project, right? I know for a *fact* that she went home to Ohio after two years of trying to make it in LA. Just went home and gave up and got a job at Kohl's before she got a call back from her agent.

Artists like Victor!a and me, we earned our spot here.

But then here comes Ryan Holding, all sweet and perfect, beloved by all. Okay. And I did my best to be open minded, but you know what? I think she thinks she's better than us.

In fact, I *know* she does, wherever she is. Even now. The first time I met her at a party, she was gushing all over me, *Oh wow, it's so cool to meet you, I can't believe I'm actually talking to Helladonna!* And I was like, okay, we're laying it on a little thick. But whatever, she was young and eager.

And then later that night, I'm walking back from the bathroom and what do I overhear? Ryan's talking to her friend Mary or Martha or whoever and thinks no one's listening, and she's like, "Oh, Helladonna? No, I haven't heard any of her albums, you know I don't listen to pop. But you've gotta pretend to be a fan of everyone around here if you know what's good for you."

Yeah. The two of them laughed their heads off like it was the funniest thing they'd ever heard. And just a few years later she's calling *herself* a pop star?

You'll excuse me if I'm underwhelmed.

She always had that big goofy grin on her face, acting all polite and interested at parties—until she'd drop it and roll her eyes when she thought no one was watching, usually after talking to those model girls. Like, that's venomous. I'm not saying I could stand those catty bitches any more than she could; they'd put me down too. Plenty. Said my themed shows and costumes were tacky and I looked like a clown in all my stage makeup.

Which, by the way—you know I did all that first, right? I was here creating elaborate productions in sold-out stadiums before anyone knew Ryan Holding's name. My Candy Wonderland tour grossed $52 million in 2012, way before Ryan started up on her derivative vaudeville bullshit. I just think it's . . . *interesting* how some of our ideas have overlapped.

Anyways. Just don't be *fake*, you know? Don't act like you think someone is the shit and then turn around and mock me to your little hick friend from Massachusetts.

I got the sense she felt she wasn't "like other girls." We know the ones, these days—they call them pick-me girls. I mean, Ryan's whole second album had all these songs about being different, being the one the guy was *supposed* to be with instead of his mean-ass girlfriend, right?

Not a girl's girl. Not in that era.

With the party stuff, though—you don't want to imbibe? No pressure. Everyone can do what makes them comfortable. But Ryan was like this, this almost comical Southern belle, *Oh my me, I couldn't have a seltzer! I'm not of age!* Give me a break. We're all drinking, we're being shitty youths, you're not special because you—I kid you not, she actually fucking did this once—you brought a *crossword* to a *house party* and sat down on the couch while everyone did shots around you.

I mean, just don't come if you don't want to be there?

I don't know, man. I'm sorry that whatever happened to her happened to her. My grandma always said not to speak ill of the dead, and . . . I mean, do we know for sure she's still earthside? Did they ever arrest that McCarthy guy?

They'll slander me for that, but it's good for my engagement. Keep it coming, Ryde-or-Dies.

She wasn't my cup of tea.

NICK HOFFMANN, *songwriter and guitarist of Socket Plug*

I did first meet Ryan at a party. It was in Vegas, a particularly rowdy one. I was playing a show there when she was touring for her first album, and a buddy of mine was dating someone in Kylie Cameron's crowd, so I tagged along.

It was in a suite that someone rented out at the top of the MGM Grand, overlooking the city. We took the elevator up, and you could hear the music pumping before the door even opened.

A lot of big names were at that party—Desiree LaBelle, Rodrick Flores, Helladonna. I'd heard of Ryan but hadn't given her much thought. I mean, I'm a rock guitarist. I don't know if I'd heard any bluegrass in my life up to that point.

But I remember that I got there and got my beer—I was trying to take it easy, I had a rehearsal the next day, and amps are hell on a hangover—and walked around to find this really pretty girl curled on the sofa talking to one of the models. She had a magazine in one hand and a glass of wine in the other and looked for all the world like she was spending an evening at home. Like she wasn't even part of the party.

I recognized her hair first. She was wearing this drapey metallic shirt with tight black pants, and I made the connection from a photo I'd seen in one of the tabloids.

I waited until the model went for a refill before making my way over to Ryan and saying, "Any good stories in there?" I don't think I'd ever seen someone read a magazine at a party.

She looked up at me and shrugged, and said, "It's just a tourist thing, so no. Sounds like there are some good museums around town, though."

Ryan flipped the cover closed to show me the title: *Las Vegas Life*. It had this couple who was dressed to the hilt, reacting with shocked, gleeful faces at the results of a craps table.

"This could be us," she said, raising her eyebrows.

I laughed. "Yeah? You like craps?"

"No." She laughed too. "I've never gambled in my life. I'm completely out of place here."

It seemed like a true statement on more than one level. But . . . it was kind of cute. "I mean, if there's anywhere you should gamble, it's here," I said.

"I know, I know." She made a face. "My band has already made the rounds at the casinos."

"Your band—you're Ryan Holding, right? I'm Nick Hoffmann of Socket Plug." I realized I still hadn't introduced myself, and I sort of felt like an ass. I didn't want her to think I expected her to know everyone on sight.

But she smirked and said, "I know. You guys just headlined Coachella, didn't you? That's pretty epic."

I was impressed and, again, felt kind of guilty that I didn't know anything about her genre. I said that we did, and asked, "You keep up with a lot of rock news over in bluegrass world?"

"I don't live under a rock," she said. "Plus, I think Kylie's friend Savannah has a huge crush on you; she goes on about Socket Plug all the time. I probably shouldn't even be talking to you."

"Oh, I see," I told her, acting like I was super interested in the news. "Tell me more about this Savannah girl."

Ryan leaned back on the sofa and clasped her hands together over her knee like she was giving an interview. "Well, she's older than me. She models for Versace. She can do that thing where she ties a cherry stem with her tongue."

I smirked. "But I bet she doesn't know where all the best museums in Vegas are."

Ryan shook her head. "I wouldn't count on it. And she's missing out—there's one that's completely devoted to bobbleheads."

"No way." I grinned. "Like baseball-player bobbleheads?"

"Baseball players, politicians, Mickey Mouse . . . you name it."

"I've never heard of such a thing," I said.

"Believe it," she said. "You want me to point it out to you?"

She stood with her glass of wine, and I realized she meant I should come with her. It was the most interesting conversation I'd had at a party in a while—most parties in those days didn't involve conversation at all—so I was happy to follow. Instead of leading me out to the balcony like I thought she would, we wove through the crowd and out of the suite entirely.

I thought I understood then—I thought she was leading me back to her room, and that did make me feel both thrilled and nervous. Celebrity that I am, I've always been more awkward than my bandmates about that side of the rock star lifestyle.

But no, Ryan surprised me again. She pushed through a door that almost certainly should have been locked and led me to the roof of the building, complete with an empty bar and deserted patio. We were partying on a Monday night, did I mention? Weekends and weekdays don't exist in jobs like ours.

It was . . . breathtaking. Big carpet of neon spreading out before us, and then this blank, dark sea beyond that where the desert stretched into nothingness. It gave me this crazy feeling in my chest. Ryan went right up to the edge and looked out over the railing with the wind whipping all her hair around her face.

She set her wine down and pointed north. "You see the Eiffel Tower over there?" she said. I did. "Okay, follow the road beyond that and look at that tiny red light next to the tall building there, with all the lights off. See that?"

"I think I do," I said. I didn't.

"That's the bobblehead museum."

I squinted. "No way you can tell from here!"

She said, "Yes, I can."

"No, you can't."

Ryan turned around and leaned on the railing and smiled wide. "You're right, I can't. I just wanted an excuse to bring you up here."

I should've been more used to flirting by then, but it felt like my stomach had slipped off the rooftop. I asked, "Is that so? Why me?"

She shrugged. "Guys don't usually like to talk *to* me at these things. They just sort of talk *at* me and try to get me to dance with them until I walk away. It was nice to have a fun conversation for a change."

It didn't hit me then, but it really sucked that she had to deal with that. And looking back, she was a kid. I wasn't much older—the youngest in my band, I want to set the record straight on that. But it's a bummer what she had to go through. I thought of a couple of my other friends downstairs who were probably being douchebags to other girls like Ryan as we spoke.

"I'm sorry you've met so many morons," I said. "I try not to be one."

"You're doing a good job of it."

And then she tugged the front of my shirt, gently, and pulled me forward to kiss me.

~

Exclusivity is . . . kind of a weird thing to navigate in these careers, especially when you've grown up with so much relationship instability like Ryan and I did. You're constantly moving around, working with different people, seeing your team shift; it's hard to know when to get close and when to move on. How do you date someone who lives in a different state and has a tour schedule opposite yours? It's even weirder than long distance.

Ryan and I spent as much of the next two days—and nights, if I'm being honest—together as we could. "Neon Dreams" on the *Firebird* album? Not to brag, but yeah, that one was about me. We did, in fact, "walk down those Las Vegas streets like anything was possible and nothing was real."

But we both had to head out of town midweek. Socket Plug was going back to LA, and Ryan was set to play her last show in San Francisco. We very bravely and, um, passionately said goodbye and promised to meet up with each other the next time we overlapped.

If I'd known back then what would happen in San Fran, I would have gone with her. I wish I had.

SKIP

It's unfortunate that you can't really see the loopholes in the security system until something like this happens. Things like OSHA, you know, are written in blood—it takes mistakes to understand what we could be doing better.

And really, it was a sign that Ryan was starting to get so big that she needed a more robust security detail. But I still felt goddamn guilty that it had to happen at all.

JASMINE

Simon McCarthy was some creep in his thirties who'd been attending every single one of Ryan's shows—we saw that from the ticket records afterward. Like, literally following her on every stop of the Southwest tour; the guy must have been shelling out for planes and cabs left and right. Ugh.

But the San Francisco show was the first time he managed to get one of those VIP june-bug tickets. I don't know why it didn't raise eyebrows when a man of that age got in the backstage line all alone. I mean, Ryan welcomed everyone, but that should have put the bouncers on alert.

SKIP

McCarthy struck up a conversation with some other girl waiting to get backstage and walked in with her. Security thought they were together, so I guess they stopped keeping an eye on him? I don't know. We ended our contract with that company after the incident, I'll tell you that much.

Anyway. He acted normal for the first half hour or so, and then . . . well, he slipped something in Ryan's Diet Coke. The fucker must've had a lot of practice. You could hardly even catch it in the security footage afterward.

She sat down to watch the other fans play *Guitar Hero*, and after a while you see her sort of start to slump, start to rub her forehead. That's when McCarthy steps in, starts asking Ryan if she's feeling okay, if she needs anything. Yeah, she needs you to get the fuck away from her.

Sorry. It gets me riled up even now.

I have no clue what his plan was. This dude tries to lead her out the back exit like no one's going to stop him, says Ryan needs some fresh air, when security *finally* gets off their asses and asks where the hell he thinks he's going.

I mean, that was that—you could tell by one look that Ryan was pretty out of it. Security restrained him, the cops were called, Ryan was rushed to the hospital, the whole ordeal. Thank god it was just a small dose of GHB. She recovered quickly—I've never been more grateful.

MARI

McCarthy was a complete and utter idiot. But Ryan was extremely lucky that, one, he was caught on camera, and two, the drug was still in her system when they tested her at the hospital. Otherwise there might not have been enough to charge him. He didn't even get the second felony charge for attempted sexual assault because they couldn't "prove intent."

Bullshit.

They did arrest him, though, and they did charge him with one felony, yes. He got three years.

All the "amateur sleuths" on Reddit act like McCarthy is the be-all and end-all in Ryan's disappearance. He's got obvious motive, they say. He'd tried it once before. Then there was that stupid viral photo going around of Ryan at the VMAs, and everyone *swore* you could see McCarthy in the background, until a second photo taken from a different angle proved that the first was doctored. It was actually Martin Scorsese in bad lighting.

In fact, that was another one of your photos, wasn't it, Elyse?

Anyway. I mean . . . did I try at one point to track down where McCarthy was the night of the VMAs? Yes. I admit it. I wanted to put the rumors to rest.

Could I find a good alibi for him? No.

But for me, it boils down to this: McCarthy is a *complete and utter idiot*. No asshole who tries to roofie a seventeen-year-old in a room full of fans and security has the brains to kidnap her *without a trace* when she's older and exponentially more recognizable and protected.

I have to believe that.

JASMINE

Ryan took two weeks off after the McCarthy thing, which was the most I'd known her to rest while we were actively working on an album.

Well deserved, though. I wish she'd taken more.

MARI

I flew back to Austin to be with her again. It was fall break for me, anyway, and I wanted to make sure she was okay.

I didn't know if Ryan wanted to talk about it or not, so I didn't press. But when we were curled up on the couch watching TV my second night there, she said, "I didn't even know what was happening."

I paused and turned to her. "With the . . . the roofies?"

She nodded. "I didn't even know I was in any trouble. I remember this little girl, Eliza, was just about to get a twenty-note streak, and I was really excited for her and trying hard to focus. And then . . . I was in the hospital."

I said, "That's really scary, Ryan."

"Yeah." She stared straight ahead. "If I didn't know what was happening this time, how will I protect myself if it happens again?"

I put my arms around her. "It won't happen again."

"I don't want people to have to hover over me," Ryan said, rubbing the back of her hand across her eyes. "I want to be able to take care of myself. I want to be able to take care of *others*. All those girls could have been in danger. And I didn't—I didn't even realize it."

"How could you have?" I said, and I squeezed her tighter.

It wasn't exactly the most helpful response—I think she was looking for actionable advice—but, hell, I was just a teenager too. I didn't know how to deal with roofies. I had to believe it wouldn't happen again, though. Skip was already putting preventive measures in place: contracting with a different security company, placing more eyes in the VIP lounge, adding lids and straws to all drinks.

But I think it was starting to dawn on her, and on me, too, that this was how it would be for the rest of Ryan's career. She'd have to be subject to more protection the bigger she got, always looking over her shoulder for someone who might have it out for her.

Or for people close to her.

"Is it worth it?" she murmured.

"Only you can answer that," I told her. "And if someday you decide it's not . . . then that's it. You can do something other than music."

Ryan shook her head. "I can't do anything else. I've barely even finished high school."

I held her closer. "You could. It's never too late."

She let out a big, long sigh. "This is still what I want. It's still worth it to me. I've got a lot of ideas I haven't even tried yet."

EIGHT

SKIP

When Ryan got back from her little hiatus, she had a meeting with me, Jas, and Serge, the film producer we'd hired to do her music videos for *Firebird*. We'd done a very simple one after releasing "Shoes on the Dash," just a two-location shoot with Ryan playing her banjo on an Austin rooftop and standing next to an old Buick—close-ups, lots of hair flips, early 2000s oversaturation. You know the kind.

But our budget for this sort of thing had grown. And so had Ryan's ambition.

We had five singles planned for *Firebird*, and videos to go along with each: "Neon Dreams," "Blue Jean Baby," "Didn't You Realize," "Whiskey and Wine," and finally, "Alcatraz." There was a lot of creative opportunity there—Ryan asked if she could be more involved this time around, and I said of course.

She came ready to that first meeting.

"'Shoes on the Dash' was good," she said. "But what if we did more storytelling? All these songs would be really great for a short film format."

I was already seeing dollar signs—but in our expenses, not our bottom line. "What do you have in mind?" I said.

Ryan raised her eyebrows at me. "What's our budget?"

I shook my head. "How about you write a proposal first. Then we'll see what's possible."

Well, shit. Little did I expect her to pull out this huge manila folder, all fat with notes and screen directions and these crazy collages made out of magazine clippings.

I remember just looking over at Serge—this very serious, cerebral, well-respected director who had clawed his way up to the VMAs from Staten Island, where he'd spent his childhood filming the neighborhood with a Super 8 camera—and I wondered, *What the hell could he be thinking?*

SERGE CHIRKOV, *film director and auteur*

She had grit. I remember watching her lay out all these, well, scrapbook pages, essentially, and hearing her talk through her ideas for each video.

A young girl her age, I would have expected them to be just that—ideas, and nothing more. But Ryan Holding had envisioned the piece from beginning to end.

People see a difference between cinema and music videos. Perhaps they think of the type of music video that is simply a stand-in for a live performance, such as Ryan's first foray, or the many videos of the '80s and '90s in which the artists sing to the camera and do little else. But Michael Jackson, Duran Duran, Madonna—I think Ryan took great inspiration from these. "Material Girl" was most certainly included in her printouts.

The music video *should* be a little gem of cinema.

And no, Ryan was not an expert in what she was trying to convey. I know there has been criticism that she was never formally trained in film, yet she received writing and directing credits for some of these videos, culminating, of course in the magnum opus that was "Hear Me Now."

But racking focus, depth of field, mise-en-scène—this is not what matters for a successful piece of media. Ryan was a storyteller.

"What if the video for 'Neon Dreams' features two lovers?" she said. "They've come to Las Vegas together—maybe back in the '60s, so we can have all this original *Ocean's Eleven* glamour—but their fate changes, and they have to leave separately."

Her eyes had this light to them as she spoke. It was the look of someone who truly believed in what she was selling.

"What causes this change?" I asked.

"Maybe he loses all his money and can't bear to face her," she said. "And she wins big, but before she has the chance to tell him, he's gone."

"Ah," I said. "Very tragic. So they have both lost, in the end."

"Yes!" Ryan seemed to be pleased I understood.

She was able to convey the feeling, the thrust, the patina of the story that she wanted to bring to life, which is much harder to teach than technical skill. And that is why her music videos were beloved.

SKIP

With Serge's buy-in, we were able to strategize. To keep costs manageable, "Blue Jean Baby" and "Didn't You Realize" would be these sort of fun, homegrown videos. Ryan was on a soundstage for "Blue Jean Baby," with a set that we could put together by hand; we ordered a few pallets of fake silk flowers and had her sing against a really colorful background. "Didn't You Realize" was a cakewalk: just a video montage of Ryan's performances to date with shots from fan meet and greets and exclusive backstage footage of her having fun with folks in the VIP lounge, goofing around with Dust and Roses and Montana Line.

This meant that the remaining three videos would receive a very polished, high-production-value treatment with all the stops pulled out: "Neon Dreams," "Whiskey and Wine," and "Alcatraz." In fact, Ryan had an overarching vision for these three, a trilogy, if you will: They'd follow the same couple from their fallout in Vegas. It wouldn't be overt, but she wanted fans to be able to figure out the throughline if they were paying attention. "Whiskey and Wine" would feature the man in a dingy piano bar in LA, where he'd run away to work after losing everything in Vegas. His paramour or what have you, the woman from "Neon Dreams," finally finds him there, but it's too late—he's planned a robbery in an attempt to regain some of his former financial stability, and he's going through with it.

I mean, you know where this is going. He gets caught, and "Alcatraz" is the final installment. His lover leads a daring jailbreak, and they ride off into the sunset. I've gotta hand it to Ryan, though—she nailed that ambiguous ending.

JASMINE

I loved that final shot of "Alcatraz." You have this action-packed story arc, these star-crossed lovers that you're just rooting for—and this badass female character who turns the whole damsel-in-distress trope on its head.

But just as they break out of jail together and you think it's gone the way of your typical love story, the camera pans from the man, who's smiling out the passenger window, over to the driver's-side window. You see Ryan's reflection, and the smile slowly fades from her face as she looks at the road behind her.

It's a great moment. Is she regretting going to such dramatic lengths for this man? Is she wondering what she left behind? What will become of her now that she's a fugitive too? We'll never know.

People talked a lot about that trilogy after Ryan's disappearance. It's been picked apart for clues, just like her other videos. They say she knew she was going to disappear even then; that she started leaving secret messages for those who wanted to find her.

Do I believe those theories?

No. I'll tell you that right now. I don't, I can't . . . because Ryan was so so smart, and if she genuinely wanted to be found, I believe she would have been found by now. I really do.

Either she went away without the intention of ever coming back, without telling any of us, and without contacting us since, which I find hard to believe, or . . .

I'm sorry, this is hard for me. Still.

Or something happened to her. I know that's very much in the realm of possibility. She stepped on a lot of people's toes.

So.

MARI

Ryan was encouraged by the secret messages she put in her first CD booklet; I think a lot of the fans told her about their experiences deciphering them. It sounds like there was even a Myspace forum for people to talk about the different quotes and discuss what they meant. So she wanted to give them even more for the videos.

There are breakdowns everywhere online of the *Firebird* arc, but the major ones are the bouquet of bluebonnets the gambler character brings Ryan in "Neon Dreams," a nod to her Texas home base and first album; the Massachusetts state flag in the background of the "Whiskey and Wine" piano bar; and the Alcatraz inmate that has *Ryde or Die* tattooed on his arm in "Alcatraz." Ryan really cemented the fans' names for themselves with that inclusion—people went wild on Myspace.

People have theories about the other video singles and say that the plastic marigolds in "Blue Jean Baby" spell something out or that there's secret messages in the scrapbook pages her character is crafting. I remember stumbling into some really weird chat rooms when I'd procrastinate writing my college application essays. There were these guys who were dead-on *convinced* the marigolds spelled *OBEY* and that Ryan was part of this government operation to rise to fame and control young minds. Another group had dedicated themselves to picking apart every shot of the "Didn't You Realize" montage to look for Simon McCarthy and, I don't know . . . prove that he was at her shows? We already knew that. I sat in the chat room for a while and watched them debate the "evidence" ad infinitum—he was there in the front row in San Diego, he brought a friend with him in Las Vegas, there was a whole trafficking plot in the works.

I couldn't stomach much of it and hoped Ryan was too busy to see anything like that. I mean, these chat rooms were definitely fringe groups, but looking back, they were a sign of what was to come. And you have to remember that she wasn't even eighteen yet. There were already people who were too online back then, who would rather sit in a basement on a desktop and analyze footage of a teen star's concert to try to find a predator.

I told myself to look for a silver lining. More and more people were finding Ryan's music; the videos got into the CMT rotation and started to reach a larger audience even outside of the country sphere. I even heard the stoners at Hamilton-Wenham who only listened to rock and metal talking about the prison-break scene in "Alcatraz" and how it was similar to *Shawshank Redemption*.

For the record, there weren't any Easter eggs in the other two video singles, unless you count the old Hamilton and bluegrass festival clips in "Blue Jean Baby"—at least nothing intentional. And I know for a fact that Serge and Skip were careful not to include *any* footage of McCarthy in "Didn't You Realize." Those claims are bullshit.

My favorite Easter eggs, though, were the ones only we would know: the cabbie wearing a newsboy cap, Frank's signature hat, in "Neon Dreams"; the I Survived Storrow Drive shirt, a nod to Boston; the characters stopping for the Italian ice that Ryan and Jas loved on their way out of town after the jailbreak.

And a harp charm on Ryan's character's bracelet in "Whiskey and Wine," just for me.

SKIP

Those music videos were gold for *Firebird*. They built hype and intrigue that we could never have managed by repeating the first album's marketing strategy alone. I know I talk about momentum like I'm a broken record, but the beautiful thing about it is that the more bulk you add, the more you build on your existing success, the faster you climb. You know those spinning merry-go-rounds on kids' playgrounds, those metal death traps with hardly anything to hold on to? Once you get them going, it just takes a little push to bring it to breakneck speed.

I was still working with other artists, of course. Madcap had a full roster to cultivate. But it was becoming more and more clear to me that Ryan was our diamond in the rough.

We released *Firebird* in September 2008 and planned it so that one video of the trilogy would drop per month to build anticipation, with "Blue Jean Baby" and "Didn't You Realize" falling in between to keep them satisfied.

The buzz built itself. People were buying the album just to see if they could guess what would happen in the next video.

Ryan headed out on tour again in November, this time for a coast-to-coast run with a brief holiday break that would hit LA, Vegas, Austin, Chicago, DC, New York, you name it. We pulled out all the stops.

At our little team Christmas party that year, I gave Ryan a tiny box with a ribbon on it. She opened it to find the Post-it I'd folded up small.

She read it. "Eight weeks?" she asked.

But Jas looked over at me and raised her eyebrows. "Does that mean what I think it does?" she said.

I nodded. "*Firebird*'s been top of the *Billboard* 200 for eight weeks now," I said to Ryan. "Know what the record is for a female country album?"

"What?" She sat ramrod straight.

"Ten," I said. "So if you can keep this up . . ."

"Do you think I can?"

"I do," I said. "But you've already broken your own record, and that's pretty damn good in my book."

It ended up being just before the Austin show that we got the news. I told Ryan just before she went on, and I swear she had tears in her eyes.

When she finished "Neon Dreams," the first number, she indicated that the band should continue to vamp, and she went to the edge of the stage.

"Austin," she said. "You know what I found out just before I walked out here?"

A roar went up.

"I just found out that *Firebird* broke the record for the *longest-running* female country album at the top of the *Billboard* 200! That is because of *you*! You are my heart and my everything!"

She brought the house down that night. She'd made it.

PART II

NINE

JASMINE

I still count the *Firebird* tour as one of Ryan's best, hands down. I didn't come along on all of it, but when I did, the energy was electric.

There's a sweet spot an artist hits when they're growing fast but not quite mainstream, an exclusivity and hype that can't be manufactured or bought.

And Skip wanted us to harness that as best we could.

SKIP

Andre and I had been talking about expanding operations out to Los Angeles for some time, and Ryan became the impetus to do that.

I think we all saw it coming before she did—the inevitable identity crisis she was about to have.

Look, I'll say it bluntly: Ryan was outgrowing bluegrass.

There's nothing wrong with the genre. It was her home. It was where she was comfortable, and I think she felt she owed a lot to Frank, to the musicians on the festival circuits, to bluegrass fans—and rightly so.

But I could tell, and Jas even more so, that Ryan wanted to experiment. She wanted to push those boundaries. Hell, press the mute button when you're watching the *Firebird* trilogy and you'd never know they're supposed to be music videos for bluegrass songs. The cinematography, the styling of those videos, was all Old Hollywood in my opinion. And Serge agreed.

There was a natural separation that was becoming clear: Andre had our older mainstays in his portfolio, I had Ryan and our other young eclectics. LA would not only help them grow, but it'd double our entry points for discovering new talent. The cost of doing business in California was higher, obviously, but Ryan had earned us the means and the money, and it was worth a shot.

I talked through it with Ryan and her parents over dinner. Don't get me wrong, I wanted it to be everyone's decision, not just mine. If Ryan wanted to stay in Austin, so be it.

But as I suspected, she liked the idea. LA would open us up to a wider range of resources—particularly film. It was decided that she and Barb would find an apartment out there, and John would stay behind in Austin to maintain the house and property, keep working. Their marriage by that point was, well . . . Ryan didn't talk about it much. But this decision was telling to me.

~

By the time we set up the Madcap offices in Los Angeles, we were starting to look a little more like the major labels Andre and I had left all those years ago. We didn't sell out, I'm not saying that. But I mean, we got *interns*, man. We got Ryan a proper tour bus and, most importantly, a more permanent band. We trimmed the fat of the backup musicians who just weren't cutting it and held auditions for the ones who could really jell with Ryan.

It was another step toward an expanded, versatile sound for her. This was no longer your bluegrass jug band; not to be pejorative, but—you know. These were professionals who had longtime experience as backing musicians. That crew was razor sharp. We managed to poach Kelly Clarkson's bassist Jared Angel, and we had Celine

Williams on electric fiddle, Elliott McNeal on drums, Chris Murano on keyboard, just to name a few.

Oh, and Wilder. Of course.

MARI

It really was a happy coincidence that I ended up at UCLA. Honestly, the closest place to home that I even applied was Duke, and even that was pretty half-hearted. It's funny that I ended up back here because, at that point in my life, I wanted out.

It wasn't that I disliked Hamilton and the East Coast—I love it, obviously. But seeing everything that Ryan was doing made me want to leave home too. To be at least a plane ride away.

I wanted to be far-flung, and of all the colleges I went for on the West Coast, I got the best scholarship from UCLA. When Ryan told me she'd be there, too, it was like the stars had aligned.

I was working toward a double major in English and business with a minor in music education—the harp had played a role in the scholarship. I didn't know exactly what I'd do with any of that. But I'd liked the few conversations I'd been able to have with Skip about music production and thought there might be a role for me somewhere in the industry.

It was fascinating to me the way that Ryan's presence grew online—by the time I got to school in 2009, everyone knew her most popular songs and videos. She still interacted with fans directly on her Myspace page back then, and YouTube was taking off. Facebook was really blowing up. You had more access to these artists than ever before—you could actually talk to them, if you were lucky.

And the pictures that were published, the videos, the content—it was all free. It was only the beginning.

NICK

I was really glad to hear that Ryan was coming to LA. Yeah. I mean, it wasn't like I'd waited for her or anything—I'd seen a few other girls since Vegas, but the timing worked out that I was just doing my own thing when she moved to town.

She called me first, and I liked that. We were taking a break in rehearsal, and my phone rang with her number—when I answered, she said, "Guess where I am!"

"Where?" I was smiling like an idiot already, it was stupid.

"Pasadena."

"What the hell are you doing there?"

I heard her laugh through the phone. "I live here now, and I'm having a housewarming party this weekend. So if you feel like stopping by . . ."

She didn't have to ask me twice.

~

It was wild; we were able to just pick up where we left off. I went to her shows, she went to mine; we partied with Kylie's crowd and hit the LA nightlife every weekend. I think she was still getting used to the attention in those days.

It was cute how shy she was. She'd hide her face behind a menu in a restaurant or duck down in my car driving back from the movies.

I just smiled and waved to the paparazzi. Sometimes I even walked us to the car on a longer route so they could get more pictures. I was used to it, and I wasn't shy about having someone that good-looking going around town with me. Sorry, but is it bad to want to show off your hot and talented girlfriend?

Look, we didn't . . . we didn't really talk about what our expectations were about the relationship. We were "seeing each other," but I assumed she understood the way tabloids put you under a microscope out there. I thought she understood the loyalty we needed to have to our fans too.

Obviously, that was my mistake. You know what happened next.

JUSTIN

No, I did not go to UCLA just because of Ryan. Have people even looked at the timeline? She moved to Los Angeles *after* the fall semester had already started. I swear, no one actually researches this shit. They parrot each other until they're all whipped up into a hissy fit.

Mari and I were in the same English class at Hamilton-Wenham, though, I'll admit that. We went to the same college fair. She and I talked about screenwriting, and she told me they had a good film program, so I applied. Sue me. There was a screenplay I was working really hard on, this idea I had for a sort of tragicomedy portrait about a man who devotes his whole life and all his savings to finding Bigfoot. I wanted to see if I could find a home for it out in Hollywood.

It was a coincidence that the three of us ended up in California together. I hadn't talked to Ryan in years.

But did I ever wonder if I'd run into her around town?

Sure. Sure, I did.

TEN

KYLIE

When Ryan moved to LA, I was like girl, okay. We need to sit down and have a serious talk. It was all good when we were meeting up and partying between tour stops and modeling shows, but if she was going to hang around me and the girls full-time, she seriously needed to let her hair down a little bit.

I asked her outright one day when we were hanging by my pool: "What is with the crosswords anyway? The magazines? It's weird, Ryan."

She frowned at me. "I just feel . . . awkward," she said. "I don't know what to say to anyone. It's loud, and I can never hear myself think."

"You don't have to say anything if you just drink and dance," I said. It was like she wanted us to be having dinner parties, which—yes, she did end up throwing after we broke off from the model crowd. And I'll admit that they were incredibly fun. But that was much later.

"Aren't you worried about all the drinking?" she asked me. I should have been, but I wasn't, not then. "What if something . . . happens?"

I peered through my sunglasses and saw that she was looking out at the pool. I felt pretty stupid, then—obviously, she was thinking of the McCarthy thing. She was probably afraid to drink anything anymore.

I reached over and squeezed her hand. "If something happens, then I'll beat the shit out of whoever's responsible," I told her. "So, okay.

Pregame with me instead, and then do your own thing. But the way I see it, you never look like you're having any fun, and that . . . brings other people down."

Ryan sighed and said, "Sorry."

There was something I wanted to get across to her, but I wanted to word it carefully. I said, "Listen, you should be yourself. The advice from kindergarten is still true. But think of it as, like—networking. The parties are how you get to know people and how they get to know *you*. And they form opinions about you, like it or not. And that can hurt your opportunities. This is a small town."

"Helladonna's already formed her opinion," Ryan said, and she looked genuinely injured. There had been a profile on Helladonna in *People* a few weeks before, and seriously, it was hardly anything—they were talking about personal style, and she said something about how she'd never be caught dead in silver cowgirl boots.

"That's another thing," I said. "Stop feeling sorry for yourself. Not everyone's going to like you. Are you going to mope about it, or are you going to let it roll off your back?"

"She's a huge artist," Ryan said. "I really respect her."

"And you're starting to be a huge artist too," I said. "So focus on that. Be secure in yourself, bitch. Cut loose at a party, flirt with some guys, for god's sake."

She looked reassured, but not at my last comment. "That wouldn't be fair to Nick," she said.

But it wasn't long before we learned that she should kick Nick to the curb along with all her other hang-ups.

NICK

So, yes, the optics were bad. It's cliché to say that it wasn't my fault, but I stand by that.

The guys and I were celebrating wrapping up our tour at Les Deux, and things were getting wild. Ryan was invited, obviously, but was running late at the studio. She did that a lot. I was kind of irritated with her and was already two rounds of shots in, so that didn't help the whole situation.

These girls came up to us and were so excited. *It's Socket Plug, holy shit!* And they were asking us all about touring and what it was like to be in a band and everything. One of them said it was her birthday and asked for a picture with each of us. I mean, sure. But when she got to me, she asked if she could have a kiss on the cheek—it was her birthday, after all.

What the hell, I said sure. But when I bent down, she moved her head, and I sort of kissed her neck—I don't know. It was just my luck that Ryan walked in that same moment, and me getting my picture taken with my arm around this random woman and my face in her neck probably wasn't how she expected to see me.

Of course I apologized. I explained what happened. But having that image plastered all over the tabloids the next day with a big stupid headline that read HOFFMANN'S NEW HOTTIE? sort of put the nail in the coffin.

"It's not just that, Nick," she had said. "I think we want different things. And I need to focus on my album right now."

Yeah, okay, Ryan. That's probably why you went on to date seven guys in two years after you broke up with me.

SAVANNAH D'ALESSIO, *Versace model*

It was five guys, but still. I don't know what Ryan was on in her early LA days, but she started acting like she was the hottest shit ever. She went from guy to guy to guy like it was a game. Nick Hoffmann, then Jason Alvarez from *Rodeo Nights*, then Tyler Michaels—she only dated him for *two weeks*—who else? Oh, the one who was in that episode of *Big Bang Theory*. And finally Evan Henderson.

The *Big Bang* guy was weird, you know? A lot of these dudes were. Not Nick, but I mean, you get it. I'm not trying to victim-blame. But the more you fool around in public, the more you open yourself up to any guy who thinks he can get a piece. And, like, you just can't judge these people's true intentions. I tried to look out for her, but she made a lot of enemies, and she made a lot of men feel like they were entitled to her attention.

If you're a woman in the industry, you learn how to shut them down without making them angry. But Ryan was a massive flirt who had a hard time saying no.

TBH, I think that's what did her in.

Listen, I tried to defend her. Lots of people were calling her a slut, but I was like, guys, we don't know what she's going through. I mean, obviously there were some daddy issues going on. It was like John had abandoned her—who stays in Austin when your daughter is running rampant around LA?

I should've known she was trouble when she stole Nick from me.

MARI

I think Ryan was sort of—well, making up for lost time, I guess. I'm not saying I personally started any of this, but I do remember a conversation we had after she'd split with Nick. She was really broken up about that. I was over at her place—she and her mom had a pretty nice townhome in Pasadena then—and we'd made this huge nest of blankets in her room with massive bowls of popcorn, Reese's cups chopped up and thrown in. Highly recommend.

"I feel like I overreacted," she had said, about the whole incident with Nick.

I shook my head. "Nah. I'd go berserk if I saw Ben kissing some other girl's neck." That was where I slipped up.

Ryan sat up straight and asked, "Who's Ben?"

Ben was a guy I'd started seeing at UCLA; he was sweet and quiet and hardly listened to music. Which was good, because I'd had more than one guy get really weird and clingy when he found out I was best friends with Ryan.

I told her, and I saw her expression change—there was a certain guilty look she got whenever she realized she'd missed out on something big in my life.

"Stop," I said when I saw it. "I kept it from you on purpose. There's nothing to tell."

"What about in high school?" she asked. "I know you went to prom with Dean Blainey, but was there anyone else?"

It took some prodding, but I finally told her that yes, there was also Tony Baratta.

"Tony *Baloney*?" she screamed.

Yeah, the very same kid who had been teased mercilessly because he always brought a plain bologna sandwich for lunch. Like I said, kids are stupid. He was fine. In fact—oh god, he's not going to read this, is he? He volunteers for the North Shore Music Theatre now, and we're on friendly terms. And he is *more* than fine now.

I shouldn't have said that. You're not going to print that I said he was more than fine, right?

Okay. Anyway. I told Ryan to calm down and said that yes, Tony and I dated, but we went our separate ways for college. And after she got all the Baloney jabs out of her system, she was quiet for a long time and then said, "Do you think I missed out on having normal relationships?"

I shrugged. "What is normal?"

"Something that doesn't involve the press literally following you around."

"Maybe," I admitted. "Maybe that will just be what's normal for you eventually. I don't know if a regular relationship would have been enough for you. Remember Justin? Didn't you feel like he was holding you back from all the festival stuff?"

I shouldn't have brought him up. I know that now. Maybe all this is on me.

But she said, "Oh yeah, William. He was sweet, though. I feel bad about what I put him through."

And again, I opened my big mouth and said, "He's here in town, actually. I think he's studying film at UCLA."

That's all I said. I just offered the information. Nothing happened right at that moment, but she did say, "Oh, really? We should have him over sometime." She thought awhile longer and changed subjects: "I don't think I knew what I was doing with Nick."

"How could you?" I asked. "You've never dated a celebrity before. I would have no idea how to handle that."

"I guess I need more practice," she said.

And I laughed, but that was how Ryan approached things: with laser focus. Dating was affecting both her quality of life and her career image. She needed to up her game, so she was going to do the damn thing.

JUSTIN

Yeah, I was really happy when Ryan reached out. I honestly thought she was a scammer at first—she called and left a voicemail, and I thought it was someone pranking me.

But no, I called her back, and it was really her. After all those years.

Okay, okay, looking back at everything I said, I know I was kind of a dick the way I talked about me and Ryan in our early days. But I was genuinely glad to hear from her. Seeing her again for the first time . . . I don't know, it did jar me. I had this version of her that I remembered from middle school and this version I'd seen in the media since, and neither of them matched up with who she really was then.

Things had been tough in my first year at UCLA, I can't lie. I felt like everyone around me had more money than me. I'd brought my cousin's junker car out west, and it broke down the first week of school. Taking the bus in LA is a bitch, man. The whole city is built on cars, and while I was able to bum rides from my friends, it didn't feel great. My parents said they'd help me pay for a new car, but I had to raise half, and the jobs I could find hardly paid anything. I was really hoping to land something with one of the film studios; I'd been working hard on my screenplay and, yeah, I know now that it was a naive dream, but I thought if I could just get some studio exec's eyes on it, maybe it would have something. Instead, I found myself flipping burgers and working for the university's telethon call center. I must have cold-called hundreds of alums that semester who rarely picked up the phone.

I was hoofing it in the meantime. When Ryan said we could catch up, I offered to meet her downtown and take her to the beach, to In-N-Out. I thought that maybe I could get away with just walking everywhere. That maybe she wouldn't notice.

But instead she sent a car—a literal tinted-window sedan—that brought me to this big house. I still thought I might be getting punked.

But Ryan came out and smiled and hugged me, and said, "Hey, William!"

No one had called me that old nickname in years. I liked the way she said it, I don't know. Like she'd been looking for me the whole time. She had a way of making you feel that.

~

Ryan had kind of a lot of guys in rotation, but that was fine. I was just glad to be able to spend time with her. And I wanted to be there for her when these other guys let her down.

Because something told me that they would.

TYLER MICHAELS, *music producer*

I would say my one regret is dating Ryan Holding. The whole thing was a game to her, man. We met at a party, and she was *all over me*, laughing and talking and touching my chest—she knew what she was doing.

She always knew. This disappearance? I think it's a whole publicity stunt, man. You wait, she'll pop up in Dubai or some shit as soon as some trendy little pop star is about to steal her title and drop the hottest album of 2036 or whatever. Ryan never did shit unless she could see dollar signs. Mark my words.

Sure, I was into her at the time. She was hot. Before I knew it, we were going everywhere together: Santa Monica, Les Deux, Beacher's Madhouse. Photos of us all cozy in the tabloids. Ryan was always kissing me in public, in full view of everyone.

Then I say one little thing about how her lyrics could be more mature, that some of the harmonies on *Firebird* sounded muddy—just my professional opinion—and she goes ballistic. Full-on tears at the Bourgeois Pig sidewalk café on Franklin. Everyone's staring.

The next day, *bam*, what do I see? TROUBLE IN PARADISE splashed across every goddamn newsstand, me glaring at Ryan like a monster while she's crying these big beautiful tears and struggling to keep her chin up.

It was a racket. I'll say it: I don't care what her cronies think. It was a publicity stunt at my expense. You've heard "Count Your Days"—*I stared at your red flannel / While you pared me down, pushed me to the ground / Well, I'm not going to let you walk on me / Leave me in the street / You're not so special now.*

Yeah, Ryan, real subtle when I was wearing a red flannel at the café. Don't fuck with Ryan Holding, they say, or she'll write a song about you. I was one of her first victims.

What?

Oh—the DUI? Yeah, I regret that too.

BRADEN PETRI, *former cast member on* The Big Bang Theory

I don't want to generalize. But Hollywood women? They all want something out of you. And Ryan was no different.

I went into my acting career with an open heart and an open mind. I knew Hollywood was morally bankrupt when I set out, but I thought I could do some good and bring some wholesomeness to cable TV. And

I was really excited when Ryan showed me some interest at a concert we both attended—she was such a sweet girl when she started her singing career, and I'd been as concerned as everyone else when she started down that dangerous path. When will women get it into their heads that partying and serial dating just isn't attractive? Fame corrupts all.

Anyway, I invited her out on a *real* date to a nice restaurant, and thus began our relationship. Things were wonderful at first. She was beautiful, and she was really interested in my work on *Big Bang*. I could talk to her for hours about the stage play I was writing and my childhood growing up on the ranch.

But then Ryan started wanting more. She wanted to go out dancing—I do not dance—she wanted to take day trips, she wanted to go shopping on Rodeo Drive. I told her, I simply cannot afford to do all this. She said she could pay for it. She said her income was three times what I was making. Can you believe that? She took every opportunity she could to humiliate me.

I finally had enough. I had to tell her it was over. And let me tell you, I did not feel remorse when she continued on her downward spiral, spinning her little web of lies.

Have you read my book *The Big Braden Petri Theory* as part of your research? I would highly recommend it. There's a full chapter in there about Ryan.

I would love to believe that she saw the light, like when Justin Bieber spent a year off the grid in 2019 to reconnect with his faith. Maybe Ryan realized the error of her ways and left it all behind to live in simplicity and humility. She did say, "I hope this has all been worth it" in her VMA speech, didn't she? If her fame cost her her soul, well, I don't think it was.

I hope that she's okay wherever she is, and that she didn't end up—you know. Down below.

TEEN STAR MAGAZINE, August 2010

BARELY "HOLDING" IT TOGETHER?

Country music star Ryan Holding stumbled as she left a party at best friend Kylie Cameron's Calabasas summer home this week, a telltale red Solo cup in hand. The "Shoes on the Dash" singer owes her soaring fame to young girls all across America who have followed her swinging and upbeat bluegrass music from Hamilton, Massachusetts, to Austin, Texas, to the City of Angels.

"She's my role model," says Kennedy Robins, age 7. "I asked for silver cowgirl boots for my birthday. I want to start banjo lessons, too, just like Ryan."

Ryan's popularity is without question. But do her recent appearances at LA's most infamous clubs—and her never-ending roster of beaus—spell trouble for her young fans?

"I see her turning a new leaf, and it's not one I appreciate," says Donna Meyers, an Orange County mother of three. "My daughter and I used to sing her songs together on the way to school. Now my girl comes home from school every day with gossip about who Ryan's dating. I mean, what's that teaching her?"

"Ryan's got a responsibility to these girls," says Kathy Perkins, school counselor at Long Beach Preparatory. "They are watching her every move. And right now, the message is, 'It's okay to drink at parties. It's okay to behave badly. It's okay to date more guys than anyone can keep track of.'"

Sadly, it appears the steady, wholesome relationship these women hope for will have to wait. Ryan and her latest fling—*The Big Bang Theory*'s Braden Petri—seem to be on the rocks. The stunning starlet is rumored to have been seen leaving Club Blue hand in hand with actor Evan Henderson, an older man. It remains to be

seen whether he can lock Miss Holding down.
In the meantime, *Teen Star* looks forward to hearing the song that Ryan writes denouncing Mr. Petri.

MARI

The press would never give her a fucking break. First of all, Ryan could have had anything in that Solo cup, and what she did in her love life was her business. Tyler Michaels got an actual DUI, did you ask him about that? He nearly hit a *person* flying down North Garfield with a blood alcohol level of 0.14 percent and there was, like, one story about it.

Ben had to hear me rant about it until I was blue in the face, and he'd always say, *Yes, Mari, you're preaching to the choir.* In fact, he'd endured seeing my own unflattering paparazzi photos in the press alongside Ryan's, which jarred him quite a bit.

But it was true. Ryan walks out of Hyde looking slightly tipsy, and oh, stop the presses, shame shame shame, how could she do this to America's girls?

She just . . . broke down one night. I was having dinner at her place, and she was paging through an issue of *People* while our pasta boiled. Ryan flipped to an article and suddenly yelled, "You have got to be *fucking* kidding me!" and I knew she was raging mad.

"What?" I asked.

She didn't answer—instead, she marched to the living room and back, slapping an *LA Today* magazine next to the other one. "Look."

I compared them. Both were fashion blurbs; one had a picture of Ryan in shorts and a crop top while shopping on Rodeo Drive, and the caption was something like Rodeo Risqué—Is Ryan showing too much skin for a Tuesday shopping trip?

In the other picture, Ryan wore a pair of sweatpants and a gray sweatshirt with her hair tucked up under a baseball cap. I remembered when it was taken; we'd just gotten back from a trip to Portland and were stopping for gas. That caption said, Nice groutfit, Ryan! We guess the star's stylist is off duty. Or maybe Ryan's been hitting the donuts a little too hard! or something equally stupid like that.

"What do they want from me?" she asked. "Skimpy or modest? Style or comfort? Skinny? What? I can't do anything right."

I threw both magazines in the trash.

Whenever celebrities get big enough—and women in particular, but not always—people stop seeing them as their own person. It's like they felt like they owned Ryan, like they had bought her with her music. To some extent, it's fair. I mean, no artist is anything without their fans. Music is made to be listened to. But they owed Ryan a lot more grace than they gave her.

I was trying to give her grace too. I was glad she was meeting new people, but I was bound to disapprove of some of them. Tyler Michaels and Braden Petri were obviously bad, but Evan Henderson was . . . I don't know. He was worse for her in a subtler way. I thought so, anyway.

But then, I wasn't in her relationships with her.

That's the problem with this project, isn't it? That's why I didn't want to do this. You can hear everyone else's chatter, but Ryan doesn't get to tell her side of the story.

Did you ever consider that maybe she doesn't want it told?

EVAN HENDERSON

I figured you'd get around to me eventually. But I don't know what to tell you. Ryan and I had a relationship back around 2009–2010, just before she released her third album.

She was unlike anyone I'd ever met. Bright, thoughtful, funny . . . a lot of the other women her age that I dated were just . . . I mean, sue me for saying it, but they were boring. And I don't blame them. I blame the industry for making them that way. I'll be the first to admit that these female musicians, actors, artists have to work twice as hard as the men to make less pay. It's the sad reality. They have to be liked to keep making money.

So you find a lot of yes-women. Honestly, a lot of the people you'll interact with in Hollywood are saying what they think you want them to say. We talk about valuing authenticity, but we don't really mean it. Look what the tabloids did when Ryan lived her authentic life: judged her, beat her down, tried to get her to conform to their idea of what a young woman should be.

Yes, she was young. I was twenty-eight when we started dating; she was nineteen. People get all up in arms about age gaps these days, but they don't understand how small the dating pool is in our industry. Also, all throughout history, there have been married couples who are ten, twenty years apart, even more. I'm not saying it's right just because it's what we've always done. But, you know.

None of that mattered at the beginning. Ryan wasn't like other girls her age—she was brilliant. I was working on the biopic about Winston Churchill's early life back then, and she was genuinely interested in the history around the movie, the portrait of a global and complex leader we were trying to evoke.

We would talk for hours about art and music. We traveled. I took her to my family's summer home in Malta, and we would take the boat out into Mellieħa Bay and just float. She told me how much she missed her father and that she didn't know why he was pulling away from her and her mother. She told me about growing up in Hamilton and about Mari and Jas and Skip. I listened. I wanted to be there for her.

I told her about growing up in London and the culture shock moving to Los Angeles to pursue acting. We talked about my own struggles with my parents after my father died when I was young and my mother threatened to cut me off when I emigrated.

We were vulnerable with each other. I don't know what happened.

I mean, I do. I guess the problem, as it so often is, was that we were at different stages of our lives. I had a responsibility to my career, as did she, and it meant I had to miss some of her important milestones because of the biopic—we were in Europe for filming when Ryan won her VMA for the *Firebird* video trilogy. But she was on tour when I was home for my birthday.

Our time together was limited and precious. And yet, the things she wanted to do when we *were* together felt like a waste of time to me. There was a big Pacific Northwest camping trip with Kylie Cameron and all those friends that she wanted me to attend with her, and I thought I would rather chop my fingers off.

Ryan struggled with my friends too; we liked to have these big dinner parties where everyone would bring a dish they'd made themselves. Ryan brought brownies. They were classic, a very lovely gesture, but alongside my colleague's wife's duck à l'orange . . . I don't know. My group were either married or in long-term relationships, and I think that may have intimidated Ryan. Some even had kids.

I would always think things were going great, and then we'd get back to my place and Ryan would be in tears, talking about how I ignored her all night, how no one spoke to her. I would tell her that she just had to give them a chance. Did she even try engaging in conversation with the others?

And there was one night when she was so upset. She said, "You never ever talk about my music to your friends. Not once have you ever done it."

I didn't see how that could be true; surely I'd talked about it at some point. But even if I hadn't, it seemed pretty immature to keep score like that. I'm not proud of it, but I did raise my voice, and I said, "Is that all you care about? Being the center of attention?"

And Ryan said, "Why are you even with me if you have so much contempt for me?"

I didn't know what to say to that. Of course I didn't have contempt for her; I loved her. But she could be very frustrating sometimes.

Things just . . . fizzled after that.

I didn't hear anything from her after our breakup, not until her third studio album, of course, when she wrote the extremely personal and scathing "Angeline."

It made a lot of people think I cheated on her. But no. *Angeline* was the name of my boat in Malta.

It was there for me when Ryan wasn't, I'll say that much.

ELEVEN

JASMINE

Ryan's third album was the first time I saw her focus waver. I understood. It was something I'd seen with a lot of new stars—you get big, and then, as Skip says, people's expectations are up. To produce a whole album is a miracle in itself. Now do it again. And again. And again.

I'm surprised she didn't crack earlier than she did, honestly. Does that sound unkind? I don't mean it that way. I just mean that I like my behind-the-scenes job for a reason—I couldn't stand folks analyzing my life the way they went after Ryan's.

I tried to be there as much as possible for her. We established regular coffee dates—ordering from the drive-through, since it was getting tough for her to just go to Starbucks without being swarmed by then—where we'd sit on Madcap's rooftop patio and chitchat. All work talk was off the table, and I'd just listen.

Her parents were divorcing. I think I can say that now. They didn't want to make a big public deal about it back then and draw even more unwanted attention in the press, but I think . . . her mother and father had different ideas about how Ryan's life should be handled. John didn't agree with all of her career decisions, and Ryan was having a tough time with it.

It's easy to vilify John, but I can't say I completely disagree with him. If I had a daughter, would I want this life for her? No, I'll tell you that right now. But I also know I couldn't stand in the way of her dreams.

She might have been thinking more about family in general back then, especially because of what was happening to her parents. I remember her asking me, "Have you ever fallen in love, Jas? You or Skip?"

I laughed and said, "Not with each other."

She gave me a sly look. "That isn't what I said. I just mean in general. Neither of you are married, are you? Neither of you have kids?"

I shrugged. "No, no kids. We've both had people in and out of our lives. Skip would probably say he's married to the job."

"Would you ever want to have a family?" she said.

"Maybe someday." I looked over at her. "Where's this coming from?"

This time she was the one who shrugged. "I guess I'm just wondering . . . do I do this for the rest of my life? Madonna's still performing, and she's in her fifties. Do I just keep going until I can't anymore? Are people going to get sick of me?"

"Hey, hey," I said. "These are big questions. No one can answer them. But you're too young to be worrying about stuff like that. I'm an old crone, and I'm not even worried."

Ryan laughed a little then. "Yeah, but you don't have people trying to guess your boyfriend's addresses on the internet," she said. "I feel like you could have a regular family. I'd be worried about the press getting involved in mine . . . It's been hard enough keeping the divorce quiet. I can't imagine how I'd feel watching my spouse and kids on TV in real time."

"Me neither," I said quietly. And then, after a moment, "But other celebrities make it work."

"I guess," she said.

It wasn't my place to tell Ryan what to do. But it was my job to support her, professionally and personally. That was a job I was happy to have.

MARI

I think a lot of little things sort of started to eat at Ryan. She and Barb had moved to a bigger house in Malibu, and while it was amazing—I mean, swimming pool, wet bar, home theater—it was a big change. She made a few comments about how bizarre it was that *she*, Ryan, had bought the house with her own money.

Then there was . . . everything else. Ryan would complain about these people who would come into the VIP lounge after her shows just to get her to sign as much stuff as possible. In fact, concert operations ended up instituting a limit of three items per person for signing.

The paparazzi and media were predictably bad, she had expected that, but fans would mob her when she was out. I'd be shopping with her and see people pointing from across the street or whatever and think, *Shit, here we go again.*

The worst for me was catching a cell phone camera pointed at me—people always thought they were being so subtle, but no. It's weird how normalized it is now, but I remember getting this jolt the first time I realized someone wasn't holding up their phone for a signal but taking a picture of us without asking. It was a wild sense of entitlement, like people thought they could take stuff from Ryan whenever they wanted. And she had signed up for it by daring to be famous.

There was one day when we were down at the Santa Monica Pier, celebrating Ryan's breakup from Braden Petri. I was supposed to have gone camping with Ben that weekend, but this was more important. We were just goofing around and playing the carnival games, and I won a little stuffed unicorn for her from one of those claw machines. This guy came up to us and convinced Ryan to give it to him for his hospitalized daughter, who was apparently a huge fan of Ryan. Asked for a picture too. I thought I smelled bullshit—and sure enough, I found the stuffed toy listed on eBay the next day for $1,200, photo and all. It was incidents like this that should have made us more wary of Justin. I was . . . I feel like it was my fault. I should have been more of a mama bear. But we *knew* him; he was one of us. He was from home. Sure, he'd been sort of annoying in grade school, but he'd grown up, and I'd had plenty of normal conversations with him.

He was as normal as any guy studying film at UCLA can be, which is to say still sort of annoying and pretentious, but harmless.

Ryan did end up reaching out to him. I think all the dating turmoil was making her feel what I'd also felt when I'd gotten to California and become surrounded by tan, slender people with green smoothies and not one cable-knit sweater in sight: that I'd do anything for a little taste of home.

It came at a cost.

JUSTIN

Ryan and I mostly just hung out at her place a lot. It was hard for her to go anywhere without getting recognized, and she didn't want to pull me into that. I appreciated it, although I wouldn't have minded a little more exposure that might've helped me make a name for myself.

Going over to Ryan's helped me hide my money troubles from her. You'll learn something if you hang around rich people enough: They don't notice what's going on in your life. They forget that not everybody lives like them.

I don't mean to be snarky about that—it's just the truth. Her reality was different from mine.

We'd sit out on this massive deck she had overlooking the ocean and talk about what was going on in our lives. She told me about the music videos she was working on. I would've given a lot to be a part of that production and was working up the balls to ask her for a job before, well . . . before things went to shit.

Ryan read parts of my screenplay too. She said, "It's hilarious. It's very you."

I didn't know how to take that. "Am I hilarious?" I asked. I wanted her to get it—the story was funny on the outside, but you were supposed to feel deeply connected to this guy who was desperate to find Bigfoot. It was supposed to be a commentary about striving and striving for something you can never get.

And she said, "You're sentimental. Remember when we were dating? You were always so sappy."

Ryan laughed. She was smiling at me when she said it, and I smiled back, but I think that was the first time I realized we remembered our first years together very differently. I don't know, I'd thought about our middle school relationship as—as my first experience with these really powerful emotions, this pure feeling of being turned upside down by the thought of someone and knowing they felt the same. But maybe she'd viewed it as just that: a stupid middle school relationship.

"Maybe I've gotten better," I said. I dared to say it.

"There's only one way to find out," she said. My stomach dropped. We looked at each other for a minute and my mind was racing, I was like, *What did she mean by that? Does she want to try again? Does she want me to kiss her?*

Two more seconds and I would have leaned forward on my deck chair and done it. We were that close.

But instead she started humming and walked over to pick up her guitar. She would play for me sometimes, especially when there was a melody she was working through. Ryan started strumming and looking off into the distance.

"That's pretty," I said.

She looked at me. "I can't figure it out," she told me. "It doesn't sound like my normal stuff, but it's been stuck in my head, and I don't know what to do with it."

"Does it have lyrics?" I asked.

She shook her head. "Not yet."

"You'll have to sing it to me when it does," I told her.

And she grinned and said she would.

JASMINE

It seemed like Ryan was feeling unsteady in a lot of her personal relationships, and that was aggravating the doubt she'd expressed to me back in Austin about where she was going with her music. Skip and I both knew it. You could just tell she wanted to try out something different but was afraid to swerve from her lane.

So I tried a different tactic. I said, "Why don't you see what your fellow musicians think? It's always good to avoid working in a vacuum. Why don't you run it past them?" Skip and I were trying to push her to not be such a lone wolf with the songwriting—well, lone except for me, but I wanted her to get fresh eyes on her ideas. She and I had been locked in the studio together for too long.

The band was made up of people who were musicians first and foremost, of course, but a couple of them had a knack for songwriting too.

Celine was one, and Wilder—as you know—was the other.

The three of them worked well together. Celine was older and had grown up in the music industry, with her dad being half of the Walker Williams Band, of course. Wilder was closer to Ryan's age. He was also a bit of a gamble in Skip's eyes, I think, as a kid from out east with minimal industry experience, but for his audition he played this incredible remix of Joe Maphis's "Flying Fingers"—the kind of song that's just pure showing off. His guitar was like an extension of his own body. He was completely at ease with it.

I remember I sat in on one of their sessions, and the three of them were jamming together, creating this free flow of music that was just so cool. They came to a natural pause, and Ryan said, "That felt a little more like pop, didn't it?"

Wilder shrugged and said, "Did you like the way it sounded?"

She said, "Yeah."

"So go with it. Who cares what it is if it sounds good?" Wilder said.

And to my surprise, Ryan grinned and went with it.

That was the beginning of what ended up being "Mine All Mine."

MARI

I really liked Wilder. He just seemed like someone who was excited about life. And that big mop of hair he had back then . . . he was a sweetheart. There are a million examples I could give you. He organized a surprise birthday party for Ryan that summer, and we all went up to Big Sur. He remembered everyone's coffee orders and favorite ice-cream flavors. He always had a joke ready when you needed it.

I remember thinking that Ryan and Wilder would make a cute couple. I kept waiting for it to happen, honestly.

But for some reason . . . it ended up being Justin who caught Ryan's eye after she and Evan Henderson broke up. I'm convinced she was rebounding. Justin came with us to Big Sur, because why not? Everyone was inviting their friends and family, it was a big group. Ben came too—although we'd started to have some arguments about how we hung out more with my friends than his. I made an effort to spend time with his buddies even though I didn't have much in common with them—I really did. But there's only so much discussion about *World of Warcraft* that a girl can take.

We rented this lodge on Carmel Bay, and I swear, Ryan and Wilder had been sitting with their heads together talking in the back of the car the whole drive up. But when she said she was going for a walk down to the beach that evening and I said, "Ooh, with who?" she shrugged and said, "With Justin."

I remember sort of frowning at her and being like, "Justin? Why?"

She got red. She said, "What do you mean? I invited him on the trip. It's just . . . nice to see him again. We've been catching up."

"Yeah, I know," I said. "But a walk down to the beach sounds kind of . . . romantic."

Ryan made a face, but I could tell I'd hit on something. "It's just Justin," she said.

I took a chance and said, "From what I saw today, I thought you'd rather do something like that with Wilder."

I thought I saw her flinch. She'd been open with me about all the other guys she'd been going around with, so I wasn't sure why she was being so cagey now. It was like our roles had reversed.

"Of course not," Ryan said. "He's like a brother or something, I don't know. Plus, I'm sort of his boss."

I snorted. "Skip is his boss."

She rolled her eyes. "Yeah, but we have to work together, and there's a weird power dynamic, isn't there? He's just—he's off-limits."

"Does he know that?" I asked. "He planned this whole thing for you."

"Of course," she said again, and I could tell she was getting irritated with me. "He's just a really nice guy."

"Okay, okay," I said. "Well, have a nice moonlit walk with Justin, then."

"Shut up," she said. But she was trying not to grin.

SKIP

I was never worried about Ryan's new sound. Jas and I encouraged it, if I haven't already made that crystal clear. There was one afternoon I walked past the studio lounge and heard this new, complex pop-bluegrass fusion. Ryan's and Wilder's voices came from inside, laughing and singing, and I just stood outside the door and smiled to myself.

That was it. That was what Ryan would be known for from here on out.

Of course there was chatter. I tried to shield her from that. We released three singles in early 2012 ahead of the full album: "Count Your Days," "White Lace," and "Angeline." I remember I saw an old country buddy of mine at a happy hour in downtown LA, a very down-home Texan who was real into the old outlaw ballad days. No hate to him—I was too. That's what got me into this career. But he said, "Another country producer turned pop, huh? Los Angeles will do that even to the best of us."

I was like, "Man, what are you going on about?"

"Those singles ain't country," he said. "And I won't be the only one to tell you that."

I just laughed. "But are they good?" I said.

He grumbled something into his drink and didn't have much to say back to me.

MARI

The pushback was there, but it wasn't as bad as I had expected. Sure, I came across some rants online—*Ryan's abandoning her original fans, these songs aren't country, I don't recognize this music anymore.* There were a few opinion essays in smaller publications saying that she was selling out on the music tradition that had brought her her fame, and that the move to LA and the slippery slope of more alternative country pop-rock would dilute her into another Hollywood clone. They used a lot of big scary words.

But the genuine fan base that Ryan had built, the Ryde-or-Dies and even more casual listeners who just liked her style . . . they weren't swayed at all. They liked her for *her*. They appreciated what she was doing and wanted to see more.

And it didn't hurt that her technical skill was rock solid either.

ROLLING STONE, published March 2012
A NEW SOUND FOR A NEW ERA?

Young bluegrass aficionado Ryan Holding has worked hard to establish herself as a fresh new fixture in a genre overwhelmingly composed of young bucks and old crooners. With an innocent charm and a glittering stage presence that's supported by fretwork that would make Earl Scruggs proud, some have gone so far as to call this young banjoist a prodigy.

Holding built an ironclad reputation for herself both on the South and Northeast bluegrass circuits that was ratified by her signing to Austin, Texas's Madcap label, a partnership that skyrocketed her to the top of the charts. And country stood supportively behind this little lady like a proud parent.

But Holding is growing up. Madcap's expansion to Los Angeles has sparked rumors about whether the bluegrass star will cut ties with her country roots, and the concern isn't without basis.

This month, Madcap released "Angeline," Holding's third single ahead of her forthcoming *Diatribe* album—and it's number three in a line of tracks that have sounded decidedly more pop than country.

Rolling Stone has reviewed each single independently: "Count Your Days," a fiery hell-hath-no-fury tirade of a scorned woman, almost approaching metal at times; "White Lace," a soulful lament that the singer may never find true love, accentuated by a '60s-style jazz organ; and now "Angeline," a ballad-length exploration of a complex romantic relationship accompanied by equally complex electric guitar riffs—and, most notably, very little banjo—courtesy of Holding's newest backup virtuoso, Wilder James.

These are a far cry from the sweet, clear-eyed "June Bug" or "Shoes on the Dash" of Holding's debut album. It's a grittier sound, born of an increasingly complicated musical identity and plain-old growing up; still young at 22, Holding already has more than seven years of industry experience under her belt.

It's this critic's prediction that *Diatribe* will be reflective of Holding's nuanced development. Her background provides a depth that artists trained strictly in pop or rock can't match, an unusual flavor for which listeners seem to be hungry. She won't stick with bluegrass forever.

Nor should she, if "Angeline's" number one spot on the charts for the third week in a row is any indication.

TWELVE

JASMINE

"I want to call it *Diatribe*," Ryan told me one day. "I have something to say, and people are going to hear it, whether they want to or not."

The press around that album was great—and for that reason, we wanted to keep things as under wraps as possible. Helladonna had her whole discography leaked by a hacker earlier that year, and while it was still a great record and did go platinum, stuff like that is going to affect sales. It affects the way that artists approach their work too. It's just not the ideal situation.

So Skip put us on lockdown. Only authorized personnel in the studio; he did a security review with our IT guys, met with our distributors and vendors to make sure all their policies were up to date and the recordings would be safe. And for the most part, they were.

With . . . one exception.

SKIP

Obviously I'm not the jackass who actually did the leak, but I blame myself. Ryan had always had access to tracks that others didn't, of course, and as we moved into the mixing process, there would often be a few she wasn't yet satisfied with. The three singles were already out in the world, done deals. But on *Diatribe*, with one month left before the release, Ryan still wanted changes to "Dangerous," "Listen!" and especially "Mine All Mine."

I could be sympathetic as to why. Look, I wasn't in her head, but they seemed more personal than a lot of the music she'd put out. More reflective of her current feelings about this career, maybe. Jas would have the best insight. They were all purportedly about relationships, but I wondered if "Dangerous" was more about taking this step toward a new sound—how it felt exciting but dangerous. And "Listen!" was firm and a little angry, the lyrics telling someone to *Shut up, shut up, just for one minute / Let me get the story straight before you try to spin it / I can't hear myself / I can't even think / With you and your words always talking at me.*

It was "Mine All Mine" that was the genuine romantic. *If we had met differently / In another life / Would you make a promise to be / Mine, all mine?*

That one could've made the toughest son of a bitch melt. It's beautiful, earnest, sad. The singer is falling for someone who's off-limits—as much as she wants him, she can't have him. So she imagines a parallel world where they're different people.

Hey, I guess my insight's not so bad. Or maybe I'm full of bullshit, who knows. They were just songs.

But they were important to Ryan. And while I thought all the tracks sounded great, she wasn't satisfied, so I let her take the mixed files on a USB drive to listen to at home. We'd always done this with either CDs or thumb drives, now that they were easier. I didn't give it a second thought.

Until T-minus two weeks before *Diatribe*'s release date.

It was early morning and I was in the shower; I could hear my cell ringing and ringing on the bathroom counter, and I thought, *Oh hell, what's this all about?* I had a whole smattering of messages from my PR team, but the first callback I made was to Andre, who never got in touch this early, even by Austin time.

He said, "Have you seen the news this morning, Skip?"

And I said, "Give it to me straight."

Leaked. Three tracks: "Dangerous," "Listen!" and "Mine All Mine." The three that just happened to be on Ryan's personal thumb drive.

JASMINE

Skip called an emergency meeting that morning. To this day, I don't know how much Ryan knew beforehand, but it couldn't have been everything. Because when he told us which three songs had leaked, her face just crumpled.

JUSTIN

So.

I'm not proud of it. But I'm not going to say I regret it either. I've asked everyone to hear me out, and with your permission, Elyse, I'd like for them to finally listen.

Two things happened leading up to the leak. One: After weeks and months of applications, I finally got a job on a medium-budget movie set. They wanted me to be a location scout, and I lied, okay? I told them I had a car. I didn't think things through, but I knew for a *fact* that I was not going to let this job pass me by.

I needed money. Badly.

Two: Someone stole my screenplay idea.

I'd sort of been buddies with this hotshot trust fund guy at UCLA. And I'll name names—it was Austin Proust, the son of director Thomas Proust. He made a big secret of this indie film he was doing and invited everyone in our major to the screening.

What do I see? A poignant story about a goddamn accountant abandoning his family and his careful life to hunt down Mothman.

You just . . . you don't know what that feels like until it happens to you. It was like I was sinking into the floor, *through* the floor. I didn't know what to do.

So, yeah. Maybe I was already on the defensive when I went to Ryan's place that week. We were on the couch together watching *Twilight*, and she was comforting me. She said, "I always hated Austin Proust. He was an asshole to me at a party once."

"I'm sorry," I said. "He was an asshole to both of us."

Ryan grinned and leaned her head against mine. She said, "Want me to try to get him blacklisted?"

She was joking, but it was nice to hear. "I wish you would," I said.

I was feeling pretty good. I thought I might even get to kiss her tonight. Ryan said, "I have something that might cheer you up." She pulled out her laptop and plugged in a USB drive she had, then opened a track. She smiled at me.

"I finally finished the lyrics," she said.

"Oh yeah?" I asked. I leaned back and listened.

Your hummingbird heart / Always moving, full of art.

First red flag.

I looked at Ryan uncertainly. "That sounds really nice," I said. "Like my poem, huh?"

And she said, "What poem?"

Second red flag.

"The poem I gave you when I asked you to be my girlfriend, back in middle school. *Hummingbird heart.* I wrote that."

"No . . ." She looked confused. "Is it that similar? You didn't *write* it . . . I mean, I wrote the lyrics because they reminded me of you. But it's not like—"

And I said, "No, Ryan, I wrote that. I wrote that line."

I felt all hot inside. First Proust, now this. I couldn't believe what I was hearing. "I still have my notes about the poem, but I gave the final draft to you. You still have it, right? I'll show you."

Her face became closed off, and she leaned away from me on the couch. "No, Justin," she said. "I'm sorry, but we've moved around so much that I think it's gone. I didn't mean to hurt your feelings."

Well, she did. "Okay, well, those are my words," I pushed. "Could I . . . get a writer's credit or something?"

"I don't know," she said. "It's kind of late in the game, but I can see. I just don't know."

I was about to press back on that—how long does it take to add a credit to a CD booklet?—but then Ryan got a call from her dad. She picked up the phone and walked away.

I was not feeling great in that moment. I had no money, my screenplay was dead, another one of my creative pieces had been ripped off by someone who I thought cared about me, and Ryan hadn't saved my poem.

That one stung the most.

I sat there and stared at the laptop screen and worked myself up into this fury. And then, suddenly, the answer to at least one of those questions became clear.

I opened up an email to myself on Ryan's laptop and made it happen.

THIRTEEN

MARI

How much of Justin's story are you actually including? Because he does not get to make this about him. He does not deserve whatever platform you're already giving him by devoting even an ounce of attention to what he did.

I don't want to spend too much time on this for multiple reasons—one being that it was a difficult time in my life as well—but Ryan was gutted by Justin's betrayal. I kept calling her that morning until I got through; I think she was in crisis mode with Skip and Jas for most of the day.

"How bad is it?" I remember asking. "Can you still launch the album if it's only three songs?"

"We're pushing back the release date," she said. And then, "Mari, I can't talk. I think I need to take some time off to clear my head."

And I said, "Okay, of course. This is a lot to deal with. Let me know how I can help; I'm here for you."

But she closed herself off instead.

SKIP

I mean, talk about a mess. That idiot Justin had sold the tracks to some skeevy music-sharing site—he probably got a fraction of what he could have if he'd shared it with a proper black-market dealer.

We could've released the album on schedule as planned, but the awkward thing was that our whole marketing campaign was based around the tracks being a secret. I mean, it doesn't sound very artistic to say, but Ryan was truly starting to have a "brand," so to speak, and the music videos, graphics, everything, was informed by her call. We were happy to give her that creative power.

Two of the three established, released singles had music videos; we were wrapping up editing for the third that would drop after the album. She liked to do things in trilogies, though *Diatribe*'s videos were more subtly connected than *Firebird*'s were. "Count Your Days" was stylized like a '50s sock hop; Ryan's love interest takes her to the dance but then leaves with another girl, so *she* challenges *him* to a rumble. A lot of fun cameos in the sock hop—Kylie was there again, Mari, Jas even got in on the fun. And Justin, unfortunately—I would've had Serge cut his frames if we'd had our own crystal ball.

We filmed a scene with Ryan in a greaser look, leather jacket and bright-red lip down below the First and Sixth Street bridges where the *Grease* car race was filmed. They end up opting for a game of chicken, and he swerves first, but Ryan keeps driving.

Then you have "White Lace," which seems to be set later on in the '60s, but Ryan drives up to a fortune teller in a beat-up car that's the same one from the end of "Count Your Days." You can just see her leather jacket in the back seat if you're looking closely too.

The other Easter eggs I can remember were about *Firebird*; I mean, the car is a 1967 Pontiac Firebird, so it was anachronistic, but that was the point . . . The fortune teller has all these papers and charts hung up behind her, so there was a lot of opportunity there. We had the secret messages from the debut album's packaging up there; we had Polaroids from the tours and ticket stubs and press clippings all connected by red threads. Some early footage from "Angeline" flashed through the crystal ball when Ryan bent over it, trying to learn if her character would find true love.

Anyway, all that is to say we built the campaign around all this mysterious fortune-teller imagery. What's coming? What's going to happen next? The graphics all had ornate question marks and a bit of a tarot feel—without going so far as to ruffle feathers of people who still remembered the satanic panic.

So, the mystique was somewhat ruined.

JASMINE

Albums can perform just fine after a leak, and I'm still not convinced we did the right thing by pushing it back. But we could all feel that the momentum had stalled.

In a team crisis-control meeting Skip called, he said that Justin could be subject to a civil lawsuit for what he did. "It's theft, plain and simple," he said. "And Ryan, you probably have plenty of evidence on your side."

Ryan shook her head, looking numb. "He deleted the email he sent himself from my account," she said. "I don't know if I can prove he did it."

"Oh, he'll crack." Skip rubbed his hands together—I'd rarely seen him so vindictive, but if I didn't know better, I'd say he was relishing the idea of bringing Justin to the breaking point.

"No," Ryan said, and for a moment everyone was quiet as we looked at her. "Call Anaheim Studios." I'll never forget the hard look she had on her face. Usually Ryan is quick to smile, but that day her expression was completely rigid.

Skip asked, "Who's that?"

And she answered, "They hired Justin to be a location scout. Tell them what he did, and they'll fire him. That's more than punishment."

There was a long silence in the room before Skip said, "Okay, Ryan. I'll do that."

~

I'm not sure what happened after that meeting, but the next thing I knew, Ryan was in Seattle. I don't know if Barb or anyone went with her, but I do know Mari was blindsided by it. We didn't hear from Ryan over the weekend, and the following Monday, she said she still needed some time.

Unfortunately, there wasn't anywhere she could go to escape the press.

IN AN LA MINUTE spot, *aired March 2012*

ANCHOR: . . . and in music news, bluegrass star turned pop sensation Ryan Holding became yet another victim of a music leak ahead of the release of her third album, *Diatribe*, which was set to drop next week. Can the young star handle this setback with grace? Our correspondent Stefan Barnes caught up with Ryan on the streets of Seattle, where the "Shoes on the Dash" singer has escaped to clear her head.

[Footage cuts to a handheld camera; Ryan is squinting into the reporter's light on a dark and rainy street as the camera follows her.]

STEFAN: Ryan! Ryan, can you tell our viewers how you feel about the leak?

RYAN: It's not a good time to talk right now, I'm sorry.

STEFAN: What does this mean for *Diatribe*? Will it still release on time?

RYAN: I don't know.

STEFAN: Is it true that you were dating Justin William Ayers, who leaked the tracks? What did you say to Justin when you learned what he'd done?

[Ryan stops and glares at the correspondent.]

RYAN: How do you even know about that? That's private, no comment.

STEFAN: Ryan, you've known Justin since childhood, is that correct? Did you ever think he was capable of something like this?

[Ryan turns to duck into her hotel, and the correspondent reaches out to grab her arm; Ryan whirls around and throws him off.]

RYAN: Shut UP! Can't you leave me the f— alone?

ANCHOR: Moms, cover your children's ears—Ryan Holding isn't the sweet Americana singer she once was.

SKIP

You'd think they'd have some more decorum. I mean come on, Ryan was still a kid. She was upset. I'd given her that tough love, taught her to expect them to put her under a microscope with a career like hers, and she always said "Occupational hazard" when there was a salacious article or crazy fan.

"Occupational hazard," with that wry smile of hers. I miss that smile.

She took it on the chin. But . . . a person can only take so much. Have you ever heard of a fugue state? It happened to Agatha Christie, dissociative fugue. Sometimes, if a person is under enough pressure or suffers a trauma, they just sort of . . . leave it all behind. Forget who they are.

Old Agatha turned up in a spa miles away calling herself Teresa Neele and truly believing she was someone's mother from Cape Town.

I'm not saying that's what happened to Ryan after the leak, and I'm not saying it's what happened after the VMAs. I tell myself it's a reasonable theory, and then I remember that it would be impossible for Ryan to get anywhere without being recognized.

But sometimes people just snap, change their appearance, slip into another life as a Walmart cashier in Kansas or some shit. Stranger things have happened.

I've tried to find her, Elyse, I have. I've used all the resources that are available to me.

Wherever she is, I hope she's not alone.

MARI

The week or so after the songs leaked was . . . a weird one.

I had no idea Ryan went up north. I still don't know why she did it. She wasn't answering my texts or calls, and I started to get really worried, so I called Jas to see if she knew anything.

"I think she went to Seattle," Jas said. She sounded surprised that I didn't know where Ryan was, and for some reason, that hurt the most. Like, yes—if anyone in the world knows what's going on with Ryan right now, it should be me.

I would feel that weird guilt and fear times ten a few years later.

But yeah, Jas said that Ryan had mentioned Seattle. And then I saw that *LA Minute* clip and found the hotel where she was staying.

So I went.

Even when I got to town, Ryan wouldn't tell me her room number until I was actually in the lobby. I was super worried for her, but after spending my money and my weekend to make sure she was still alive, I was starting to get a little pissed off. My emotions were all over the place by the time I was pounding on her door. I felt wired.

How much do you want to know? I'm not here to give you some bullshit account of a catfight, if that's what you're looking for. That's what the tabloids always wanted.

But yes. We fought.

She opened the door with this sullen look on her face, and I said, "Thank god. What's going on? You have to talk to me!"

"I don't know what's going on," she said. She didn't invite me in. "I just need a break from everything. Is that allowed?"

I didn't like her tone. I could have been more understanding, I know—she was going through something rough—but come on, I'd come to help.

"Of course it's allowed," I said. I looked past her shoulder into the room and saw a blue duffel bag I didn't recognize. "You're not alone, are you? You shouldn't be alone right now."

Ryan crossed her arms. "No. I'm not alone. I'm fine."

She was being cagey again, and that set me off. Why not let me in? Why not let me help? You can't just vanish when things get difficult. She was always bad about that. So I said something that I knew was just a bit over the line: "Yeah, I can tell you're totally fine by the way you disappeared from LA and screamed at a journalist and didn't answer my calls."

She glared at me. She said, "I'm sorry. I don't know who I can trust right now."

That literally made me take a step back. "That doesn't include *me*, right?" I asked. "That doesn't include the one person who's had your back for more than, what—more than eight years, does it? Who's gone to all your shows, all your tours and events and stupid-ass parties with girls you say you hate but can't seem to stop hanging out with?"

"You seem to benefit from it enough." Ryan couldn't look me in the eyes when she said it. I'll give her that much.

"Ryan!" I just said her name, really sharply. I didn't know what else to say.

"You were the one who said I should reach out to Justin again," she muttered.

"That's not what I said. I never said that."

"Well, that's what it felt like."

I stood rooted to the ground, just staring at her. I felt empty inside. Then I said, "I don't even know who you are right now."

And I walked away.

FOURTEEN

Reddit user u/kill_bill

There's no way Justin didn't murder her. Take a coddled white man who already feels entitled to this woman and acts like he owns all her creative ideas and then have Ryan ruin his life—there's no way he takes that lying down. We've seen the pattern again and again.

Justin claims he was at his job in Encino the night of the VMAs, but we know that he didn't show up to his shift at Shake Shack (thanks to u/ancient_jellyfish and their amazing network of fast food friends! You guys rock!).

Justin STILL WORKS at the Shake Shack on Ventura Blvd in Encino if any of my LA friends are brave enough to confront him!!!

#RescueRyan

JASMINE

Ryan and I had coffee again when she got back from her hiatus in Seattle. We sat on the rooftop patio at Madcap, and I waited for her to go first. The smog was particularly spectacular that day—I could hardly even see the First Republic Bank building. Lovely.

When Ryan didn't say anything, I asked, "Are you feeling better?"

She shrugged. "I guess."

"Do you want to talk about it?" I asked.

"Not really."

"You have people in your corner," I said. "It's not always gonna feel that way, but you have to remember that. You're not alone in this."

Ryan took a sip of her coffee and then looked at me. I could tell she was trying to frame what she wanted to say, and to be careful about her wording: "But very few people know what it's like, right? You don't get mobbed. Mari doesn't. I was hurrying to my hotel in Seattle, and this dark car pulled up out of nowhere; two men got out and started running at me. I didn't know it was the media until they pulled out the microphone.

"I don't want to feel sorry for myself for being famous," she went on. "It's not that. But . . . sometimes it does feel like I'm alone."

I nodded, and we were both quiet for a long time. She was right. I didn't know how that felt. Neither did Skip.

Finally, I asked, "What do you want to do next, Ryan? It's up to you now."

She thought for a moment and then finally gave me just a hint of a smile. "I got some good advice from someone one time," she said. "I think I'll turn to my fellow musicians and see what they think."

SKIP

While all the celebrity news junkies and crackpots got off on Ryan's *LA Minute* outburst, the more serious publications laid off. Ryan was included in a few articles about music leaks and data security in the industry, a piece about the media pressure on young female artists in the age of the internet. But those were good. They made her a sympathetic character whose boundaries were overstepped during a very bad day in her career.

And even better was the fact that other artists knew what she was going through. They'd had music leaked or been threatened by the same risk.

So when Ryan came to me and asked, "How fast can we get some guest artists on this album?"

I said, "Tell me more."

"People have already heard those three tracks," she said. I could tell she'd come back from whatever ledge she'd been on, because her momentum was starting up again. "I'm not in denial about it—I know they're everywhere. The lady at the check-in desk had it playing on her laptop, for crying out loud. And they've heard the singles, so . . . that's more than half the album."

"Yes," I said.

"I worked hard on those songs. I'm not going to let them go to waste." She looked me straight in the eyes. "But we can make them fresh and new."

MUSIC NOW MAGAZINE, May 2012

"Count Your Days," music thieves, because Ryan Holding isn't going to let you stand in the way of success.

After a recent three-track leak ahead of the forthcoming release of *Diatribe*, Holding's third studio album, Holding and her label Madcap Records have decided to rebuild anticipation of the drop with a little help from friends in the industry.

The label announced Tuesday that a last-minute list of guest artists will sing on the album, adding new voices to the leaked tracks as well as the record's three singles, which will be rereleased.

The stars lending a helping hand include such former tour mates as Dust and Roses and Montana Line, but

> the lineup also boasts new and unexpected collaborations: rap artist Tame J, pop sensation Victor!a, indie rock band Brace for Impact, and—perhaps most surprising of all—model Kylie Cameron, who recently released a number of self-produced songs on her social channels.

KYLIE

The whole music-leak thing was where things started to crumble between me and the girls. I mean, they were all *so* judgmental of Ryan when she yelled at *LA Minute*. They were all like, *Why is she so angry? Look how red her face is. Nothing is tackier than screaming in public like some cokehead.*

Savannah was especially bad. I don't think she ever forgave Ryan for her fling with Nick Hoffmann—which, fair. That was kind of shitty of Ryan.

But it wasn't an excuse to bad-mouth her as terribly as any of them did. I was like, you guys, we know what it feels like to be painted in a harsh light by the press. For Chrissake, Savannah'd just had an exposé written up about her supposedly cheating on Nick—who she was dating at the time—with the male model on the Versace fall campaign. Just because they'd gotten dinner together after a shoot. God forbid a woman eats with her coworker when she's hungry.

Plus, I did feel . . . really shitty about what Ryan was going through. We've all trusted guys we shouldn't have. We've all worked really hard on a project just for something to go wrong. And I thought the girls would be more understanding.

They weren't. They laughed at her any chance they got—not to her face, but that made it worse—and they would play the leaked tracks at parties just before she arrived, and then giggle behind their hands all night whenever she would look at them and say, "What?"

I should have called them out on it earlier. But I did finally tell Savannah, "What's your goddamn problem?"

We were sitting out by her pool, and she was reading some smear piece aloud about how female artists can't handle fame, how girls like Ryan are too delicate and sensitive to do their jobs well. And she looked at me and said, "What's *my* problem?"

"You should be supporting her," I said. "Someone could write a piece like that about us in a heartbeat."

She snorted. "Oh. So because I'm a woman, I should be supporting some other woman's shitty behavior, just because we've both got boobs?"

"No, but we're supposed to be her friend," I said. "And I don't want to be friends with a bitch."

And I got up and went to Ryan's.

It took a second for her to let me in at first—I realized when I was standing at the door that she hadn't been to the last few of our gatherings, and I felt like an idiot for not noticing it. She'd been avoiding us. Of course she knew what Savannah and everyone were saying behind her back.

But Ryan still smiled when she saw me and said, "Hey, Kylie. How are you?"

I said, "I've been an asshole, Ryan. I'm sorry."

SAVANNAH

So I guess you just have to grovel at Ryan Holding's feet and you'll get a collab. Some people have no backbone.

VICTOR!A, *pop vocalist and songwriter*

It was a great experience singing with Ryan! I loved the raw, unleashed feel of "Listen!" Look, I've experienced some shitty career setbacks, too, and when she and I got in that booth together, screaming *Shut up, shut up, just for one minute!* it was the best feeling ever.

She was my homegirl. I hope she's okay, wherever she is.

GAVIN

It was wild to see how much Ryan had changed since the Southwest Sands tour. Her whole demeanor was different—less bubbly, more businesslike. Even "Angeline," which we sang on, was nothing like her old bluegrass.

And maybe that's just part of growing up. Montana Line sounds a lot different now than we did in the early days, I'll tell you that. But Ryan was so carefree when she was just a little thing doing all those crazy tours, and during the *Diatribe* sessions, she seemed . . . guarded.

There was just one moment when we were killing time in the studio, waiting for the tech guys to work out some problem they had on the soundboard, that us guys were messing around telling each other our stupidest jokes. *A blind man walks into a bar. Then a chair, then a table.* Or, *Why do divers fall off the boat backward? Because if they fell forward, they'd still be on the boat.*

And Ryan's guitarist Wilder comes in and says, *What do you call a chicken looking at a bowl of lettuce? . . . A chicken sees her salad.* Without missing a beat, Ryan cuts through the groans and says, "Caesar? I hardly know her!"

It was so stupid and goofy and she knew it, and we all busted out laughing.

I was like, yeah. There's the Ryan I remember.

JASMINE

Sure, she was learning, but I've come to be convinced that Ryan was often very aware of what she was doing. She ended up being more strategic than Skip and me combined.

The collabs were exactly the right move to reignite anticipation around *Diatribe*. Even the bad press was good press.

And Skip and Mari don't like to dwell on it, but there was plenty of bad press—articles about Ryan not picking a genre, commentary that her glitzy performances and videos disguised what was actually mediocre music, critics trying to discredit her and her fan base. That was a big one. It's just young girls who listen to Ryan Holding, right? So it's not serious music. Teen girls can't tell the difference between cheap, flashy glamour and quality sound. Her lyrics are all about boys and high school and petty girlie rivalries. And if you like Ryan Holding, you're not a serious musician either.

It's the same age-old bullshit. They said it about Beatlemania, about the Monkees. *Only things that men like are serious things, hurr-durr.*

So I think Ryan's collaboration with this slate of "serious," well-respected musicians ruffled some feathers. It suddenly gave her a lot of credibility. And all their fan bases would have to admit—hey, I like Brace for Impact. I like Dust and Roses. And if they like Ryan, maybe she's onto something.

Skip pulled me into his office one day, and he had that wild look in his eye.

"Artist of the Year?" he said to me quietly. It was like he was afraid to say it loud enough for the universe to hear. "Do you think we could do it?"

I smiled. I said, "We know she's got the chops. All you can do is put her name in the hat."

We both knew what it would mean. Ryan's fan base wasn't going anywhere—that was solid. Some strong recognition from the Academy would be gold for truly cementing her fame, putting her up into that upper echelon of music industry legend.

I crossed my fingers.

MARI

I don't know who Ryan spent her time with after coming back from Seattle, but it wasn't me. Kylie Cameron, I guess. And Wilder. I saw her out with him once or twice and walked the other way.

It was . . . a tough time for me. I still wasn't completely sure what had happened between us. It was summer, I was working hard at a marketing internship in downtown LA, and my boyfriend, Ben, was back home for the break. So I kept busy and tried not to think about it.

I barely saw anything of Ryan until the promos for *Diatribe*'s launch came out—they'd reshot the whole campaign when the guest artists came on.

I remember standing on Spring Street in Chinatown and staring at the billboard with my jaw hanging open.

Ryan's red hair was cut and straightened into a chic long bob and bangs. Her signature red lipstick and cat-eye liner had been exchanged for soft pink and natural bronzer.

Her look had completely changed, and she'd changed along with it.

FIFTEEN

TATIANA DEGROODE, *RYAN'S PERSONAL STYLIST AND FASHION CONSULTANT*

I'd been working with Ryan Holding in the background for many years—specifically for her tours—but it was the *Diatribe* album when Mr. McIntyre approached me and extended my contract to full-time.

Ryan wanted something fresh and new for this album. The curly mass of hair, the red lip, the overdone eyes—it had taken her as far as it could. She and I had many talks about her philosophy behind it. We reworked the material for the album and then made a plan for the year forward, the year it would earn her the nomination for Artist of the Year. Because yes, she did receive that nomination.

It was 2012 then: a time of great shifting in the celebrity landscape, I felt. Katie Holmes's split from Tom Cruise, Miley Cyrus's controversial pixie cut, Whitney Houston's death. Beyoncé, a mother. You feel these things, you know. The energy was ripe for Ryan to step into a new era of her career.

Diatribe was no longer bluegrass, and Ryan had come to grips with that. This would be her first album as a full-fledged star, a woman. No longer a teenager, no longer the Ryan she had been when she started out. And all the guest musicians on the album attested to that.

The hair—yes, the hair was the biggest part. That was a clear change. We cut it, added bangs, made it sleek and elegant. We colored it closer to a brighter red, almost a strawberry blond, removing the lowlights. Ryan and I examined the look she had created thus far, this sort of 1940s chic, and asked ourselves: *How could we bring it into the future?* 2012 was more pastel, more soft, understated. We went more natural and smoky; she did not need the stark makeup. She was confident in the woman she had become.

And if not, then it would only be a matter of time. The look would make it so.

Because it was a style fit for *the* Artist of the Year.

SKIP

I remember when I got the call from the AMAs. I was making coffee in Madcap's little kitchenette, and I recognized the number on my cell; I answered so fast I knocked the pot over, and it spilled all across the counter. There I was, talking with the head of programming at the American Music Awards, who was telling me that Ryan had been nominated, nodding along as I'm sopping up scalding coffee from the floor.

I had this feeling like I wanted to tell Ryan right away. I don't know—this was the first album where things had felt really tough, like there was a lot riding on it, and she'd worked her ass off. She'd really turned it around. So I wanted her to know that it had worked.

I ran all over the goddamn studio until I found her shut up in the lounge with Wilder, the two of them working so hard on something with their heads bent together that they jumped when I barged in.

"We got it, Ryan," I said. I must've been grinning ear to ear. "Well—*you* got it."

"No way," she said. She stood up. "The AMAs?"

"Believe it, kid."

And she screamed.

TATIANA

We dressed her in a champagne gown. She is so tall, that one. A long ball gown of taffeta with a tight bodice and dramatic skirt, and big diamond earrings. Hollywood, the old Hollywood she loved, but understated. The dress had a slit that went all the way up her left leg. Tall nude heels. She towered like a Venus but held herself well—I had to tell her early in our relationship, stop hunching, stop hunching, don't apologize for the space you take up. I will not work with women who hunch.

Back straight, chin lifted, or the clothes will wear you. Move deliberately and with grace, and no one will be able to deny you.

Stand tall.

MARI

I watched from the TV set in Ben's apartment. We were supposed to be having a night in together, and he was . . . getting irritated with me.

"If she was a dick to you, move on already," he said. "Why keep dragging it out by watching her every move?"

"That is *not* what I'm doing," I said. "I just want to see if she wins."

He said, "What do you care? What has she ever done for you?"

He wasn't necessarily wrong, but if fame made Ryan selfish with her attention, it was because she had to be. It was all-consuming. Most of us don't have jobs that center around us, ourselves, being a brand.

It had been clear to me when I saw Ryan's billboard in Chinatown that she was becoming her own brand. She had been a brand for a long time.

"I won't watch the whole thing, I just want to see what happens," I sort of snapped at him. "Calm down."

Ryan was still my friend. I knew she cared about my life even when she forgot to ask. So even though I was mad at her, even though we weren't talking, part of me still wanted to cheer her on.

Plus, I got this weird thrill of vindication when I saw Kylie Cameron there with her on the screen.

KYLIE

I got to be Ryan's date to the AMAs that year! Well, a lot of that had to do with the fact that I had no one else to go with. And neither did she. Ryan was taking a break from all boys after the Justin fiasco. Even though she kept texting someone and hiding her phone, so I don't know if there was a mysterious lover . . .

The stylists got us ready together, and we blasted Socket Plug's new album and laughed about our exes together. She put on *Eternal Sunshine of the Spotless Mind*, which I had somehow never seen before, but I was like, wow. That is a great movie.

I'd never been someone's *guest* to an awards show. It was actually kind of fun not to be the center of attention for once. We had dinner together and took our seats and waited for the broadcast team to do their final check.

"Are you nervous?" I asked her.

She made a face. "Only about the fact that Helladonna is presenting my category," she said.

Yeah. Oof.

MARI

Ben had made this whole penne alla vodka recipe and was dishing it up in the kitchen while they were counting the categories down. Ryan had already swept the Favorite Country Album category, which would be controversial, and Favorite Country Female Artist. It was the last time she won either of those categories.

I was standing in the living room with the remote in my hand; I told Ben I'd mute it while we were eating, but they were down to Favorite Duo or Group, and something in me couldn't turn away. I could hear him dishing up in the kitchen, and the clanging of the utensils sounded very pointed.

As I placed my thumb on the mute button, Helladonna walked onto the stage in this fiery-orange ballgown.

HELLADONNA

I said what I said. Did anybody disagree with me? No.

AMERICAN MUSIC AWARDS BROADCAST, *November 18, 2012*

HELLADONNA: . . . Thank you, thanks, everyone! Okay, it's the part of the night y'all have been waiting for! I'm here to announce the 2012 American Music Awards Artist of the Year. Our nominees are: Victor!a. Lady Gaga. Ryan Holding. Tame J. And Rhianna. And the winner of the 2012 Artist of the Year is . . .

[Helladonna opens the envelope, and her shoulders visibly slump. She rolls her eyes.]

HELLADONNA: Oh, come on. It's Ryan Holding.

[The crowd breaks out in applause and jeers as the camera cuts away from Helladonna to Ryan, who looks uncertain. She walks to the stage amid the entrance music and awkwardly takes the pyramidal glass trophy from Helladonna. As the music swells, one more comment from Helladonna is audible: I'm just saying what we're all thinking! *Then Ryan stands at the mic, and the crowd grows silent.]*

RYAN: I want to thank you all, but I also want to take a moment to say something important. I am not here to be belittled. I have been stalked, physically attacked, harassed, criticized, and made fun of, just for pursuing the career I love. That is what it is to be a woman in this industry. And for some twisted reason, so much of that hate comes from other women. From my peers. Helladonna . . . I know you've been through the same challenges. You've had a difficult year too. And I see and respect you. I only ask for the same thing in return.

[Ryan pauses to look down at the award in her hands.]

RYAN: It's a privilege to be able to do this work, and I want to honor every artist here tonight who has fought tooth and nail to be in this room. I am with you. I celebrate you. Thank you for recognizing me too. Stand tall.

[Ryan holds the award aloft. Thunderous applause roars from the crowd.]

JASMINE

I was standing with rest of the team backstage as they led Ryan over to the wings. She came immediately to me and threw her arms around me.

"Did I do okay?" she asked. I could feel her heart beating fast, *boom-boom-boom*, through her dress. "I was so scared. I forgot to thank you all. I didn't know what to do."

I squeezed her tight and said, "You were perfect."

SIXTEEN

TEEN STAR MAGAZINE, November 2012

Pop star Ryan Holding isn't going to let the haters hold her back!

The 23-year-old "Mine All Mine" superstar got some serious side-eye from Helladonna when the "Candy Wonderland" legend presented her with the Artist of the Year award at last week's AMAs.

"So much hate comes from other women" like Helladonna, Ryan said in her acceptance speech.

But this catfight ended with claws safely sheathed. The strawberry-blond bombshell seized the moment to preach girl power to the people and share the challenges she faces as a "woman in this industry." In a chic champagne gown and pumps to die for, she encouraged artists to "stand tall."

Hopefully she can find a man who can handle her new heights!

MARI

Ben and I broke up shortly after the AMAs.

It wasn't just about my relationship to Ryan's fame, though I would be lying if I said that didn't play a role. It was a lot of things. He was looking to settle down and have kids, and I still didn't know what I wanted out of life, where I'd like my career to go.

And I did want a career. A good one.

Without our weekly dates and his constant presence around my apartment, I realized that my life was . . . quiet.

I had a few friends, no one close—a lot of them were hangers-on who wanted invites to Ryan's and Kylie's parties and sort of faded when I'd had my argument with her. I had decided to stay on campus over the holidays because I would start applying for summer internships over the winter and wanted to get my portfolio in order. Also because Ben and I were going to spend them together.

But without him, I was looking down the barrel of a very long and empty few weeks.

And that's when Ryan called me.

"You want to come over?" she said.

~

When I showed up at her house, I stood on the front step, and she opened the door and said, "Hey."

I said, "Hey."

Then she said it all in a rush: "I can't believe I accused you of being as bad as Justin. I was a wreck, and I was out of my mind with the whole situation. If you can ever forgive me, I'll never let you down again."

I said, "You can't promise that." I smiled. "But I forgive you."

And she pulled me into a bear hug.

"I missed you so bad at the AMAs," she said into my ponytail.

"I missed you too," I said.

We spent the rest of the afternoon making pizzas from the Pillsbury frozen dough and watching HGTV and painting our nails together.

She caught me up on everything that had happened at the end of the *Diatribe* recording sessions and the AMAs show.

"And you brought Kylie," I said. I didn't mean to sound so whiny. I didn't really mean to say it at all, but it just sort of came out.

Ryan looked at me. "You know, I actually think you'd like Kylie," she said. "She apologized to me, and she doesn't hang out with the other models anymore. She's nice."

"If you say so," I said. But I was surprised; I had thought Kylie was as bad as the rest of them. In fact, I thought she'd weaseled her way onto the "White Lace" track rather than Ryan inviting her.

"How are things with Ben?" Ryan asked.

I made a face. "Over."

Ryan stopped as she was spreading marinara on her pizza. "No," she said. "Why? I thought you were so happy with him!"

"I mean, I was, for a little bit," I said. "But then it just got sort of . . . blah. We wanted different things."

"Shit. I'm sorry." Ryan didn't say anything for a moment. Then she asked a question without looking at me: "You don't think . . . *I* made things harder for him in any way, do you?"

"What? No." I shook my head. "How could you have?"

"I know he was pissed in Big Sur. Wilder didn't let him invite his buddies."

I sort of laughed, but that was news to me. "I didn't even know he tried to bring them," I said. "I mean, I don't hold that against either of you. You didn't know his friends. That wouldn't have been cool."

She bit her lip. "But all the times you were there for me instead of him, all the weird pressure about keeping things quiet, navigating the press . . . that must have been a strain."

I considered it. "Maybe a little. But there were other things, and the right guy wouldn't care about that stuff anyway."

"It's valid to care, though. That's a reasonable boundary to have in a normal relationship." Ryan leaned back against the counter and ran her hands through her hair, clasping them behind her neck. "I don't want to hold you back, Mari. That sucks. I don't want to make your life any harder than I already make it."

I shook my head. "That's just what friendship is, Ryan. I know you have my back too."

"I've dragged you into enough crises already."

She looked into the distance a moment as I watched her, my hand halfway in a bag of mozzarella cheese.

"You're making me second-guess my plan to make things up to you," she said with a wry smile on her face, turning back to me at last.

"Why don't you let me hear it before you change your mind?" I said.

She nodded. "How'd you like to leave UCLA and come on my world tour with me?"

SKIP

I remember those few months after the AMAs as a real high point in Ryan's career. We were all riding the high of her Artist of the Year win and the accolades that came after her speech—shit, I don't know where she pulled that from. She's always been bright, don't get me wrong. But she couldn't have planned that better if she tried. People were calling her bold, classy. She was speaking truth to power and was an icon for sticking it to Helladonna.

We booked Ryan's first world tour for the following year, shortly after the awards show—we would head west and continue around the globe: Singapore, Hong Kong, Berlin, Paris, Madrid. The list went on. Not every show sold out—Belgium was less keen on her, for whatever reason—but most of them did.

About 1.4 million people in attendance and a gross over more than $150 mil. The numbers were staggering. I told Ryan as we neared the end of the tour, and she said, "There's no way you counted that right. Try again."

And I said, "These are the numbers straight from the finance department, kiddo. Believe it."

JASMINE

I mean, hell yeah, I went on that world tour. I wasn't going to pass up on an excuse to visit Seoul and Helsinki in one trip. Plus, work for Ryan's next album started right away. We'd got into a good rhythm, I could feel it, and I knew that we both wanted to harness the energy that had come off the AMA win like lightning.

It was . . . interesting. Ryan didn't date anyone throughout that whole world tour. She told me, in fact, that she was "seeking herself."

"The thing with Justin taught me that I need to be careful not to get swept up in a relationship," she said. "The tour is a good time to work things out with myself."

And yet, the songs she was producing on the road were so romantic. These lyrics were pouring out of her like water. *Someday, will you take me / To that house upon the hill? / Save me and remake me, lover / With flowers on the sill.*

And *Come back, baby / Call my name / I die a little / Cold and brittle / Every time you walk away.*

I wondered. But I didn't see her sneaking off with anyone new.

Anyway, it was none of my business. My business was her music, and I was proud of that—Ryan was no longer shying away from the new stuff. She leaned into the pop, the rock, the alternative. She and I developed some really excellent instrumentals with Celine and Wilder, just really deep, soulful stuff. One of my favorite riffs of all time is still that magic Wilder worked during "Flowers on the Sill."

Soon we had enough drafts for another album. It was a new era.

MARI

It took me a long time to break the news to my parents that I'd dropped out of UCLA. Well—not dropped out. I was able to work out a deal with my counselor that I could continue to work toward my degree through online classes. Because who was she to argue that working on the marketing team of one of the fastest-growing stars wasn't a good career move?

I served my time; I started as a marketing assistant and went through the proper professional development. But traveling with the Madcap team and navigating an international campaign was the best experience I could have asked for.

And I mean, I was traveling the world with my best friend. Ryan, Wilder, and I would hit the streets after rehearsals and working hours and find food, go to museums, just be tourists. It was really freeing for Ryan, I think—sure, there were people who recognized her, but it was nothing like the US. Especially if she had a hat or sunglasses on. Asia and Europe were the final frontier of her fame.

I still wondered if there was something going on between her and Wilder. It was more in how they *didn't* look at each other than how they *did*, like they were always trying not to be obvious.

There was one night in Berlin when the three of us went for a walk near the Berliner Dom after a rehearsal. We went through the park, and it was just stunning—cold and crisp, but a beautiful night with crocuses just starting to come up and birds in the fountains. There was a cart selling pretzels, and I said I'd get some for us.

When I paid and turned around, I saw that Ryan and Wilder were standing with their backs to me, facing the cathedral. They were looking at each other. But they were standing too far apart. It's such a weird thing to remember, but I thought to myself, *That's farther apart than normal friends would stand. Why are they keeping that distance from each other?*

I don't know. Maybe I was reading into it. When I brought it up to Ryan, as casually as I could, she looked at me like she didn't know what I was talking about.

ELYSE JAMES, *author*

While Ryan was touring across Europe, I was grinding away at my job as a staff photographer for the *Los Angeles Times* and missing my brother.

I had followed him out to LA, in fact, even though I was older and should have been the one to go first. But all those Pittsburgh shows and vinyl records in McKees Rocks got their tenterhooks in him, and he and a friend took a van out west as soon as they could leave town.

I followed him a few months later. My photography gig wasn't taking off like I'd hoped, but it did land me a photojournalism job with the *LA Times*, and I jumped at the chance. I wanted to tell stories. To meet new people other than the ones I'd grown up with.

I remember calling Wilder about my plans. "I won't be in your way," I said, worried he'd think I was hovering. "You just made the sunlight sound so nice."

"In my way?" he asked, always kinder than I gave him credit for. "You'd better hope I'm not in *yours*! I have, like, twenty different places I want to take you to already."

He followed through. We met up most weeks, and Wilder took me to see the Route 66 sign, the Warner Brothers studio, Topanga Canyon.

I had coworkers I was friendly with, but Wilder was the one I felt closest to.

"I'm glad you're here," he told me once. "It's easy to get swept up in . . . I don't know. All of it. Everyone's so 'West Coast' out here, and it's nice to have people around to keep you grounded."

"Same goes for you," I said. He'd always been like that—an idealist, getting so excited by one plan or another that he jumped into things feetfirst. I let him believe I was there to be a big sister.

But the truth was that he was one of my only friends.

Plus, I was feeling protective of my brother. He'd gone from bumming around the LA music scene to getting hired by a major music act in the span of a month, and on top of that unlikely timeline, he'd met someone.

He was coy about it. He talked about her all the time without saying her name, only that she worked in operations on these live shows; I had my suspicions but came to refer to her as "the Mystery Girl" when he and I would meet up for ramen every Wednesday night.

I watched him flourish and trusted him and hoped he was taking care of himself.

It wasn't until I was flipping through a copy of *Vogue* on my lunch break and stopped dead in my tracks that I knew.

There was a picture of my brother, in a splashy centerfold shoot of a live show in Paris, gazing at Ryan Holding as he played his guitar opposite her, neck taut, fingers in motion, close enough for the two of them to be in one portrait frame.

And she gazed back, caught in the heat of performance, looking directly into his eyes with an adoration that would be unmistakable to any professional photographer.

My brother, Wilder James.

SEVENTEEN

From: <wilderjames91@gmail.com>
Sent: February 11, 2015, 6:03 a.m.
To: <elysejames711@gmail.com>
Subject: I can explain

Look, sorry I hung up on you. She doesn't want anyone to know and I respect that. Literally NO ONE, not even on tour, and that means *please* keep this to yourself. I know what you'll say but she's right, it's better to keep a low profile. Honestly, it's the only way she can be in an authentic relationship at this point—she's trying to protect both of us. No one bothers us in public. I don't have any randos coming after my personal information. Or yours!! You'd get mixed up in stuff too if people knew R and I were together.

And I know how weird this sounds but it just feels . . . right. It's a really good relationship, Ellie. We didn't mean for this to happen but in the end there was nothing we could do to stop it. She's brilliant. She's an endless well of ideas. When we play our music together, just the two of us, it's like we're speaking this language that no one else understands and nothing else in the world matters.

Sorry, I know it's cheesy and you probably don't want to hear it but that's just the truth. It's a feeling that defies words. I've tried to write about it and it all comes out wrong. She's the lyrics genius anyway. I just bang on my guitar.

I didn't want to keep it from you or fib but the privacy is very important to us. It also helps R trust that I'm in it for her, not for the fame or money or anything else, which—how could I ever be when she's in the picture? This tour has been some of the happiest months of my life, Ellie. I'm serious.

I'll talk to her, okay? You two could get to know each other better once the tour is over. You'll love her, I promise.

—W

MARI

The smooth sailing never lasts for long, does it?

My first real challenge came near the end of the tour, when Ryan was beginning her shows in Helsinki. I'd gotten much closer with the marketing team and saw a lot less of Skip and Jas, but I still remember the chill that went down my neck when I passed Skip backstage at the Savoy Theatre.

He looked like he'd barely slept and pulled at his mouth as he went.

"Watch out," he said. "Andre just told me that fucker's back on his bullshit again."

HOLLYWOOD REPORT MAGAZINE, February 28, 2015

There's two sides to every story. And when it comes to the high-profile lives of celebrities, the reality is that—all too often—we only hear one.

It's the philosophy that our editors pondered when Justin William Ayers, of leaked-*Diatribe* notoriety, reached out to see whether *Hollywood Report* would be willing to share the scandal from his own perspective.

And when we agreed, we got more than we could have bargained for.

"It was a misunderstanding," Ayers said. "I thought I was doing what Ryan wanted me to do."

That course of action, he alleges, was to intentionally leak the three tracks that were made available to the public ahead of the album's release.

"She'll be after me for saying this, just watch," he said, speaking with our team in the *Hollywood Report*'s sunny downtown offices. "But I want to come clean. I want to tell the truth."

Ayers says that Holding invited him to her Malibu home to play the three tracks for him.

"I mean, that was when it first started getting a little weird," Ayers said. "Because 'Mine All Mine' sounded awfully familiar."

He brought our editors a shocking piece of evidence. It was the draft of a poem he'd written for Holding back when they were childhood sweethearts in Hamilton, Massachusetts (see insert). Scrawled on the back of his parents' old water bill dated 2003 (*Hollywood Report* called the utility company to verify its legitimacy; "My parents used anything for scrap paper," Ayers said), the draft makes for a compelling argument that Holding's lyrics for the song may not be entirely her own.

"'Your hummingbird heart, always moving, full of art' is mine," he said. "There's no question about it. She took that line word for word."

It was the first red flag, Ayers claims. "She showed me the songs, and I wasn't too thrilled about hearing that," he said. "And then she tells me: I want you to leak them. I was like, *what*? But she said yeah, you know people at UCLA, right? We need to build as much hype as possible, and I think this is the way to go. You saw what that did for Helladonna's album."

Ayers also produced emails sent to him directly from Holding's personal account with the three tracks attached. While the *Hollywood Report* will not publicly produce them here, our team has verified their legitimacy.

At time of publication, Ryan Holding's team at Madcap Records was unavailable for comment.

JUSTIN

She wanted to play hardball. Okay, maybe I shouldn't have leaked the tracks, but maybe *she* shouldn't have stolen my work and gaslit me about it. And got me fired from the film job I'd been working so, so hard to get.

After that, I had nothing. I was working a busboy job in some sticky bar and grill while she was making millions off *Diatribe*. I was clearing a table one night while they had the AMAs going on the TV in the corner, and I remember I spilled gravy or some shit all down my pants. It looked like I had thrown up on myself. And I'm sopping up that shit with napkins and getting wet, shredded napkin bits all over my clothes, and in the background Ryan is making this impassioned speech about *being a woman in this industry*.

Something in me just snapped. All those leaks did was make her album better. And my punishment was to go back to the trenches while she got to live her dream and rake in the cash? No. I knew that wasn't right.

And you know what? I stand by what I said. I'm not convinced she *didn't* want me to leak those songs. Why would she leave them right there when she knew I was upset?

Why did she leave me alone with them for so long?

Was that even her dad on the phone?

SKIP

Everyone went about everything all wrong. If that Justin bastard would have come to Madcap when he got his boxers in a twist about "Mine All Mine," we would've given him a songwriting credit, whatever he wanted. If *Ryan* had come to me before the leak, we could have fixed it together. I mean, these things happen, it was a genuine accident. Jas could tell you as well as anyone that it's hard to know where exactly you're pulling these lyrics from, and you can't ever be 100 percent certain it's not something you've heard before. There are systems in place to mitigate that—we vet thoroughly before publishing. Obviously a poem written by a horny thirteen-year-old on the back of—what was it, a bank statement?—is not going to be in the ASCAP database. So we need that communication wherever we can get it.

But Ryan was embarrassed, hoping it would all blow over. And I'm not free of blame, either, not at all. I should've gone through the proper legal channels right when the leak happened rather than going along with Ryan's goddamn tit-for-tat revenge plan. Momentary lapse in sanity on my part. That's all I can say.

Once that article was out, though . . . the damage was already done. And Justin was veering firmly into libel.

We had no choice but to sue.

Online post samples compiled by Mari and the Madcap marketing team

rydeORdie_1990

justin is lying thru his teeth. u think u can trust anything he says???? ur probs a liar too!!!!

blazerunner_38

no star gets this big w/o stepping on the necks of other ppl. Sry not sry but Ryan has probably stolen from a lot of ppl over the course of her career. Time she finally gets hold accountable

junie_bug

Leave!!! Ryan!!! Alone!!! what has she ever done to u

WhenInTexasss

truly can't believe Ryan did that to Justin. super cruel, tbh. Like sure ur album got leaked but is that really so bad 4u?? Oh no, you still got a ton of money while the person who inspired your song is doomed to poverty. honestly srsly disappointed in ryan, idek if I can listen to her music anymore

sam_123984

it's all a distraction. Look at the clues. when the idols fall its a sign of the new world order, Ryan's been trying to tell us all along. justin knows what hes doing too

MARI

I mean, it was the best trial by fire that I could've asked for in my career. We were doing damage control left and right, coordinating with the PR team. They had her do that special Oprah interview, but I think it was a misstep; she came off looking more defensive than injured. So they dialed down any live appearances after that. And once the court case started, we couldn't comment on it publicly at all.

Ryan was just . . . extremely angry. You could feel it radiating off of her like heat. In the rare moments when she and I would have free time together, she would spend all of it scrolling her phone, reading the awful posts.

"Stop," I would tell her. "You have to put it down."

And she would for five minutes or so before picking it up again and scrolling.

"They talk like they know me," Ryan would say. "There are people defending or criticizing my character like we're close personal friends when I've never even spoken to them in real life."

I never knew what to say. She would spiral. I'd usually respond with some form of "Parasocial relationships are a bitch."

"You know what they'd say if I talked about how hard this is?" Ryan said once. And she laughed. "They'd tell me to go cry into my money."

Then she sighed and slumped down in her seat. We were having coffee on Madcap's roof.

"I didn't mean to take his line," she said. "And I do feel bad about getting him fired."

"Are you going to be able to prove that you didn't send the emails?" I asked. I worded it very carefully; although Ryan and I had made up, I did feel very gun shy of criticizing her after she'd blown up at me in Seattle. She had that power over people, even if she didn't realize it.

"It's less about proving that I *didn't* send the emails than proving that I *did* want the songs leaked. Justin has no evidence that I orchestrated the leaks. If he can't produce any, it's slander."

"And then you get your payout," I said.

She nodded. "My one-dollar payout."

"Can you last that long?"

Ryan didn't look at me. She said, "We'll see."

JASMINE

It was messy. I can't lie. Skip and the legal team opted for a symbolic one-dollar payment even though we could've pressed for a lot more. But instead we were fighting an uphill battle to put the optics back in our favor and help the public to see that, actually, Ryan's the victim here.

Justin had no proof. I mean, come on. It's obvious looking back. But he had the element of surprise on us, and his sob story was a good one. He played it well: *Poor me, Ryan broke my heart when I was just a boy and then she stole my song. I was just doing what she told me to do. I wanted to help her even though she'd hurt me.* There was this whole down-home regular-Joe thing he had going on, like he was some starry-eyed kid who got swept up in big bad Hollywood drama.

It wasn't until he got served that he really started turning nasty. And he got others involved too.

TEEN STAR MAGAZINE, July 2015
JWA TELLS ALL!

"We loved each other," Justin William Ayers said of his childhood sweetheart turned rival, Ryan Holding. The young man from Massachusetts, who moved from the East to West Coast to pursue a film career, saw one dream crushed after another when his original script was heisted.

"Austin Proust stole my screenplay," Justin said. "But Ryan stole my future."

He had high hopes when he finally reconnected with superstar Ryan, with whom he'd grown up in their hometown of Hamilton, MA.

"I used to help her write songs back when we were in school. I mean, I was happy to lend her some of my ideas—I didn't care that she wasn't giving me credit. I was just glad to see her succeed." Ryan told us his story with gleaming eyes that turned misty when he spoke of Ryan's betrayal. "But 'Mine All Mine'—that had a special verse. I don't know, it was personal to me. And hearing that, hearing she didn't even realize it was something I'd written for her, it made me understand how much free labor she'd gotten out of me over the years. I wondered if she'd been doing the same thing with other guys. Maybe she was using all of us—and that's why she moved through us so quickly."

Braden Petri, one of Ryan's former flames, agreed. "Anything I did for Ryan was never enough. I felt like she was taking advantage of me. She was like a spider, spinning her little web until you were caught in her trap."

"I mean, she used our whole relationship to write a song," said Tyler Michaels, another victim of the Ryan revolving door. "That should tell you all you need to know."

When Ryan asked Justin to leak her songs for her, he was shocked.

"It's something the old Justin would have done for the old Ryan without a second thought," he said. "I said, 'Is that even legal?' Ryan said, 'Does it matter? I'll sleep with you if you do it.' And hey, come on . . . I loved this girl. I'd been wanting to get with her since I was barely thirteen. And even though I trusted her, and I did what she asked, I had this little voice in my head, you know? It was telling me things weren't right."

Mere days after the leak, Ayers says he was on his way to Ryan's house to finally make their relationship official—just as she had promised—when he received a call from Anaheim Studios, where he had been hired as a location scout.

"They fired me," he said, "because Ryan had told them to. I was supposed to take the blame for the leak all along. I was her fall guy."

"Ryan was the victim of a personal attack on her intellectual property," said Ryan's legal team when *Teen Star* reached out for comment. "We intend to prosecute Mr. Ayers for his actions to the fullest extent of the law."

No wonder she's still single!

MARI

I told *Teen Star* to use our PR statement. "Ryan is deeply pained by this difficult situation and only wishes to walk away with a verdict that is fair to all parties and a friendship that is still intact." I told the lawyers not to talk to the press.

Did they listen? No.

The public ate it up. And if they could slut-shame her, all the better. #MeToo didn't really come around until about a couple of years later—maybe they would have seen through Justin's accusations if the timing had been different. But as it was, it . . . wasn't great.

SKIP

That fucker made way more on his little press tour than he would have as an assistant location scout in a whole year. And let's be clear: He was an *assistant* location scout, okay? Actual scouting is a job that takes skill and experience that *he did not have*. Jesus Christ. He was one step away from an unpaid intern, and he's acting like it was his dream career.

Anyway. We won the battle but not the war, not exactly. Justin didn't have any solid evidence for his ridiculous claims, and we got our one dollar. Plus several thousand in damages from the lawsuit for the leak that I finally pushed once I got my head out of my ass. I think the Prousts slapped him with a fine too.

But the press was really hard on Ryan. Really unfair.

I found her in the studio one day just poring over all these tabloids with tears running down her cheeks. I said, "Hey, come on."

She looked up and I grabbed all the magazines; I took her hand and brought her up to the roof. We had a little firepit up there that we never used. Dropped most of the magazines in there.

"You know what I think about all this bullshit?" I said.

"What?" she said, really quiet.

I took my lighter—I still haven't been able to quit smoking, don't tell Jas—and I lit a scrap of paper and dropped it in the firepit with the rest of those rags. We watched them burn together.

"That's what I think. And that's what you should too."

And we just stood there together. Until all those nasty words were nothing but ash in the wind.

From: <wilderjames91@gmail.com>

Sent: January 8, 2016, 8:47 p.m.

To: <elysejames711@gmail.com>

Subject: Thanks

Hey Ellie,

Thanks for dinner last night. I know I wasn't very talkative. I'm better at putting my words down in writing than talking it through, yeah? You know that about me.

It's just been hard. I've tried to be there for her through all of this but I feel like she's pushing me away. She's been terrified of someone finding out about us with all the bad press, terrified that I believe that bullshit story or that I think she's whoring herself out or something.

I'm hurt she would think that I'm as bad as everyone else. That really stings.

It would be pretty rough if people found out, sure, but I wouldn't care. She thinks it would break up the band, and I say first of all—no it wouldn't, I'm not going anywhere. And second of all—if it did . . . would you care more about the band than me?

I want to be there for her but she'll avoid me for days before turning around and needing comfort like she's never needed before. What am I supposed to be doing? Like, from a woman's perspective, how do I handle this? How does anyone handle this? What am I doing wrong?

I don't mean to dump this all on you, Ellie, I'm sorry. I'm just ready for this to all blow over so things can go back to normal.

Thanks for listening anyway.

—W

EIGHTEEN

IN AN LA MINUTE SPOT, *AIRED APRIL 24, 2016*

The segment opens on the exterior of 1Oak, with correspondent Stefan jogging toward Ryan as she emerges from the club.]

STEFAN: Ryan! Ryan, Stefan from *LA Minute*. Are you enjoying a night out on the town after winning your trial?

[Unlike in Seattle, Ryan turns to him and smiles widely.]

RYAN: Oh, hi! Yeah, I'm taking a night out with the girls. No boys allowed tonight! Or maybe ever.

STEFAN: Have you had any contact with Justin since the trial?

RYAN: No, but I wish him well.

STEFAN: What do you have to say to people who sided with Justin in his betrayal of you?

RYAN: I'm not bothered. I'm focusing on myself and my career and moving forward from all this. I guess I'd say: Get a life, honestly! I mean that with love. I decided to get one myself.

STEFAN: What's next for you? Are you going to write a song about Justin?

[Ryan winks.]

RYAN: I guess you'll have to find out, Stefan!

MARI

I was with her that night at 1Oak. We were leaving the club because she was having a panic attack.

She had been stressed all evening while we were getting ready.

"We don't have to go out," I had told her. "Let's just stay home, okay? We can watch *House Hunters*. Just you, me, and Kylie."

Kylie had brought homemade brownies to our last hangout, and I was starting to warm up to her in spite of myself.

But Ryan said, "No, no—if I don't show my face, they'll say I'm hiding. I have to go out, and I have to have fun."

So we did. But we did not have fun.

> *TEEN STAR* MAGAZINE, June 2016
> RYAN'S REVENGE?
>
> Pop icon Ryan Holding strutted down Santa Monica Pier Saturday afternoon in a barely there gingham shorts and crop-top set. The "Count Your Days" singer laughed with friends as she won a Skee-Ball game and celebrated her recent court victory over Justin William Ayers, who claimed to have leaked three of her tracks at her own request.
> Ryan seemed to be showing off the win as she paraded around town with model-turned-popstar Kylie Cameron and BFF Mari Stevens.
> Better luck next time, Justin!

JASMINE

It was . . . tough to see Ryan's mood after the trial concluded. I was back in the studio with her and Wilder the following week, at Ryan's request, and there was a very weird feeling there. Everyone was so muted. Ryan and Wilder were sitting far apart from each other, and I wondered if something had happened between them. Both of them were keeping their heads down.

We usually started with a bit of jamming to warm up, she and I humming anything that came to mind, but as soon as Ryan put her fingers to the fretboard and started playing a few chords, she stopped and let both arms hang over the banjo.

"Do you think people like my music?" she said.

"Of course they do," I told her.

"I think they used to," Ryan answered. "But do they like the *music* anymore, or do they like it just because I made it? Do they like me, or do they like the idea of Ryan Holding, the pop star?"

"Does it matter?" Wilder said.

I swear I saw this shadow pass over Ryan's face. She said, "It matters to me."

"Do you need them to like you?" I asked, trying to get over whatever weird energy the two of them were putting off. "Did you start writing music because you wanted to draw a crowd?"

Maybe I shouldn't have tried to talk her around it; sometimes people just want to vent. But she gave a sigh and said, "No."

"Why did you start writing music?" I asked.

She ran her finger along the edge of the banjo drum. "I don't know. Because I felt like I had to. Because I got these ideas, and they needed somewhere to go."

"What's changed?" I asked.

"At first—" She shook her head. "At first I felt like a water tower. Like all these songs were building above my head, and I had to channel them out or I would burst. Then I felt more like a well, like one of those old ones with the pump, you know? My grandpa used to have one of those on his farm in Kentucky, I remember from when I was little. It took more work to get them out, but there was still plenty down there, and I could pull them up whenever I needed to."

The three of us were silent for a moment.

It was Wilder who spoke first. "And now?" he said.

"And now I feel like an empty barrel," Ryan said quietly. "There's nothing in there. And I don't know what to do."

I sat back in my chair and allowed her a minute or two. Then I said, as gently as I could, "You've been through a lot of stress, Ryan. It's just writer's block, okay? You're more than your music. You need to give it time."

SKIP

Jas talked to me after that first studio session. I called Ryan into my office and I said, "You're fired."

And she said, "What the hell?"

I said, "I'm temporarily firing you. Take a few months. Let that feeling come back to you."

She looked at me with these dead sort of eyes. It's hard on an artist—musicians, especially. You know, you put your whole identity into your work, and then when your brain won't cooperate, you feel broken. I would've given my other artists some tough love, but the kid had been through enough.

"What if it doesn't come back?" she asked.

All right, so I couldn't resist razzing her a little bit. I said, "Then you already have enough money to retire decades early. Who cares? You should be doing it because you love it."

"Are you saying I'm already washed up?" She was glaring at me, but I could see a little bit of her old self coming back.

"If I was, I'd be a hypocrite, wouldn't I?" I said. "The washed-up old producer that I am."

Ryan rolled her eyes. "I can't make any promises."

"You don't need to," I said. "Your head's big enough to be a water tower again. Just gotta let it refill."

Finally, she cracked a grin.

KYLIE

I was glad to be able to spend more time with Ryan after the trial. She seemed really down, that summer of 2016. I'd take her shopping, drive her up to my family's lake house in Tahoe, go to the pier with her. I picked up a lot of the slack because Mari was working overtime to finish classes and manage press coverage from the end of the trial. She and I got closer, too, I'd like to think. We don't talk so much anymore, but back then, it was Ryan who held us all together.

Mari was always like, "Keep the magazines away from her, keep her off her phone." And I did my best. But it was everywhere, you know? Even in the rustic little shops up at the lake, there would be tabloids with pictures of her. And it seemed to send her into a funk every time.

There was one particular criticism that stuck with her around that time. It was something I think Tyler Michaels first said, and then a bunch of other publications ran with it—something about Ryan being a spider. Like she was just trying to trap you in her web. Helladonna was dating Tyler by then, and she released some song about the "Itsy Bitchy Spider" that had everyone talking. It was on the radio, in the mall, in commercials—like you could not get away from this snarky, catchy-ass song. I'm sorry, but yeah, it was catchy. That was part of the problem. I'd get it in my head, and then I'd have to stop myself from humming it around Ryan.

There was one day when we were up at the lake sunbathing on my parents' dock, and everything was quiet and beautiful. I was like, finally. Mari would be proud of me.

Then this stupid boat zooms by blasting "Itsy Bitchy Spider" at full volume.

Ryan sat up in one motion and ripped her sunglasses off and literally threw these Versace frames into Lake Tahoe.

"FUCK!" she yelled.

I had to start laughing. I'd never heard her swear like that.

I was like, "YES, let it out, girl!"

She stood up. She said, "They want a spider, huh? They all fucking want a spider? I'll give them a spider."

I didn't know what the hell she was talking about. I'm *terrified* of spiders. But I told her I'd support her anyway.

TATIANA

It was the Met Gala of 2017, yes. Ryan approached me with this idea, and I said, my girl, you are crazy. I do not pretend to understand what this is supposed to be. But for you, I will make it happen, and I will make it good.

The look was a deceptively simple one. Big black ball gown, structured strapless bodice with boned ribbing, big bustle, swaths of dark silk all slippery and shining and draped over her. Morticia Addams makeup, back to the red lip, bright and bloody.

But the cape was my crowning achievement, Ms. James, oh yes. I could not find fabric that behaved the way I wanted, so you know what? We made it ourselves. Me and the seamstresses working day and night, knotting this shimmery gossamer thread by hand into a 180-inch cape that floated over her shoulders and the red carpet.

HOLLYWOOD REPORT MAGAZINE, May 2017

The fangs were out for Ryan Holding at Monday's Met Gala, with an ensemble developed by fashion giant Tatiana DeGroode that barked as loud as it bit. Holding wowed on the red carpet in a black Jean Paul Gaultier gown and classic Louboutins that flashed a matching red to her femme fatale pout. The look was completed with a spidery silken cape that clasped at her throat and gave her the air of a vampiress about to strike.

It's been a quiet year in music for the singer of

Diatribe fame, who released one independent single in January, "Go Home," which is rumored to directly reference the star's recent legal difficulties and fallout with Justin William Ayers.

Holding notably attended the Gala alone and set herself apart from her contemporaries who graced the promenade.

Perhaps she is taking her role as a black widow to heart.

NINETEEN

MARI

It was strange how easily I was able to separate Ryan in my professional life from Ryan as my friend. I think that bothered her too. There were times she'd come down a floor to the Madcap administrative offices to talk with me, and I would be like, I can't take a break, I'm in the middle of something, I'm literally trying to sell *your image*, and you need to give me a second.

I don't know why she asked me to come work for her team. Maybe she thought it would be different. Maybe she wanted to help me jump-start my career. But sometimes I wondered if she just wanted another friend on the inside to talk to.

It was also—I don't know. It created kind of a tough dynamic. I mean, she was the *star*. She was *Ryan*—everyone referred to her by first name only. *Ryan liked this. Ryan didn't like that. Ryan wants a Diet Coke, can someone run it up to her?* She was above all of us, literally. She was other.

And I was working a really cool job, *way* cooler and better paying than anything my old UCLA friends had snagged, but it was still a job. I did my taxes. I filled my car with gas at the station on Washington Boulevard. I separated my whites and colors for laundry.

Ryan had someone to do all that stuff for her. She didn't in the early days, but she'd begun her career so young that now, being so prolific felt normal to her. And sometimes I think she forgot we were living different lives.

Anyway, she learned to leave me alone when I was at work and to spend time with me when she normally would have outside those hours. Except one day when she came down and sat in the cubicle next to me and pulled a chair over.

I pulled myself out of whatever I'd been looking at—probably invoices for social ads. I booked a lot of those—and I said, "Yeah?"

"I want to go home," she said.

"What," I said. "Like the song? The one you wrote about Justin?"

She shook her head. "What do you think about a tribute to Hamilton? What if we shot something there?"

It took me a second to figure out what she was talking about. She had so many high-level conversations, and I was always in the weeds. "Is this a Serge conversation you're trying to have with me?"

"Stop being corporate, Mari," she said, snapping her fingers. "I need you to be just regular Mari right now. My friend."

"Sorry," I said. "What do you have in mind?"

"I had this weird dream last night," Ryan said, and she wasn't looking at me anymore. "I went home to Hamilton, and nobody knew who I was. I mean, not even my parents. Not Frank. Not you. Have I changed that much?"

I said, "Well, you've changed. But you're supposed to. When's the last time you even talked to Frank?"

It came out more accusatory than I meant it, but she was the one who'd brought it up. "Maybe a year or two ago. He called me to congratulate me on the AMA win."

"That was about five years ago, Ryan."

She stared at me. "No."

"Yes."

"When's the last time *you* talked to Frank?" she asked. "He's still—?"

I had to laugh. I said, "He's not *that* old, Ryan. I think I sent him an email last year on his birthday."

Ryan shook her head and said, "Shit."

I didn't tell her about how Frank still asked how Ryan was doing after all these years or that he'd mentioned to me that he listened to her every song.

"You've been busy," I said. "He understands."

"It's not an excuse," she said. "That settles it. We're going."

JASMINE

It was late summer—when Ryan, Wilder, and I were having coffee up on the rooftop again, during one of our little low-stakes hangouts that had replaced our studio sessions—that she got her creative momentum back.

She and Wilder seemed to have gotten over whatever issues they'd had and were sitting on the wicker couch across from me again. I once joked to Skip that those two would make a good pair, but he said, "Don't you dare speak that into existence. We can't lose that guitarist." Ha. So I dropped it.

Ryan had a look on her face like she had a secret, and she gave me a small smile as she set her phone on the table.

"So . . . I've been working on a little something," she said, and tapped the screen.

Her voice sang out a little tinny through the iPhone speakers, just her and the banjo.

Wake me when you're lonely / Don't pace the floor alone / Keep me like a secret, baby / I'm waiting by the phone.

And there was another: *Someday will you take me / To that house up on the hill?*

I grinned at her. "Sounds like we're back."

A third song started playing automatically. *Just a whisper in the night / That's how all of this went down . . .* but Ryan picked up the phone and winked.

"That one's not ready yet," she said. "That's for the next album."

It was a recording of what would eventually be "Hear Me Now."

SERGE

I was surprised when it was Ryan who called a meeting with me, not Skip. In fact, looking back, I am not sure he even knew about that meeting—she told me he'd gotten busy and she wanted to get started talking about the next project, but I didn't really connect with the others about it until later.

But she was always a step ahead. So I suppose it shouldn't be a surprise.

She wanted it to be what I would call an "autobiographical allegory." No clear through line of a plot with this one, but a cacophony of imagery and symbolism that was representative of her life and career up to this point.

Hamilton would be featured significantly, and she asked whether I'd be willing to make a trip with her and the others to do some early location scouting.

"It will be a big project," I said. "But you came to the right person."

We left for Massachusetts soon after that meeting.

FRANK

Mari orchestrated the whole thing. It was a beautiful moment. Oh, it was beautiful.

She invited me out to coffee to get me out of the studio. There we were, at Halligan's on Bay Road once again like no time had passed. I couldn't believe Mari was back in town! I was so glad to see her, told her how much her folks missed her, how quiet it had been around Hamilton since Ryan had left, and then her. Asked after her harp practice.

She laughed and said, "Still shooting for half an hour a day, Frank, scout's honor."

I told her I was still the same old same old. Mari was the one with this glittering new life on the Gold Coast, not me.

"That's good you're working with Ryan," I said. "She needs you in her corner. I hope she's doing okay out there."

"I hope so too," Mari said.

"You don't know?" I asked. "You should know better than anyone."

She sighed and said, "I know. But she's changed a lot. She had a dream about this place the other week, and it rattled her a little. I think remembering her roots is making her realize how far she's come."

I winked at her. "You've changed too."

It shouldn't have come as a surprise to her, but she sort of frowned and said, "I guess I have."

I could have sat there catching up all day with Mari and been content. But when she said, "Can we swing back to the studio?" I knew she had something up her sleeve.

When I walked back into my shop, it had been transformed.

There was space cleared, a little stage set up at one end of the barn, lights hung, and a group of chairs set out. And in the middle of it all was Ryan.

I don't even know what kind of exclamation came out of my mouth, but she came up and gave me a hug—it was so good to see her. She had become so *tall*. And she did seem different, in a way. Like Alice in Wonderland when she has those snacks and becomes too big for her surroundings. I wondered if Hamilton felt too tight on her now, like it'd shrunk around her.

But when she smiled, she was the same old Ryan.

"I'm here to make up for all the times I said I'd call you back but didn't . . . or missed your birthday . . . or lost track of time," she said. "Can I play something I wrote just for you?"

I'm not ashamed to admit I got choked up. "You've already taken over my studio, so you can do whatever you want," I said.

She played a whole little concert for me and for the others who were there—Mari, her songwriting partner Jasmine, someone named

Sarge, I think? And that young guitarist of hers was there too. He was a handsome young man, and I raised my eyebrows at Ryan when she introduced us.

She gave me a *look*. So I knew they must have been together.

None of my business, though!

MARI

I let Frank believe that we were there just for him—I didn't tell him about the location scouting or the music video or any of that stuff. He needed his moment with Ryan, and he got it. She played her exclusive show, and we spent the rest of the night with him talking and catching up.

I was watching Ryan closely the whole time we were in Hamilton. We stayed with the rest of the crew in a hotel over in Hathorne—that's Hamilton for you, no hotels—but she and I took a walk down Bay Road like we used to as dusk came on and the others went to pick up dinner.

"Is it like you imagined it?" I asked her.

"It's nice and quiet," she said.

I'd forgotten how much I missed it. I missed *seasons*; I missed the smell of pine trees and that faint sea air you could feel even fourteen miles inland. The empty street was a far cry from downtown LA.

But I imagine Ryan meant the solitude too. We'd been lucky in keeping this visit under wraps, and I'd struck a deal with our local outlets that they would get exclusive content as long as they waited to publish until after we were gone. It felt strange, in fact, to walk down the street without worrying about someone coming after us.

"I never thought I'd be back," she said. "At one point, I thought I'd want to settle down here. But after I'd been in LA long enough, I guess I sort of . . . forgot about it. I remember growing up here like it was a different lifetime."

"I do too," I told her, and the second I said it, I was surprised to realize that I meant it.

"Sometimes I wish we'd never done it," she said suddenly, stopping short.

"Left Hamilton?" I asked.

"Yeah," Ryan said. "What have we become?"

It's strange, but I knew what she meant. Standing there on Bay Road, it was like I was seeing Ryan again for the first time in a long time. The Ryan I used to know.

The path she had chosen for herself, the fans she had amassed, the media—it had built her up into something almost inhuman, more than human. She wasn't just a cog but a full machine of her own creation, chugging along at full speed, unable to stop her own momentum. It was the billboard in Chinatown. It was the merchandise we churned out through marketing. It was the snap assumptions people made when they read any headline about her, misleading or not.

"Would you have been happier if we hadn't left?" I asked after a moment.

"That's the problem." Ryan sighed. "I know that I wouldn't have been."

I wrapped my arm around her shoulders, shorter than her though I was. "Then you're right where you should be," I said.

~

When we got back to Frank's shop and said goodbye, we all split up in separate cars to drive to Hathorne.

Listen, I thought Ryan was going to ride with me, but she got lost in the shuffle. And I didn't know exactly where she was when I got a text from her that said Stopped to pick something up soon after the rest of us had arrived at the hotel.

The rest of us, that is, except Wilder.

I do know, however, that Ryan didn't show up until an hour later, and when she got back to our shared room, it looked like she had been crying.

"Are you okay?" I asked her.

She rubbed her eyes and said, "Yes. It's this stupid town. I can't handle myself here."

"Was it Wilder?" I asked, and when she started to protest, I said, "Ryan, come *on*. What is the point of being so secretive and dramatic? You obviously drove together. Just spit it the hell out."

And—listen. I can say this now. It's in the past. Okay?

But yes. Ryan did say, "Fine! Fine. Maybe there was something between us, okay? But now it's done. So we all might as well forget it."

I left it at that.

TWENTY

From: <wilderjames91@gmail.com>

Sent: September 13, 2017, 11:45 p.m.

To: <elysejames711@gmail.com>

Subject: Hey

Hey Ellie.

Just a proof of life to prevent you from calling mom on me. Yes, I've gotten all your messages. Sorry I don't really feel like talking at the moment. I'll let you know if/when I do.

Tbh, I'm still trying to figure out what happened myself. The gist of it I guess is that she and I almost got caught together. It wasn't the first time. Maybe that was the problem. I thought I'd noticed a car following us when we came out of Logan, but when we got out of the city everything seemed fine. My mistake. That same car found R and I over in Hamilton when we split from the group. Must have tracked us that far.

We were parked on a side street, stealing more time together, and all I remember is seeing a flash through the windshield, and then she flipped. She knew it was a camera before I did. She was out of the car, running toward the guy—she paid him $700 on the spot to delete the photo and she posed for another one, making sure I was well out of frame. Once he was gone I was like why the hell are you carrying that much money on you? But she was . . . not in the mood to discuss it.

She was raging. She kept saying something like the one thing, the one thing I can't afford to lose—which I guess is me, which should make me feel great, but obviously not now.

She didn't want to lose me so she got rid of me before it could happen.

I tried to convince her. We had this whole knock down drag out fight and I'm not especially happy at how I reacted, but I was pissed. Why does it matter? Why can't you have both your career AND me? Why can't you get over your dumbass hangups and stop being so weird about a normal adult relationship?

I don't know, Ellie. It's an unbeatable gig, but I might see what my other options are. I can't bear to be around her and yet be apart from her. Nobody knows what we're going through—S and J will talk business to me like everything's normal and I smile and nod while meanwhile I'm just crumbling inside.

I'm going to have to play songs about myself, do you realize that? Our most intimate tracks, the ones we wrote together. I'll be physically closer to her onstage than I ever am off it anymore.

I'll stick out the rest of the album and tour. Then we'll see.

—W

MARI

Look. I can't speculate on what happened. That's your job, isn't it?

All I know is what I told you. And Ryan and Wilder were frosty with each other for the rest of the time that I knew them.

Both of them.

JASMINE

When Ryan got back to the studio after her trip to Hamilton, Wilder didn't join us. I asked her where he was, and she shrugged, and I thought, *Girl, we can't be having another songwriting crisis.*

I don't know what happened between them, and I'm not going to gossip about any rumors to a journalist. I did pull Wilder aside and ask him if he was okay.

"Why wouldn't I be?" he said, and even when I stared him down for a long, hard moment, he didn't break. So I let it be.

But to Ryan's credit, it wasn't a songwriting crisis. There had been a few other melodies she'd been toying with before she left for the trip. So far on the album works in progress, we had "Flowers on the Sill," "Comeback Baby," "Keep Me," "Homecoming," and "Wisteria." I pulled up our recordings to continue where we'd left off, but Ryan shook her head.

"I think I'd like to go in a different direction for the second half of the album," she said.

"Show me what you have in mind," I told her.

She began to pick out a melody on her banjo, something dark and complex like I hadn't heard since she'd started her career. It was minor, unpredictable, but something in me didn't want to stop listening to it.

"Where did that come from?" I asked her. "Play it again."

When she finished, she said, "At least I'm not having writer's block anymore. This feels . . . more like a flood."

SKIP

We ended up naming the album *Waterfall.* It was the first project where Ryan and I had a real stylistic disagreement with each other. See, you had the first half—all those lovely romantic songs, these sweet wistful melodies, what have you.

And then, after "Wisteria," you go off the deep end. It starts with that eerie, melancholy song "Ropes": *Hands tied, tongue tied / Catching in my throat / I found myself immobilized / When you drove home alone. / There's no going forward / And there's no going back / When all these ropes have got me bound like that.*

Then you have that anthemic, echoey "Way Way Down," "Deliberate," a grittier nod to old country in "Out of Gas," "Unentwined"—more rope stuff—and finally "Hush," that ends on a single haunting piano note.

It was an angsty album. And I told her, Ryan, we've got to be careful what order we put this in.

"It's in the right order," she said.

I didn't have the balls that she did, I'll admit it. But I also didn't think it was the right time to take an artistic risk.

"What if we flip the album halves, or intersperse them?" I told her. "People want to leave feeling good, not like a ghost just walked through them."

I think she took offense to that. She shot me with a glare.

"It's in the right order," she said again.

I called Andre about it. He said, "No fuckin' way. You end on the summer bop, and in this case, it's 'Homecoming.'"

"I'm telling her," I said. But she wouldn't have it.

Maybe it was my own bias. I'd gotten too soft on Ryan, I was . . . worried about her. If an unknown artist had walked into Madcap with those songs, I'd've shaken their hand and congratulated them on being the next Johnny Cash or Springsteen in their dark and moody eras.

But Ryan's songs, exceptional as they were, seemed to be coming from a place of personal difficulty.

Shows how much I know, anyway. Thank god I didn't push it.

We released the album at the end of September, and surprise surprise, it shot right up like the others always did. Sure, there were the few stupid headlines I'd been worried about, like Ryan Goes Emo or the meme that went around about her having such a hard life as a multimillionaire. But the professional critiques were good. *Rolling Stone* compared the mature depth of her voice to Adele, *Hollywood Report* said the album was a brilliant study in emotional control, how music can drag you through all five stages of grief even if you haven't lived it yourself.

She kept on gliding. It was a good year for her—Album of the Year nomination, People's Choice Award, Kids' Choice. The video for "Ropes," another very avant-garde Serge production, won Best Pop at the VMAs. I always sort of got the creeps from it, that sci-fi cinematography and all the CGI of the ropes snaking around Ryan while she walks through an abandoned research facility until she's completely bound and emerges as some *Ex Machina* sort of cyborg. But visually, it was very cool.

I remember standing onstage with her at People's Choice and looking out into that crowd, and thinking, *How much longer can we sustain this momentum?*

Where does she go from here, you know?

When you work with artists, you're always looking out for the peak. No one ever wants to reach that summit because of what's on the other side. But you will, someday. Like I said, even making one album is a miracle, and no one can do it indefinitely. You'll keep going until circumstances force you to stop, sure, but what do you do when someone newer and shinier comes along? How do you forever produce new and original and groundbreaking stuff? You don't. We all have expiration dates, and that's just the natural cycle of things. People's attention spans grow shorter every day.

I looked out into that vast darkness of the auditorium, and then I looked to my left, at Ryan, and I wondered if she felt the same thing.

And just for a moment there, she turned and looked back at me. And I knew she was thinking it too. I knew.

She smiled and nodded at me like we should set it aside and just enjoy this win. Because yeah, it was a good year for her. A really good one.

I didn't know it would be one of our last.

HOLLYWOOD REPORT MAGAZINE, February 2018

[The article is inset with a photo of Ryan on the red carpet in a long midnight-blue and gold gown, holding a gramophone trophy.]

> Following a marathon award season sprint that saw her taking home People's Choice, Kids' Choice, and Best Pop awards among many other nominations and recognitions, Ryan Holding cinched a final win with Best Pop Vocal Album at this year's Grammy Awards in January. The star's dualistic tour de force, *Waterfall*, has been described as Holding's best work to date and comes with its own complement of gripping music videos directed by auteur Serge Chirkov and Holding herself.
>
> With the win, Holding becomes the first female artist to earn the Best Visual Effects award and the first artist of any gender and genre to hold a Grammy for Favorite Country Album and Favorite Pop Album.
>
> The wins come on the heels of a record-breaking world tour that has moved the needle of Holding's wealth into the billionaire strata.

The only question now is: What's next?
"Something big," she told *Hollywood Report* with a smile Saturday evening. "The best is yet to come."
Here's looking forward to this pop sensation outdoing herself!

TWENTY-ONE

SERGE

In April of 2018, we began principal photography for "Hear Me Now." That was the first time Ryan was listed with me as director on IMDb. I may have held the title, but that project was Ryan's vision, through and through.

JASMINE

It was interesting. Everything surrounding "Hear Me Now" was . . . interesting.

Do I really believe the video has clues about Ryan's final public appearances and whereabouts, like everyone online says it does?

No. I do not. That is not to say that the composition and filming process of "Hear Me Now" wasn't unusual, though. Sure, Ryan had a very visual mind; when she was writing songs, she often had some idea in her head of the imagery she wanted to evoke, even the style of music video we might eventually create with Serge. *I want it to sound like an old Hollywood jazz lounge feels,* she'd say, or *What melody would you play if you were standing on a cliff contemplating your life, Jas?*

She made me laugh with those big questions. But they did get the results she wanted.

"Hear Me Now," though—I mean, Skip and I knew she had a music-video idea before we knew she was even composing the song. We went on the Hamilton trip, and I remember asking him, "What is this for?"

And he shrugged and said, "Hell if I know. She's never been this cryptic."

Ryan started writing the song with the line, *I've been here singing my heart out / Can you hear me now? / Will you hear me now?*

And part of me knew, by the depth of her voice and the way she closed her eyes when she sang it. I said, "Is that the one for the video?"

She said, "It is."

SERGE

It was the most intensive process of all the videos she created. Ryan was there at my side in the director's chair for every production, but this time she was in my notes, under my skin, breathing down my neck.

The band had to be completely silhouetted behind her on the stage—no features visible. The cape had to twist just so in the water. The woman pouring the bucket from the box seat needed to wear a specific shade of orange. The dress didn't satisfy Ryan? Back to the costume department.

She was tense the whole time, less friendly with her band than I've ever seen. I was surprised, in fact, to see that she talked to very few people on set, chatty as she usually was. Her mind seemed to be very far away.

I tried to keep an eye on her. I did. I hoped no one had caused her any pain. The only one I was suspicious of was her guitarist, that Wilder fellow. It was interesting; he was originally supposed to play a larger role in that video. He was meant to swim past Ryan when the theater floods and free her from the cape.

But it came right down to the actual day of filming—we had the water tank set up and all, for the rest of the scenes—and I brought him over with Ryan and talked him through what was going to happen. We had a dive specialist on set who was going to walk him through breathing and safety techniques.

Wilder had hardly heard my spiel when he said, "No. I'm sorry, but I'm not up for it."

Ryan stared at him, I swear, boring holes in his head. She did not take her eyes off him. But he would not look at her—and I wondered what that meant.

I was thrown. I said, "It's perfectly safe, Wilder. I can assure you. We have the specialist here and first aid standing by for all the underwater scenes."

But he just shook his head and said, "I'm sorry. Too little, too late."

And he walked away. I turned to Ryan to see what the hell that was supposed to mean, but she was watching Wilder go.

Finally she looked at me and said, "I'll talk to him later. What else is on the shot list?"

I did see them together when I was packing up at the end of the night, yes. Listen, I—I didn't want to say anything before because it wasn't my business. I've told myself this had nothing to do with Ryan's disappearance, but . . . I suppose it seems a lot more relevant in hindsight.

The State Theatre is a loading-dock nightmare; there's a parking lot on the same block as the building, but only one very narrow alley leading backstage that's gated on either side. We'd had to play a game of *Tetris* to move equipment, and I stayed late to map out how we'd bring in the papier-mâché tree the next day.

Everyone else had left, or so I thought. I heard voices suddenly, and Ryan and Wilder came out into the alley. I was about to say hi to them when I realized they were arguing; I don't remember word for word. I'm sorry. It was something about enough being enough—that phrase was thrown around. I think they were both accusing each other of being very stubborn. Speaking in these low, angry whispers.

It reached a bit of a fever pitch and then silence; Wilder took a step back and whispered something to her. She nodded. After that, well—Wilder sort of pushed Ryan up against the wall. And then they were kissing.

I was just standing there down the alley a ways, worrying I was going to have to make my presence known any second—I mean, they were blocking my path, and I certainly didn't want to see anything else that I shouldn't—when Wilder picked Ryan up and carried her away toward the parking lot. She was giggling by then.

I just shook my head and minded my business. I hope that wasn't wrong of me.

God knows the worst crimes have been committed when well-meaning folks just look the other way.

KYLIE

It was such a cool video to shoot. Mari and I are both in it; you can see my hand when we all pull her down the first time. I honestly think I had more fun than Ryan did. Between rehearsals, safety training with the water, and actually filming, it was about a three-week process.

But I barely talked to Ryan in all that time. Mari and I mostly hung out. Ryan seemed really busy with everything and almost sort of . . . flustered? Every time I saw her, she was running to tell Serge something or bent over sketches with Tatiana DeGroode.

The video was, like, all she could think about. I tried to tell her about Savannah and Nick breaking up, which was *huge* news to everyone else, considering they'd had a *child* together, and I swear all Ryan said was, "Do you think that black Met dress is going to be too heavy for the water?"

I was like, *Girl! I need you to freak out about this with me!*

But it seemed like she had a lot on her mind.

MARI

The video took about three weeks to shoot, all told. Ryan got very . . . placid near the end of production. I thought the stress of it must be taking a toll on her. But whatever it was, her head was elsewhere.

"You okay?" I asked her at one point. "You've been acting like you're on another planet."

It took a moment for her to register my question. "Sorry. Just preoccupied," she said.

"Yeah, obviously. With what?"

Ryan glanced at me, and her eyes were surprisingly bright. "I'll tell you later."

She never told me.

Kylie was the only one having fun with the video, because while Ryan was rushing around to produce it, I was rushing around to develop a campaign for it, not to mention acting in it myself.

I remember having a sort of pressing question when she and I were on a break together, waiting for the crew to fill and test the water tank for that final scene—something about YouTube licensing for her channel.

And in response, she just looked off into the distance and said, "Mhm."

SERGE

She solved the cape problem in the eleventh hour. She called me in the middle of the night, in fact.

"I won't put Wilder in a position he doesn't want to be in," she said in a rush. "We'll have all the instruments around me; the guitar can just be one part of it. But, Serge: I want the crystal ball from 'White Lace.'"

"Okay," I said. "What for?"

"That," she said, "is what's *really* going to save me."

TWENTY-TWO

MARI

I guess I've put it off long enough.

It just . . . it happened in a blur. It's hard for me to remember the finer details now that I'm back in Hamilton, now that the night of the VMAs feels like it happened to someone else in a different life.

SKIP

When I saw the final cut of "Hear Me Now," I knew it would be up for the VMA. We released it so close to the end of the eligibility period, but we *just* managed to sneak in there, along with an EP that included "Moonbeam," "September Rain," and finally, "Hear Me Now."

I'm not saying that to brag. It was just clear—Ryan's positioning was right, she was reaching her peak, and it was a particularly well-done video.

Hell, they love spectacle. And they didn't even know what kind of spectacle she was about to give them.

KYLIE

The 2018 VMAs was such a fun night—I mean, up until Ryan disappeared. She also threw up a little when we were getting ready, but I think it was a combination of nerves and of drinking too much. Ryan and Mari and I got ready at my penthouse in Washington Heights, and Tatiana and all our stylists came over while we blasted music and ate Doritos and shit.

Ryan came back from the kitchen at one point and had a shot of tequila—I mean, I assume that's what it was, because she was also carrying tequila for us—in a rocks glass. We knocked back shot after shot, and we were jumping on my bed, and the next thing I knew, we were flying through Manhattan in the limo on the way to the venue.

MARI

Ryan was never a pusher. But she was really pouring the drinks for us that night. It wasn't until we were jumping on Kylie's bed that I was like *Shit, I'm really feeling this.* And I climbed down and took a breather and said, "Whoa, whoa, Ryan, how many have you had?"

And she threw her head back and laughed and said, "Does it matter? I'm getting a VMA tonight!"

I said, "Yeah, and as part of your marketing team, I want to make sure you can walk to the stage to get it."

She slid off the bed and smiled at me and sort of patted my hair. "Aww, Mari. It's all going to be okay. I want you to have fun tonight—you've done so much for me."

And she poured another round of drinks.

TATIANA

I came to Ryan with my ideas for the VMA look. I thought, maybe a spin on the spidery imagery, something silver again that would be a nod to her beginnings, or an homage to her past music-video characters. My silhouettes were all the Old Hollywood that she was known for—hourglass, classic shapes, tight bodice.

But no. She said, "I want something completely different. I want modern this time." Okay, like what?

We talked and talked in circles, it seemed, and finally came around to angular, to boxy. It was a very, very different direction, but I liked it. Ryan often wanted to reinvent herself. I thought perhaps maybe she was doing that again.

So I took cues from Blake Lively, from Janelle Monáe, and suggested an oversize blazer and miniskirt. Bright red, lavish.

"Yes," Ryan said. "But let's do blue. I want it to be like my dress at the beginning and end of the video."

"Okay, okay," I said. "But we are going to make it *rock star*."

It is MTV, after all.

TEEN STAR MAGAZINE, September 2018
SOMETHING BLUE

Pop star Ryan Holding wows on the red carpet in an electric-blue Saint Laurent blazer with effortlessly chic bedhead hair.

"My shoes match my shoulders!" the "Hear Me Now" singer commented, pointing out the diamond studs scattered along her shoulders and her sparkly sky-high Jimmy Choos. What's she most excited about?

"The after-party," she said with a smile. "Whatever happens tonight, I can't wait to celebrate with my friends."

JASMINE

I wasn't surprised at all when "Hear Me Now" was nominated. But the stakes were very high. If she won, Ryan would become the youngest female artist in history to hold Best New Artist, Best Visual Effects, and Video of the Year.

Skip went as my date that night. It was sweet.

Ryan arrived separately from us—with Mari and Kylie, I think—so I can't speak to how she was before the show.

Drunk? No, she didn't seem drunk at all. The girls were definitely tipsy. Maybe more than tipsy. But not Ryan.

It was funny; actually, I just got the sense that she was feeling really alive. Really wired. She was quiet while the rest of us were talking and laughing, keeping her purse clutched to her chest and just people watching. Like she was taking it all in. I chalked it up to nerves at the time, but hindsight is twenty-twenty, isn't it?

Maybe there was something going on. Maybe there wasn't.

I leaned over at one point in the night, just before they announced her category, and asked, "How are you feeling?"

"Good," she said. "Ready."

VIDEO MUSIC AWARDS BROADCAST, AUGUST 20, 2018

[A member of Brace for Impact in a colorful paisley suit emcees, standing with an envelope before the microphone.]

EMCEE: . . . And now we come to a truly powerful moment in the night, when we honor the videos that have sparked our imaginations and pushed the bounds of creativity. Each of our nominees is celebrating an incredible year of work. But one stood out to our voters as the clear winner. And that video is . . .

[He rips open the envelope.]

EMCEE: . . . "Hear Me Now," directed and produced by Ryan Holding!

[The applause is thunderous. Ryan ascends the stage with her hand on her heart.]

RYAN: I can't tell you all what this means to me. Every day, I find it hard to believe this life is mine. But I hope—I hope it's all been worth it.

[She pauses for a moment, a long moment, seeming briefly as though she wants to say something else. Then she continues.]

RYAN: Thank you, New York. Thank you.

MARI

We were cheering and screaming for her with everything we had in us. Ryan came off the stage, and she was beaming, but her eyes were filled with tears, and she was staring right at me—we all sort of dogpiled her, but she reached out and hugged me tight.

And she spoke very low in my ear, but very clearly and deliberately, to the point where I thought, *Wait, are you not drunk? Are you completely sober right now?*

She said, "You mean everything to me, Mari. Whatever happens. Even when it doesn't feel like it. Okay? Do you trust me?"

And I said, *Yeah, of course, of course.* I didn't know what she meant. I was going to ask her later. But in the moment, she pulled back and smiled wide and started jumping up and down with Kylie. Then everyone else flooded around her as the show concluded.

FRANK

My wife and I held a little watch party of the VMAs back in the studio. I was so excited to see her win. I called her right afterward—I knew she wouldn't pick up, but I wanted to leave a voicemail saying how proud I was of her.

She never called me back.

VICTOR!A

Yeah, I did see Ryan afterward. Just for a little bit. I had to congratulate her—she killed it up there! I'm sure you know about these things, but there's kind of the preshow on the red carpet, the actual show, and then there's a valet bottleneck, so everyone hangs around for almost another hour shooting the shit, postshow, before we all head to our after-parties.

I found her in the crush of people and gave her a hug. "You did it, Ryan!" I was jumping up and down and everything, super wound up. I wanted her to match my energy, but she just smiled at me and squeezed my hands.

She said, "Couldn't have done it without you."

We caught up a little bit, even though I couldn't stay long; I was throwing this massive blowout in my loft in Dumbo and had to get over there to kick things off.

"You're coming, right?" I said.

Ryan said, "Yeah, I have something I want to do. But I might swing by later."

"Do it, definitely!" I told her. "We've gotta celebrate you."

I don't know; her vibes were sort of off. I didn't feel like anything was weird at the time, but looking back now . . . she seemed a little jumpy. Looking around and being distant. We all had drinks on us, but she was clutching that silver astronaut in both hands like she was afraid to lose it.

TYLER

If Ryan was at the VMAs that night, I wouldn't have known. I pregamed and got shit-faced. It was a great night for me.

HELLADONNA

I tried to keep my distance. What did I have to say to her? Nothing.

But Ryan did come up to me and congratulate me on my Best Power Anthem win.

"Oh yeah?" I said. I wasn't even trying to keep the cattiness out of my voice. I didn't give a damn what she thought. "Did you actually listen to it?"

I have no idea if she realized I'd overheard her that time at the party, years ago. But to her credit, she looked me in the eye and she did say, "Yeah. The bridge is my favorite, how you added the organ and synth in the background. Gives me chills."

I didn't want to thank her—didn't need her opinion—but I managed to say, "That's my favorite too. Wasn't sure about the organ, but my producer convinced me."

She nodded and started walking away. I don't know, I'm not really sure what came over me. I called out to her and she turned back. I said, "You know that Met Gala dress? The spider one?"

She looked nervous. I'm sure she thought I was going to call her out for it.

But I said, "That was badass."

She smiled and said, "Thanks, Helladonna."

What? It was. So sue me.

EVAN

I did try to talk to her, yes. But she saw me and walked the other way.

SAVANNAH

I told her congrats because I'm not petty. She said, "Thanks, Savannah. That dress is really cute on you."

But she said *cute* really patronizing. So I said, "Thanks! Yours too," in the same tone.

She smiled and said, "Thanks," and then turned to talk to someone else.

KYLIE

I ignored Savannah and Helladonna. I was ready to *go*. It was time for the after-party, and the drinks were already flowing.

Honestly, um . . . the rest of the night is kind of fuzzy for me from here on out. If you'd asked me the next day, I would have sworn that Ryan got in the limo with our group on the way to Victoria's.

And listen, it's hard to admit this, but it wasn't until, like, two days later that I realized that she . . . hadn't.

Yeah.

I still feel guilty about that. It was what helped me get my drinking under control.

MARI

There was so much going on that it's hard to remember. I'd made a lot of friends and contacts working for Ryan, too, so people were coming up to me and chatting, asking about the album, the after-party. Everyone was still drinking while we waited for the valet. The lobby was *packed.*

And then Ryan was trying to say something, leaning down next to my ear—she said, "I have to run back to the hotel first, okay?"

I said, "I'll go with you."

"No," she told me. "Go with Kylie to the after-party, I'll be right there."

It was so loud. I should have stopped her. I did ask, "What do you need? Why do you have to go?"

"I just need to work something out quick."

It was her lingo. She always needed to work out a verse, or a lyric, or pin down some tune that had been playing around in her head. I didn't question it.

"Okay," I told her. "Text me when you're on your way, all right?"

She said she would.

Our limo came, and I made my way with Kylie and the others through the crowd. I remember that I looked back to find Ryan just before I left the lobby.

She was by the stairs, looking back at me.

And that's the last time I saw her.

ELYSE JAMES, *author*

That was the moment I took my famous photograph of Ryan.

Pausing at the stairs, looking back at Mari, in her blazer of stark, violent blue against the deep red of Radio City Music Hall.

I caught her eye for the briefest moment before she descended to the lower level, not to be seen again.

She did not know me, but she knew of me. I doubt she recognized me in the crowd, but maybe there was something of my brother's face in mine. Maybe I made her think of him, just before the end.

Wilder was not in attendance at the VMAs in New York City that night, not as far as I know. In fact, I didn't know where he was.

And although I was there at the VMAs to do my job as a photojournalist, I locked in on Ryan not because she was a record-breaking music-industry legend, but because she was the woman who broke my brother's heart.

And he disappeared that night too.

From: <wilderjames91@gmail.com>
Sent: September 22, 2018, 11:37 p.m.
To: <elysejames711@gmail.com>
Subject: Quick update
Hey, Ellie. I hope this doesn't come as a major shock but I need to take some time away. I'm officially quitting the band and going to try to figure out what to do next with my life, so I might be out of commission for a little while.
If you don't hear from me, I'm fine, okay? I promise. Don't worry. If I had a crystal ball maybe I could tell you where I'm going and what the next few years of my life will look like.

I'm sorry I can't say more—it's hard for even me to see that far.

Love ya.

—W

From: <elysejames711@gmail.com>

Sent: September 23, 2018, 1:09 a.m.

To: <wilderjames91@gmail.com>

Re: Quick update

Wilder, WTF??? the next few YEARS?? answer your phone!!! now!!!!

PART III

TWENTY-THREE

SKIP

No, we didn't realize Wilder was gone—like, *gone* gone—for a long time. I'm sorry, Elyse. He submitted his formal resignation just before the VMAs, so we thanked him for all he'd done and closed out his paperwork.

I remember asking where he was headed. I thought he must have gotten a pretty goddamn good opportunity if he was leaving the pay that we were giving him, and he told me he'd gotten a gig with Les Jardins—they won Eurovision that year. I didn't know he'd been auditioning or anything, but why would I have? I congratulated him and wished him the best.

It wasn't until I received your call a few weeks later that I contacted Les Jardins' manager and asked about Wilder. She confirmed she'd never even spoken with him.

It was strange. Strange as all hell. But we got the same answer as you: Given his email stating his intent to leave, he was not considered a missing person. So I know, I know, I'm empathetic to what you went through . . . but it was a difficult case to pursue after that.

And Ryan had provided her own fallout to deal with.

MARI

Everything was a mess. There were people who said they saw her at the after-party, people who said she was at a different after-party, people who had no clue. No one had a straight answer. I personally am confident that she never showed up at Victor!a's.

I texted her at some point in the middle of the night asking where she was—no answer. It was late, we all crashed at Victor!a's, but when I woke up the next morning with a wicked hangover, I had this weird feeling in my gut. I went back to the hotel—she'd booked separate suites for us, which was odd, since we normally would have stayed together—but they told me her room was already being turned over for cleaning.

I called Ryan again and again with no answer. By that evening, I had called Skip and Jas and Kylie and anyone else I could think of. But everyone, swept up in the celebrations of the night before, had lost track of Ryan.

I'm sure you've gone over this a million times. There was no surveillance footage of her leaving the building—at least, nothing that was released during the investigation. Her house in Malibu has been left exactly as is, locked up and left untouched except for the cleaners who are still scheduled on a weekly basis. Her jet is still in the hangar, grounded. Her phone number is a dead end—no responses, no messages. Left with no direction, my team didn't do anything in particular with her social accounts, but we've monitored the floods of heartfelt messages and *Ryan, come back!*s that still roll in on the daily, if you would believe that.

The police closed the missing persons case as soon as they opened it. The NYPD had been in touch with Ryan, they said, and confirmed she was okay. In fact, they said she had stopped by the Midtown Manhattan station the morning after the VMAs, but that didn't make any sense at all. They refused to give us more information.

Everything about it was strange. If she was okay, why wouldn't she answer any of us?

Why wouldn't she have told me where she was going?

JASMINE

I didn't know what to think. The police have been wrong before, even in these high-profile cases—*especially* in these cases, in fact. There was a lot of public pressure on them to find Ryan, but they confirmed point-blank that they had spoken to Ryan and she was perfectly fine, just taking some time off for herself.

The official statement we released was very passive and generic. I mean no offense to Mari and her team—what else could we do? Going against the police would have incited a riot, and it was not a good look if Madcap had lost track of its biggest star. People were already developing conspiracy theories about the NYPD and LAPD covering up cult activity and kidnappings. We had to say *something*. But we also had to hedge our bets in case news came out later that . . . well, that Ryan was not actually okay at all. I think it was something along the lines of *Ryan is pursuing new stuff at this time and requests that you leave her the hell alone,* but worded better, of course.

It wasn't my gut instinct that she was—well, hurt, or something. Maybe I've just been in denial. But I did wonder if there had been some kind of . . . break. That happens, you know.

She had been under immense pressure, most of her life, really. And sometimes, after long enough, people sidestep from one reality into another.

HOLLYWOOD REPORT MAGAZINE, October 2018

> The music industry is buzzing about the alleged disappearance of pop singer-songwriter Ryan Holding following her Video of the Year win at MTV's Video Music Awards.

Sources close to Holding say that they have been unable to get in contact with the singer since that night, and she has not been seen or photographed in or around her New York or Malibu homes.

"The New York Police Department spoke with Ms. Holding at Midtown North Precinct on the morning of September 23," said NYPD Chief of Police Michael Holmes. "We spoke with her again by phone at the urging of her colleagues. Both times, Ms. Holding was safe and healthy, and expressed a desire to take some time off after spending many years in the spotlight."

But some say the statement doesn't add up, especially when Holding expressed intentions to attend the VMA after-party at the penthouse suite of industry peer Victor!a and never showed.

"I didn't see her that night at my place," Victor!a told *Hollywood Report*. "And I haven't been able to get in touch with her since. I really hope she's okay."

It is unclear whether Holding's label, Madcap Records, was aware of any plans by the singer to take a hiatus. The company released the following statement this morning:

"We at Madcap Records celebrate Ryan Holding's historic VMA win and the deep loyalty and touching concern of her fans. Ryan is pursuing new endeavors at this time and requests privacy and patience as she enjoys a well-deserved rest and works toward her next major creative project."

TEEN STAR MAGAZINE, October 2018
RUNAWAY RYAN?

Pop legend Ryan Holding is said to be missing after sweeping the VMAs and disappearing into the night. Is it a case of a runaway star or foul play?

"I saw her at the VMAs, and we had a great time catching up," said Tyler Michaels, one of Holding's previous beaus. "But she was acting strange, really jumpy. I wondered for a second if she might be on drugs."

"She was totally spaced out," said Savannah D'Alessio, close friend of Ryan. "She was going to come to the after-party with us, but when we got in the limo, she wasn't there. I don't know if she took something or if someone slipped her something again. It's so sad, you know, how the rules don't apply anymore once you're that rich. I'd been really worried about her. I just hope she's okay."

Fans across the nation have banded together to share clues and compare notes on social media and in person, determined to find the missing star.

"I've got my whole school involved," said Amy Waltz, 17, of Cleveland, Ohio. "We've got people DMing her on socials, trying to find clues in her music videos and press coverage, and contacting anyone in Ryan's circle they can get a hold of. It's really exciting, actually. It's like we've got our own detective agency, and we're connected to people around the world who are concerned for Ryan and want her to be brought home safe."

Will their hard work pay off? Only time will tell.

Until then, *Teen Star Magazine* has opened up our tip line and is offering a $5,000 reward for any information that leads to Ryan Holding's whereabouts.

TWENTY-FOUR

ELYSE JAMES, *AUTHOR*

I've intentionally removed myself from this narrative as much as possible because this is a story about Ryan, after all. Ryan overshadows my own career as well as my brother's. Her disappearance eclipsed Wilder's estrangement, and yet it is, I believe, the key to his departure.

While everyone was focused on finding Ryan Holding, I was trying to find my only brother. If the police were no help to a celebrity billionaire, you can bet they were no help to me. I rushed home to Los Angeles after the VMAs. When Wilder wouldn't pick up the phone, I went to his apartment and badgered the landlord until my driver's license and a photo of the two of us together, along with his final email—which suggested he was about to stop paying rent—convinced him to let me inside.

The place was clean and bare. Not empty. His quilt was on the bed, his dress shoes and a few old clothes were in the closet along with his old blue duffel bag. His cupboards held some food, but anything important or perishable had been cleared out. Nothing in the fridge. Keys and wallet, gone.

His phone, however, remained on the kitchen table, switched off.

I charged it and guessed his passcode—1612, our address in McKees Rocks—and scoured his messages and notes for any clues. There was nothing. No texts out of the ordinary, no unusual pictures, no secret apps or locked folders.

And in fact, it was that *nothing* that made me most suspicious.

Wilder had been in love with Ryan. That had been clear to me. Yet there was no mention of her anywhere on his phone, no messages to her, no photos or memories or voice recordings.

Either he had deleted everything after their breakup, or she'd been so paranoid about their relationship being discovered that she gave him whatever burner phone he was probably using now.

I hated her in that moment, I have to admit. I couldn't comprehend *why*, why Ryan was so afraid of a normal relationship, why she closed herself off, why she needed to have my brother so badly, out of all people. Because I couldn't shake the feeling that wherever they were, they were together.

So I set out to understand Ryan Holding.

I took my brother's phone home with me and scrolled through it most nights, trying to find something I had missed. I googled many different variations of his name, of names he might use as aliases, of music news across the globe to see if anything about him would come up. All of it was old information, published well before he had disappeared.

Work on the book got sidelined when the pandemic kept me inside and temporarily reduced my photojournalism career to long-range shots of architecture and landscapes. As I set up interviews and scheduled trips once it was okay to travel again, I learned about Ryan and her life, her mind, her behavior, from those who knew her best. I traveled to the places where she'd been and where my brother had gone too. Rent kept deducting automatically from Wilder's accounts, and I took that as a sign that he was still alive and well somewhere, at least alive enough to move money into checking.

Until one day, in late summer of 2022, it stopped.

Wilder's landlord called me just after I'd finished interviewing Serge and before I was to speak with Kylie the following week.

"It seems the well has run dry," he said. His name was Dale. He was a generally grouchy man with whom I'd developed a tentative friendship, once he got over his initial exasperation at my endless questions about Wilder's comings and goings.

"Can you try to run it again?" I asked him. "Maybe it's an error."

"No error. I've already tried." He sighed. "Sorry, Elyse, but I think the apartment is a dead end."

I don't know what I expected. I guess I thought that as long as his apartment was still paid for, he'd be coming back. I thought that at any moment I might get a text from an unknown number or a call from Dale and the long, bewildering wait would be over.

Instead, I found myself packing up Wilder's things for him and staring down the empty apartment alone.

"Good luck, kiddo," Dale had said, shaking my hand after helping me load the last box into a friend's pickup. "He's out there somewhere."

"I hope so, Dale," I said, and then I went home and poured myself a little too much wine.

I spent that evening scrolling through Wilder's phone one more time.

And then I saw something.

Buried way back in his photos, eleven years old, was a selfie of Wilder on the "White Lace" set. He was making a goofy face as he stared into the prop crystal ball on the fortune teller's table. I enlarged the photo and saw, at last, the person in the background: It was Ryan, laughing, almost invisible in the dark contrasted light.

It was the only picture of Ryan on his phone.

I sat up, theories pinballing around my head like I was on the Ryde-or-Die conspiracy subreddit. Didn't Ryan place great importance on the crystal ball in "Hear Me Now"? Didn't Wilder himself mention it in his final email to me?

I didn't wait until the next morning. I called Serge and talked around the tipsiness that had made my mouth feel like cotton.

"Serge," I said. "The crystal ball, the prop from 'White Lace'—where is it? Do you still have it?"

"Elyse, didn't expect to hear from you so late," he said. It sounded like I had woken him up. "The crystal ball . . . let's see. We rented props for a lot of the videos. But since we used that one multiple times, it *could* be in storage."

"Where?" I asked. "Where's the storage?"

"Madcap's got a locker in south LA. Skip might be able to let you in."

I emailed Skip that night and, after rereading the message the next morning and regretting its slightly manic tone, I called him and explained myself.

"I don't know, Elyse," he said. "I think it's a long shot. I'm not even sure if we have any video props in the locker—Serge would know better than me, but I personally have no clue where that thing is."

"Can I look anyway? Please, Skip." I didn't tell him that I would break into that storage locker if I had to.

He sighed. "I guess if it's anywhere, it would be with the rest of Ryan's stuff. All right, I'll send you the address. Yes, we can go as early as today—because I know that was your next question."

I was ten miles over the speed limit the whole time I was driving to south Los Angeles. Madcap's storage facility wasn't the typical self-serve, but gated; I gave my name and Skip's to an intercom at the front and pulled into the lot.

"You beat me," Skip said when he arrived. "But I don't want you to get your hopes up, okay?"

I laughed nervously. "We'll see."

The storage facility was rented by several other businesses, and the hallways were long, windowless, and claustrophobic. I felt my heart beat with every muffled step we took down the linoleum floor.

"Here it is," he said, pulling out a ring of keys. "This is where we shoved any of Ryan's old stuff, anyway."

Skip unlocked the heavy metal door and slid it aside, switching on a fluorescent light that buzzed over the square room. As my eyes adjusted, I saw stacks of framed posters of Ryan, bins piled high, mic stands and stage equipment gathered in one corner. Clothing racks with garment bags containing Ryan's famous costumes and red carpet outfits were tucked neatly to one side of the room. I noticed the famous Met Gala spider dress behind the clear plastic. Boxes of CDs and merchandise were everywhere, and I recognized a Ryan Holding lunch box that a younger cousin of mine had used back in 2010.

"Knock yourself out," Skip said. "The 'White Lace' stuff would probably be somewhere in the bottom of . . . that pile, unfortunately."

We dug in silence. Nothing but merch, old records, and props that I didn't recognize. It was strange to go through these things with my own hands, like I was finally encountering the relics of a strange history I'd been studying all this time. None of it was familiar to me.

Until I reached the fourth bin.

There, at the very bottom, was something spherical wrapped in a black cloth. I kept my hands steady as I grasped at the shape and shook it free of the other junk. Pulling its covering back, I saw opalescent glass and a small wooden stand.

The crystal ball.

It was smaller than I remembered, somewhere around the size of a cantaloupe. I was about to call to Skip when I turned it over and saw a small opening in the bottom where a light bulb would go to illuminate it. As I shifted the ball in my hands, something very quietly rustled inside.

I shook it. Turned it upright again.

"Shit, I remember these old magazine features," Skip said with a laugh, his back to me a few feet away. "I don't know what we were thinking, putting her in a T-shirt over a long-sleeve shirt with a vest on top, nonetheless. What the hell was up with all those layers?"

"And the plaid Bermuda shorts," I agreed, careful to keep my voice steady as I raised the ball over my head and peered inside. A tiny scrap of paper rested at the edge of the opening. I took one more glance at Skip, then hooked it with my nail and managed to pull it out without ripping it. I slipped it into my pocket.

Then I said, "Skip, I think I found it."

"Yeah?" He stood up and brushed his hands on his jeans. "Well, I'll be. I guess we do still have it."

"Yep." I turned it over, looking for any other markings, then handed it to him. He did the same, squinting through the hole with one eye.

"Nothing, huh?" he asked, looking at me. "I guess I don't know what it is you'd even be looking for."

"Me neither," I said. "It was just . . . the best clue I thought I'd gotten since they disappeared."

"It was worth a shot." Skip sat down heavily on one of the bins and ran a hand over his face. "I have to believe they're okay out there. And just choosing not to get in touch . . . for whatever reason." He sighed. "It hurts a little, doesn't it?"

I forced down the lump in my throat and nodded. "It does."

He looked at me for a moment. "Maybe we'll have some answers someday."

I met his gaze, unwavering. "I'm hopeful."

~

Less than forty-eight hours later, I was sitting on a plane, unfolding the scrap of paper that held a single word in Wilder's handwriting.

Hailuoto.

I'd googled it the second I was back in the safety of my car, waving Skip off. Hailuoto—an island in the North Bothnian Sea, just off the coast of Finland. Eight hours north of Helsinki.

It was madness to go there, to think that Ryan and Wilder could be there. But why would the note be in the crystal ball? What else could it mean?

What other options did I have?

I touched down in Helsinki later that night and booked a rental car and hotel room. I surfed Finnish channels until one in the morning, willing the next day to come, and when I couldn't stand that anymore, I lay in bed with the lights on and stared at the ceiling.

If Wilder was there, what the hell would I say?

What would he say?

The whole situation, combined with my jet lag and lack of sleep, made the drive the next day feel dreamlike. It was like many road trips I'd taken before. With the rural setting and the pine trees, I could even get myself to believe I was back in Pennsylvania, driving home to visit my brother and hear about the progress he'd made on the guitar.

If I'd been wiser, I would have stayed another night in Oulu before driving out to the minuscule strip of land where I would catch the ferry to the island.

But by the time I drew close to the northern region at five o'clock, my momentum was too great to be stopped.

I bought coffee at the tiny roadside shop next to the ferry dock while I checked the schedule, and then in almost no time I was being carried toward Hailuoto, gazing at the vast expanse of water outside my car window and feeling not a little nauseous.

I was one of only a few passengers. I had no plan for how to go about finding the brother who had been estranged from me for four years.

But with a population under one thousand, I thought that someone on Hailuoto must know where he was.

The ferry deposited me on the island's eastern shore, and I paused a moment, gripping the wheel of the rental car and wondering what to do next.

I hit the gas.

Hailuoto is a very rural and remote isle, not touristy or well traveled in any sense. I had expected some sort of town center, but tall pines lined every road, giving more of the feel of a campground than a seaside village.

At last I pulled up on a cluster of buildings and a shopping market with its lights bright in the gathering dusk. I parked and went inside, looking around the store with its few inhabitants and again feeling like I was losing my grip on reality.

"Hyvää iltaa," called an elderly woman in a green grocer's apron, smiling at me and nodding. I winced; I had meant to brush up on some Finnish on the plane, but my brain had whirred at a million miles an hour the entire flight. I clumsily tried to repeat her greeting. Understanding my problem, she tried for English. "Can I help?"

"Ole hyvä," I tried. "Please, I am looking for my brother." I took out my phone and held up a photo of Wilder and me together.

In the moment that the woman adjusted her glasses and peered at the photo, my stomach churned. What if he wasn't here, and I had come for nothing? What if he'd expected me to find the note right away, and had once been on Hailuoto, but left long ago? Where would I sleep if I could not find him tonight?

But then the woman's face broke into a knowing smile.

"Ah!" she said. "Veljesi ja hänen pieni tyttönsä. Yes, yes. He is here."

"Really? Kiitos. Kiitos!" I had learned *thank you*, at least. "Where?"

The woman pursed her lips and shook her head. She held up a hand, and my heart sank a little again as she shook her head again and walked away.

But then she returned with a piece of paper and a pen.

"Here," she said, and wrote down a collection of numbers and letters. She drew lines on the paper in a map and marked the shop where we stood with a star. Then she drew arrows down the road, left, right, straight—and another star.

His house. Maybe.

"Here," she said again, smiling and pressing the paper into my hand.

"Kiitos," I said again, then once more, and I took her hand in both of mine.

"Yes, yes," she said.

I drove with both hands on the wheel and her map held under one thumb so I could track my direction. The night was getting darker as I turned off pavement and onto a gravel road, deeper and deeper into the forest. My headlights cut through the twilight around me, and a deer stared at me from the brush line along the road.

There, at last, was a cottage in a clearing. Pale yellow with cream trim and window boxes lining every sill. Curtains obscured the view inside.

A small garage was set to one side of the yard with a few other outbuildings behind it, so I couldn't see any cars—not that I would recognize them, anyway.

But the home was occupied. Light glowed from the windows, and I could smell woodsmoke from the small brick chimney.

I turned my car off and sat for a moment in silence, hearing none of the nighttime forest noises for the sound of blood rushing through my ears.

Then I walked to the front porch and knocked on the door.

Footsteps sounded faintly on the other side.

And then I was face-to-face with Wilder, with my brother, looking into eyes that were so familiar but older and slightly more lined, as he looked back at me and many, many unspoken words passed between us.

At last he opened his mouth.

"Ellie," he said, and broke into a wide smile. "I knew you could do it."

TWENTY-FIVE

The following is a transcript from the recorded conversation between the author and her brother on August 29, 2022.]

E: What the hell, Wilder. What the hell?

W: I'll explain everything, I promise. Come in, Ellie, please. Come see our home.

E: I'd like to know more about that "our."

W: Yeah, it's . . . just come in. I told you, I'll explain. Can I get you some coffee?

E: I've come to the edge of the world to find you after four years, and you ask me if I want coffee right now?

W: Well . . . do you?

E: Yes.

W: Okay, then. Come to the kitchen.

E: Okay.

[A silence falls, and the sound of shuffling is heard, a chair scraping across the floor, the tick of a gas burner and the light clang of a kettle.]

W: We do French press these days.

[No response; the water boils.]

W: Cream and sugar?

E: Please.

W: Here we are. Just like old times, isn't it? Meeting up for coffee when you were off classes in Pittsburgh, or every other week when we were in LA, me rambling on about how my life was falling apart . . .

E: Wilder . . .

W: I know, Ellie. I'll tell you everything now. I'm just trying to figure out where to start.

E: Maybe with that little girl who looks just like you poking her head around the counter.

W: What? Lilla, you're supposed to be in bed.

L: Who's she?

E: I could ask the same thing.

W: Come here. Come on, it's okay. Meet your aunt Ellie. Say hi.

L: Hi.

E: Hi . . . Lilla, was it?

W: Lilla. It's our nickname. Her real name is Ellie—Elyse.

E: Oh.

W: Yeah. We thought—we thought it was the least we could do to honor you.

E: And "we," this mysterious and omnipresent "we" is—

W: Go back to bed, Lilla, okay? Äiti tulee pian kotiin. Voitko levätä?

L: Okei, okei. Hyvästi, Ellie-täti.

W: It's her new favorite phrase. *Okei, okei,* like she's all exasperated. I don't know where she picked it up from—probably our neighbor. They get along like a house on fire.

E: Wilder.

W: Yes. *[A pause.]* It's Ryan, okay? I'm sure you figured that out before you came here, and if not, seeing Lilla . . . that should have sealed it.

E: She looks like both of you.

W: I think she's Ryan, through and through.

E: So when—?

W: We . . . we secretly got back together after the *Waterfall* tour. Sort of. It was messy. We'd broken up, but, you know . . . it was hard to make a clean split. We were working together, practically living alongside each other still. I kept telling her every time we met up that it was the last time. She kept telling me the same thing. We were angry with each other, angry with the whole situation, and when

"Hear Me Now" started filming, I swore I'd leave when it wrapped. I told her as much. I even told Skip and Jas in order to hold myself to it. But then . . .

E: Then?

W: Ryan told me she was pregnant.

E: Convenient.

W: Don't take that tone, Ellie. I was ecstatic. Terrified but ecstatic. So was Ryan.

E: Yeah, so overcome with that motherly glow that she decided to essentially fake both your deaths—

W: Don't you understand? No, you don't, because you were always bitter toward her. But imagine, just for a moment, the kind of scrutiny under which she lived her life. The hordes of fans and critics who watched her every move. This level of invasiveness that had become *normal* for her.

E: Ryan said she could never be a mom, exactly because of that. What changed?

W: How do you know that?

E: I . . . I read it somewhere.

W: She never spoke about that publicly. I know she didn't. She was very private about the prospect of parenthood.

E: Then you must have told me. My question stands.

W: It's not that she didn't *want* kids. She thought she *couldn't* have them. That there would never be an opportunity, or a supportive enough relationship—or even if there was, that she wouldn't be able to handle the extra attention. The criticism. She really sympathized with Britney Spears, people who had broken down in public like that. She once said, "That could be me. I've almost had public meltdowns as it is, and if they came for my child, I don't know what I'd do." And then . . . when she did get pregnant . . .

E: She changed her mind?

W: Not changed. Just . . . relented. She's worked very hard to control herself and her emotions and relationships, but this was one thing she didn't want to control. Ryan wanted to give in. And when she told me, stubborn as I was being toward her . . . I wanted to give in too.

E: So you let her talk you into disappearing.

W: Ellie, I know . . . I know it was extreme. I'm not saying it wasn't. I've missed my old life; she asked for a *lot*. But Ryan is the mother of my child. And I loved her even before that became true—I had never stopped loving her, despite it all. Leaving was what she wanted. She was starting to burn out anyway, starting to wonder when people would get tired of her and move on to the next big thing. And because our relationship had always been the bigger priority to me than my career—even more so once Lilla was in the picture—I didn't mind taking a big step back. Did we disagree on how to go about it? Yes. I swore to her that our friends and family could be trusted—you, Mari, our parents, even Skip and Jas. I said you all had a right to know.

E: Yeah. We did.

W: You did. But . . . she had been burned before. And you, Mari, I mean everyone had connections to the press or was at risk of being tricked or even hurt by some psycho who wanted information. A clean break was the only way, just the three of us, and then we could reevaluate after a year. Like going on a retreat. And then a year turned into four.

E: And you forgot about us.

W: No. No, don't say it like that, Ellie. Being a dad shifted my whole goddamn world, okay? We're so remote here, and our lives changed so drastically, but it was . . . it was something that felt special and sacred for the first time in my life. Maybe I wanted to indulge in that a little longer. Is that so bad?

[A long silence.]

W: Here. Let me get you a refill.

E: No, that's—

W: What is that?

E: What? Nothing.

W: No. Your phone was behind your mug. Give me your phone.

E: Why? It's just my phone.

W: Show me the screen, Elyse. Show me the GODDAMN screen!

E: Wilder, stop, it's just my phone, it's—

W: What the *fuck*, Elyse! Are you recording this conversation? Are you out of your goddamn mind?

E: I didn't mean to upset you. Wilder, calm down.

W: Like hell! Like hell you didn't! What did I JUST SAY? I vouched for you! I swore up and down to my wife—yes, my wife!—that she could trust you. That you would never do anything to hurt us. And after four years, you track us down, you come into my home, and you SECRETLY RECORD the things I tell you and you alone, in confidence, as the big sister who's supposed to protect me—

E: What the fuck do you think I'm trying to do, Wilder? You didn't tell me any of this shit! You kept me in the dark for so long that I thought you might be DEAD! Mom didn't know, nobody in the goddamn country knew if either of you were dead or alive! Do you realize how fucked up that is? How—how absolutely unhinged and *delusional* it is for a partner to ask you to do that—

W: SHE is my family now! I have to put her and Lilla first. They are everything to me, and you, on the other hand, took long enough to figure out the message I—

E: You are not about to say that. I know you aren't about to accuse me of not deciphering your weird little riddles faster when I *thought my little brother might be having a mental breakdown*—

R: Wilder, whose car is in the—? Oh.

E: Oh.

W: Shit.

R: Hello, Elyse.

E: Hello, Ryan.

TWENTY-SIX

After my shouting match with Wilder, the sudden silence made my ears ring as I stared at the woman who had appeared in the kitchen with us. She was tall and slim, and her wavy hair was pulled back into a short ponytail, dyed dark brown.

But it was Ryan.

"How are you, Elyse?" She spoke again, as if the clear repetition of my name would calm me down. It did—marginally.

"I've been better," I said.

"I'm sure this was sort of a shock," she said. She kept her eyes on me and her movements slow as she set her purse and the bag of groceries she'd evidently just picked up on the counter. I must have missed her at the supermarket by minutes.

"She was recording my conversation, Ryan," Wilder said, a note of desperation in his voice. "She's recording everything."

Ryan turned her green eyes on me. The others had mentioned them in their interviews, and the media had certainly fixated on them in her time, but not until that moment did I understand their full effect. She looked at me with a strange mixture of pity and appraisal, but I somehow felt that she wasn't surprised. Ryan met my gaze unwaveringly. After a moment, I felt compelled to either look away or give in, and I wondered how many others had been swayed by the same tactic.

She was waiting for me to speak, but I didn't. Finally, Ryan asked, "Is that true?"

I glanced at Wilder and then held my phone up and said, "Yes."

"Why?" Ryan asked.

There was no sound in the house. Outside, wind moved through the forest.

"I'm writing a book," I said to Ryan at last. "About your life."

Wilder exploded. "You can *never* publish that!"

Ryan ignored him. "Why are you doing that?"

I faltered a little at this. No one had pressed me on my reasons yet. It was a given that the book, if I pulled it off, would be a bestseller. Everyone was willing to pay for more information about the life and disappearance of Ryan Holding. But these were not my reasons.

"Because I wanted to understand the woman who brainwashed my little brother," I said.

"How condescending can you possibly—" Wilder started, but Ryan cut him off.

"So you knew that he'd come with me? The whole time?" she asked.

I kept my phone clutched tightly in my hand. "I strongly suspected."

Ryan nodded. She looked at me for another moment, then turned to Wilder. "I think Elyse and I need to talk woman-to-woman." And when he looked like he was about to protest, she raised her eyebrows and said, "You wanted to put away the lawn furniture before the rain tonight, didn't you?"

"Yes," he said without looking at me.

"Thanks, Wilder." She watched him go. Then she said to me, "Come on to the living room. We'll be more comfortable. Lilla, you can come, too, if you're not going to sleep."

Ryan swept away while I looked around me and saw my niece, who—unnoticed by myself or Wilder—had crept back into the room and hidden under the kitchen table.

~

I followed Ryan and Lilla back to the living room. The cottage was not how I'd imagined Ryan living; I'd pictured her in a secret Italian villa somewhere with gated security and most of the luxury she'd become accustomed to retained.

But this house was on par with the other small homes on the island—cedar paneled, low lit, and snug. The furniture reminded me of the thrift-store pieces we had in McKees Rocks, and houseplants and blankets littered the space. Ryan curled up on the couch opposite the coffee table as I sank into an armchair. Lilla crawled into her lap.

They did look so alike, the now-dark-haired Ryan and the little girl with wispy strawberry curls. But my brother was there, too, in Lilla's nose and brown eyes and dark brows.

"How much did Wilder tell you?" Ryan asked. She had not requested that I stop recording, so I'd slid my phone in the breast pocket of my jacket in the hopes that it wouldn't come up just yet.

"The broad strokes," I said stiffly. "I knew most of it until you two broke up. Or said you had."

"We did break up." Ryan nodded. "I broke up with him. And it was the hardest thing I'd ever done."

"Then why do it?" I pressed. "Why not just date publicly? Unless you were ashamed of him."

She gave a small smile. "You sound just like him. But it wasn't that simple. The media pressure was hard enough on my other relationships—how can you really get to know someone when you've got a whole camera crew following you around everywhere you go, criticizing your outfits and your public affection and the way you eat pasta in print the next day? I obviously struggled with it. The men I dated struggled with it. And all of us were famous already. Wilder . . . Wilder hadn't had to deal with all that yet. And I didn't want to put him through it."

"That was his choice to make," I said. "Didn't you trust him to decide what was best for his own life?"

Ryan looked at me again with that watchful, appraising eye.

I stared back and then glared. "This is different. I thought he was dead, Ryan."

"You knew he wasn't. You knew he was with me."

I shifted on the couch. "I couldn't be sure."

"Anyway." Ryan ran her hand along Lilla's head. The little girl was struggling to keep her eyes open. "It was a mistake, regardless. I didn't want to be away from him. He tried to keep his distance. But it was a messy, messy time, meeting up in secret and then regretting it, regretting everything, not talking to each other but unable to fully call it quits. He'd spoken to Skip and Jas about resigning, and I was beside myself about it."

"And then you just happened to get pregnant."

Ryan was nonplussed by the accusation in my voice. "Spin it however you like," she said. "It was an accident. But once it happened, I realized I didn't want it to happen again with anyone but Wilder. And I thought maybe it *wouldn't* happen, not ever again. I can't explain it rationally, but it really, truly did feel . . . like my only chance."

A silence fell as the wind continued outside, punctuated softly by what must have been the sound of Wilder now digging in the garden. I allowed that we had both tried to protect my brother.

"And you wanted to protect Lilla like you protected Wilder," I said aloud.

Ryan nodded. "The thought of seeing her face in a tabloid, in a TikTok, splashed across *Teen Star*'s news site . . . it just filled me with dread. Still does. Everyone needed something from me, wanted something, all the time. I didn't even want them to think about my baby. And I wanted to be hers, and hers alone."

"How did you do it?"

"What? Disappear after the VMAs?" she said. "We had all our affairs in order beforehand. Shipped the stuff we needed here. Then I went downstairs and changed out of my blazer and used the tunnel concourse to get to 30 Rock. I thought I'd have to bribe someone down there, but it was just . . . empty. The stars aligned for us.

"Wilder was waiting for me in a rental car at the other end. We stopped by the Midtown police station so the cops could see that we were okay, then we flew commercial, intentionally made a lot of connecting flights, and just kept our heads down until we were out. We've started the naturalization process and really pushed ourselves to build our language proficiency here . . . Lilla's already got it down, thanks to our neighbors. But it'll still be a couple years before we're full citizens."

"And you got married."

"Yes. To make things easier, legally." She looked sheepish. I wondered if she knew how it sounded—how I was sitting with this news at that moment, slowly processing just how much I'd missed out on. I would never be in my brother's wedding party. I wasn't there for him when he became a dad. I didn't get to shower Lilla with gifts when she was a newborn.

I slowly shook my head and forced myself back into journalism mode before the feeling became too overwhelming. "But why the spectacle? Why not wait until you could leave quietly?"

At this, Ryan gave a small smile. "I've always liked spectacle," she said. "And I wanted—with all my heart—to accept that VMA. I would have left earlier if it wasn't for that, but . . . god, I wanted to be there. Any later and people would have started to notice. I'm shocked Tatiana never spilled the real reason for that blazer. There's no way she missed my change in measurements."

"I'm sympathetic to your fear about unwanted attention," I said. "But what kind of life is this, living like you're in witness protection? What happens when Lilla grows up? When she wants to go to school and make friends and live a normal teenage life?"

Lilla stirred but did not wake at the sound of her name. Ryan held her closer.

"We can give her most of it. Everything, really. We're set for life. And we'll move around the world as needed, showing her the best of everywhere, and eventually . . . letting her choose her own path. She'll want for nothing."

"And what about you?"

Ryan gave a little laugh. "Me? What about me?"

"You're just . . . done?" I tried to fix her with the same calculating stare she'd given me. "You're never going back to performing?"

Ryan met my eyes without hesitation but toyed with the edge of the blanket that Lilla had pulled around the two of them. "No."

"I'm surprised," I said.

She shrugged. "There was a time I thought I'd never give up my career for motherhood. But things changed. Lilla is my priority now. And I couldn't have been a normal parent for her at my level of fame. I mean . . . not the parent I wanted to be, at least. Not the mom I wanted Lilla to have, not the best version of myself."

"So, what?" I pressed. "Did you *need* to be normal? Do you have to be absolutely perfect before you can be a decent parent?"

The room was quiet as Ryan ran her hand through her daughter's hair.

"It doesn't matter now. I don't miss it."

I nodded and leaned back in my armchair. The night had darkened to indigo outside, and I could now see my face reflected in the window.

"I saw your old stuff," I said quietly. "Skip took me to the Madcap storage locker to help me find the crystal ball."

A flicker of eagerness passed briefly across her face. Ryan made a strange movement, gripping the edge of the blanket and then letting go, so quickly I thought for a moment I'd imagined it. "Did he?" she said. Her voice was controlled.

"Mhmm. It's all there, dwindled down to one room in south LA."

"Was the dress there? The spider dress?"

I nodded. "All zipped up in a garment bag."

Ryan looked somewhere past my shoulder, eyes unfocused. "That dress was such a statement. I'd never felt angrier or more badass than I did when I wore that to the Met Gala."

I found myself watching her closely. "The spider dress, all your merch, the old CDs with the secret messages . . ."

Her gaze flickered back to me, wistful. "I was so proud of those CDs. It's silly, but . . . it was fun. It was one of the best ideas I ever had."

"Have you felt any withdrawal from it?" I asked. "No one can be at the pinnacle of fame like you were and come down so easily."

Ryan's mouth twisted again into a smile, but a wry one. "I can't say it was exactly easy, going from one hundred to zero. Recovering from the burnout was something I had to do or I would've collapsed anyway. But . . ."

She looked down at Lilla now, sleeping soundly, and gently stroked her hair.

"I have so many songs about her," Ryan went on. "Pages and pages and pages. I named my fourth album *Waterfall* because I felt like my inspiration had come back, but it was nothing compared to this. She opened the floodgates. I have endless new material, living here on the island. And . . . it's a strange feeling that it has nowhere to go."

I watched Ryan watch Lilla and softened at the sight of the two of them together. I still resented Ryan for her choices. But I wondered what I would have done in her situation, a circumstance so far outside the way I lived my own life. And at once, the true regret I had been feeling all evening bubbled to the surface.

"I wish I had gotten to meet her sooner," I said around the knot in my throat. "I wish you hadn't shut everyone out."

Ryan nodded as though she had been waiting for me to say it. "I'm sorry, Elyse," she said. "I knew we would hurt a lot of people when we left. I know I caused you a lot of pain."

I halfway laughed, halfway snorted, and fought to keep the tears from coming. "It's a pretty shitty apology for all these years," I said. "No one could be sure if you and Wilder were okay, or hurt, or happy."

"I know." And she looked me full in the face. "If I consent to your publishing this book . . . will that help to make up for it? Will that be a start?"

I felt my stomach drop a little. I hadn't thought it would be that easy. And something about her giving me the go-ahead made me hesitate and wonder if publishing was the right thing to do, after all.

"Are you sure?" I asked. "What would that mean for you three? Even if I don't name Hailuoto, even if I'm vague about country and region, people will come looking."

She shrugged and looked back down at her blanket. "We can move again. We want to travel anyway. We'll be long gone from here by the time the book ever goes to print."

"But—"

"And we'll let you know where we're going this time," she added with a small smile.

"I don't know, Ryan," I said, suddenly thrown into uncertainty.

"It's the least I can do, Elyse." She fixed me in her clear, steadying gaze. "And I insist."

AFTERWORD

I stayed with Wilder, Ryan, and Lilla for two weeks before we said goodbye again. They took me around Hailuoto, visiting the seashore, the little history museum, and the hiking trails through the woods. Lilla and I waded in the freezing water of the Bothnian Sea and screamed and laughed as the waves hit our knees. Wilder made fish with herbs for dinner while Ryan hummed songs that she might have written, but ones that were unrecognizable to me. The three of them moved about with ease, relaxed and unhurried as we traipsed around the villages.

I promised to keep them updated on the timeline of the project and let them know when their whereabouts would be shared with my editor. Wilder still despised the idea, I couldz tell, but I heard snippets of him and Ryan discussing it the morning after my arrival, while I drifted in and out of jet-lagged sleep. He avoided mentioning the book for the remainder of my stay.

But Ryan helped me make plans.

"The interviewees deserve to know first," I told her, already wondering how I would break the news to Skip, Jas, and especially Mari.

"I'll write letters to each of them that you can pass along," she said. "I know I have some explaining to do."

The evenings were long and warm, and we ate our meals outside in the wooded yard. I spent many collective hours after dinner leaning back in their Adirondack chairs, looking at the deepening sky, and wondering if I was doing the right thing.

Who was I to uproot their lives again? Was it ethical to thrust this family—that suddenly seemed so new to me and so distant from the people I had once known—back into the global spotlight, even with their consent?

It was on the evening of my last night that Wilder joined me beneath the stars. He wordlessly handed me a Finnish lager with a bear emblazoned on the can. We cracked them open in unison and sipped.

"I won't publish if you don't want me to," I finally said.

He made a noncommittal movement in the darkness. "You've always wanted to write a book; I told Ryan as much. And it sounds like you're almost done. So."

"I didn't expect the subject matter to be so close to home."

"Me neither." He gave a very brief laugh. "Look, Ellie, I know it's—I mean, you have to do what you have to do. And maybe the reason I was upset had more to do with the fact that I knew this couldn't last forever. I've been living here away from real life all these years knowing it wasn't sustainable. So while I was angry that the shoe was finally dropping at first, now . . . it feels more like relief."

I nodded, quiet.

"I hope she wasn't upset with you that you'd left clues for me," I said. "I shouldn't have mentioned that to her."

Wilder frowned. "You mean the crystal ball stuff?"

"Yeah."

"Why would she be mad? It was her idea."

I paused mid-sip. "It was? But . . . why? I thought she wanted a clean break."

He sighed. "No, that was me, actually. I really was so in my head with the plans and the chaos of becoming a dad and trying to get away in one piece that I was ready to just go and figure out the rest when we figured it out. But Ryan said we should leave you a hint, at least."

"Oh." I felt something shift in the back of my mind, an odd gut feeling. "Huh."

I had a question for him, unformed, but Wilder moved in his chair before I could gather my thoughts.

"I know we all really made a mess of things, Ellie. I'm sorry about all this too," he said.

"We're okay now," I allowed. "As long as I can know you and Lilla and Ryan are happy and healthy. That's all I need moving forward."

"It's a deal."

~

I said goodbye to the three of them the following morning, slinging my lone backpack into the rental car and giving each of them a hug.

"Text me when you get back stateside," Wilder said, having given me his new number.

"I will," I said. "It was really nice meeting you, Lilla."

Ryan grinned. "Say goodbye to Auntie Elyse."

"Bye, Auntie Leese," Lilla said, waving a clumsy hand.

I waved back and turned for the car.

"Now I have an Auntie Mari *and* an Auntie Leese," Lilla said loudly behind me.

I paused, glancing over my shoulder. But Ryan just laughed and whisked Lilla into the house. Wilder stood on the step and raised his hand.

"Bye, Ellie," he said firmly.

I nodded, my question still on the tip of my tongue.

~

I kept glancing in my rearview mirror as I drove, putting more and more distance between myself and the family that were like strangers to me.

Lilla knew Mari's name. She knew it like they had met before—but they couldn't have.

Or did they?

Had Mari been entirely truthful with me in our interviews?

I steered my car onto the ferry and watched through my window as the little island of Hailuoto grew smaller and smaller in the distance.

Ryan had known that I'd always wanted to write a book. Ryan had told Wilder to leave me a secret message. And something—or someone—had convinced Mari to speak with me, when no other publication, no other reporter, no other biographer had been successful in reaching her before.

Something in me knew that I would never get the proof I needed or the straight answer I craved.

But to think what a book like this would do to build toward a comeback, the way that it would set the stage for Ryan's return to fame . . . that would be good press, indeed.

I can't make any concrete claims.

But perhaps, just maybe, Ryan Holding is the ultimate mastermind, after all.

ACKNOWLEDGMENTS

As always, so many thanks to my awesome editor, Carmen Johnson, who has the same obsessions as me! And to everyone at Little A: Tree Abraham (art director), Karah Nichols (production manager), and Rachael Clark (marketing manager). Thank you to everyone on my team at 3Arts, especially Richard Abate and Hannah Carrande, and to my family and family of friends, especially Mike and Mattie. Everything begins and ends with you. And to a certain inspirational pop star, who has provided the soundtrack of our lives.

ABOUT THE AUTHOR

Photo © 2019 Maria Cina

Melissa de la Cruz is the #1 *New York Times*, #1 *Publishers Weekly*, and #1 IndieBound bestselling author of critically acclaimed and award-winning novels for readers of all ages. Many of her more than seventy books have also topped the *USA Today*, *Wall Street Journal*, and *Los Angeles Times* bestseller lists, and her work has been published in over twenty countries. She is the author of the Disney *Descendants* series, with four of the biggest movies on Disney Channel and Disney+. Her *Witches of East End* series was an hour-long drama for Lifetime. Her Hallmark movies include *Christmas in Angel Falls*; *Angel Falls: A Novel Holiday*; *Pride, Prejudice, and Mistletoe*; and *Sense, Sensibility & Snowmen*. She lives in West Hollywood with her husband and daughter. For more information, visit www.melissa-delacruz.com.